I0668540

Continued Pursuit

By
Rachel Gripp

This novel is a work of fiction. All characters in this publication are fictitious and any resemblance to real persons, living or dead is purely coincidental.

COPYRIGHT 2014 Rachel Gripp

ISBN: 098593963X
ISBN NUMBER 9780985939632

BOOK COVER – Austin Tsosie, artist

DEDICATION

This book is dedicated to our loving parents, Vittorio, Chiarina, Leonard and Edna, for enriching our lives and making this journey possible.

This book is also dedicated to my husband, Leonard, who passed away before the completion of the first novel, and to our two sons, Richard and Leonard whose continued support encouraged my completing the sequel.

TABLE OF CONTENTS

PROLOGUE vii
CHAPTERS
ONE......................FRIENDS 1
TWO......................RECOGNITION 9
THREE..................PAST HISTORY 21
FOUR ....THE ACCIDENT 27
FIVE ....MOTEL GUESTS............................. 35
SIX ....BREAKFAST 45
SEVEN..................THE VISIT 51
EIGHT ....NEW YEAR'S DAY 63
NINE.....................DISCLOSURE 71
TEN.......................CHARLENE 79
ELEVEN ....ENGAGEMENT 89
TWELVE................REVELATIONS 107
THIRTEEN ....MEL 117
FOURTEEN ....EASTER 125
FIFTEEN.................EVIDENCE 137
SIXTEEN ....MEDOC 149
SEVENTEEN ....VICTORIA 157
EIGHTEEN.............THE SEARCH FOR JOHN 167
NINETEEN.............RAMPAGE 177
TWENTY ....STREET JUSTICE 189
TWENTY ONE ....CANDY 201
TWENTY TWO ......CONFIRMATION 211
TWENTY THREE ....INTERIM 225
TWENTY FOUR .....DEATH 241
TWENTY FIVE........JANICE 251
TWENTY SIX ....KISMET 267

PROLOGUE

The Story Begins - Approximately Twenty-six Years Earlier
Place - Pittsburgh, Pennsylvania

It was dark when the two men left the pizzeria on Larimer Avenue. They turned at the street corner and walked to a parked car, laughing about a joke they shared while golfing hours earlier. Friends since early childhood, they remained close as brothers into their adult years. Now in their late twenties, neither man knew exactly where he fit in life. The younger of the two, by only three months, worked at the Heinz plant on Pittsburgh's North Side; the other, a much larger framed man, worked as a cook at his uncle's satellite restaurant in the city's East-End. Occasionally, however, he would get needed supplies at his uncle's main operation, a much larger and popular restaurant on Federal Street, a shopping and entertainment paradise, also on Pittsburgh's Northside. But this tony location was much farther away from any of the industrial plants in the area.

The angry mood of the younger man was obvious during the morning phone call. He spoke vividly of a huge argument that had taken place with his wife the previous evening, and after a no-win exchange, he had spent the night on the front porch swing with a couch pillow for a headrest.

Upon hearing this, the bigger man felt saddened and somewhat guilty by his friend's discontent, since he had spent the night on a dark, dead-end street, having wild passionate sex with the woman he loved and hoped to marry. To assuage his own guilt and, perhaps remedy the situation, he suggested a round of golf after work, hoping to ease his friend's frustration. And at some particular point that night, his friend enjoyed a temporary release from his wife's constant harangue, his loveless marriage, and his very unhappy life.

Toward the end of the evening, when the older one was driving his friend home, a brawling street-scene near the end of a bridge and their recognition of the man being assaulted, brought the car's screeching brakes to a sudden halt. The younger one ran to the bleeding man sinking slowly on the pavement, while his tall, muscular friend grabbed the quarrelsome attacker by the armpits and lifted his squirming body high in the air, away from the almost comatose victim. As the airborne mugger struggled and swung his fists wildly, the big-framed giant whirled him farther away from the battered man and, in the hurried scuffle, the screaming attacker sailed over the bridge and onto the highway below.

Without a second thought, the two men carried the bloodied victim to the car and, after making a quick phone call, sped to a large stately home surrounded by a high stone wall. They recognized the two men who greeted them at the gated entrance and followed one of them inside the house to a room whose door was closed.

Inside the room, an older, big-framed man with dark, curly hair and piercing black eyes, sat behind an enormous desk. He listened intently to their account of the story, until he was fully satisfied with the answers to his questions.

"You both leave tonight." He slipped a fat envelope across the desk. It was not a request that needed a response: it was a directive to be followed. "You saved your cousin's life and that's all that matters right now. I will show my gratitude later." His eyes locked on his nephew as he spoke, making certain his meaning was understood. The uncle was giving them a sum of money to leave town while he handled the "bridge affair," the term he used for locating the fallen body and erasing a possible accidental death or murder charge. They would be notified when he considered it safe to return. "I will speak to your mother when she gets back," his uncle added, referring to his sister's trip to Italy with her church group. With those few words the interview was over. And within minutes, they were shown out of the large sheltered house and given an address in Youngstown, Ohio.

Hours later, after another stormy session with his wife, a very angry man revisited his front porch swing with a hastily packed suitcase and waited for his friend, who, at the point of pick-up, was seething with an anger of his own. He was unable to locate the woman he so desperately sought...the woman he loved. Since their affair had been kept secret, he had asked a female friend to make a phone call, while he stood by waiting to speak with her. After learning she was not at home, he began searching their frequent haunts and felt a gnawing distrust growing within his suspicious nature. The woman he loved had lied to him.

Where was she that evening when she was supposed to be at home? Even more important, was she giving herself to someone else?

Those two questions continued to fester inside him, and he carried one thought wherever he went. She would regret using him should their paths ever cross: she would learn the full meaning of revenge and retaliation.

***

Two young men, angered by problems of their own, are ordered to leave behind the only world they had ever known. The directive had to be followed: both men knew two unassailable facts... they could be charged with murder...and the connected uncle was trying to help them.

They rode in silence for miles, each unhappy with the outcome for being a Good Samaritan.

Little did they realize then...their exile would pass from days into weeks...and months into years...

In the end, their sacrifice was never appreciated...
From the beginning it had been a stolen opportunity...
Finally, what came around took a long, long time...
Approximately twenty-six years

Chapter 1
Friends

"You on that kick again, Hawkeye?" Cal wiped the bar counter as he watched his partner make two lemon drop martinis. "Someday you're going to screw-up, Sal."

John Calvin Burkett, known to the locals only as Cal, had witnessed that same activity for much longer than he cared to remember. He was not upset with the big man's gift. He knew about it years earlier. Filling drink orders was just a by-product of Sal's real talent, and Cal pictured the scenario in his mind.

Two people, seated in the bar lounge, finally decide on their drinks and they magically appear in minutes.

"Not a chance." Sal paused and waited for the waitress to place the bar chit. He set the two lemon drop martinis on her service tray and rang-up the tab.

"How'd you know?" The new waitress ogled him in awe.

"Same drink: different day." He walked to the other end of the long bar, dismissed her completely and, reaching under the counter, pulled a snack-size Kit Kat bar, his favorite candy, from the full bag posted there.

"You tell a good story. You even had me convinced." Cal told Salvatore Antonio Guggino when the waitress disappeared. "One of these days, the lip-reading is going to get you in deep shit."

"Yeah, yeah, yeah, I hear you." Sal took a bite of his snack bar. "Right now, I got other problems to think about." He reached into his back pocket and pulled out an envelope.

"Who'd you knock up?" Cal laughed. From his appearance alone, the guy oozed too much testosterone.

Now in his fifties, Sal wasn't exactly a ladies' man by any stretch. The man was noticeably tall and big-framed like a football player. He had very dark eyes and curly black hair that was thickly bunched all over his head while his wavy sideburns protruded conspicuously over his ears. A beard would have hidden his olive complexion but he chose an early morning shave instead and wore the remnants of a growing shadow by day's end. Handsome would not describe his face, but it was by all counts, very pleasant. However, there was much more to the man than just his physical features and salty language.

Among his many talents was his penchant for lip-reading. This gift developed over the years from a relationship with his impaired, yet trusted friend, Buddy Haskins. The lip-reading started slowly at first. But Sal was a quick study. In time, he read all sorts of conversations and related them later. So now, it was sometimes embarrassing to learn which store habitually overcharged; what was hot on the stock market; who was currently sleeping with whom; and the forever trick of setting up drinks when the patrons made their selections.

There were times when Cal thought his partner was the biggest bullshit artist this side of the Atlantic. Sal could seemingly change his personality or appearance in strange new situations, and had the facility of making people believe some made-up story that was to his liking on that particular day. This peculiar trait had the wondering minds of the locals put to rest, when they made their final decision, almost twenty-six years earlier, to live in Put-in-Bay on South Bass Island not far from Sandusky, Ohio. Sal's story was plausibly hilarious, truly absurd and very hush-hush among the locals, who had to know everything about the two men who came to live there permanently. It was their right to know these things…if the men wanted acceptance by the community. And so, Sal told the town's key players their sad tale of woe…confidentially. He knew the whispered gossip would flow… sooner or later.

Cal Burkett lost his children in a bitter divorce, initiated by his wife for no good reason. The man was faithful, hardworking and a good father. She, on the other hand, wanted a different kind of lifestyle and got custody of their children through ties with the area judges.

Rejected and broken-hearted, an emotionally whipped Cal could no longer stay in the area. He left the little place called Snow Shoe, or something like that, in the steep snowy hills of Pennsylvania, the Bass natives would recall. And although no other information was forthcoming, the townsfolk drew their own conclusions about the deviously wanton woman. Sal, who sympathized with his brother-in-law, was recuperating from a back injury and agreed to make a fresh start with him. After checking different areas and businesses, they decided to put down roots on the little fishing island that was remotely populated then.

Now it was different. The tourist trade caught on and Put-in-Bay became a haven for vacationers bent on having a good time. Working long hours, Sal and Cal's Bar concentrated on the summer tourist trade, the winter's ice fishing and the camaraderie of the locals who stayed there year round. They made money and could have taken vacations like so many on the island did. They could have escaped the harsh winters, but chose to service the ice fisherman, whose stories and singing matched the money they spent on whiskey, as an excuse to warm themselves. At least that's everyone said. But truth be told, not too much was open in winter back then. So a gathering of seasoned ice fisherman returning year after year seemed more like a reunion than a sportsman's outing. They had no problem with drunks either. Sal's six-four frame silenced the loudest and most obnoxious of any group. But that seldom happened with the returning regulars. If someone passed out, Sal would let him sleep-it-off on a couch that was set-up expressly for that purpose.

Despite his body mass Sal was a light-footed chameleon. His steps were seldom heard coming down the hall of their apartment above the tavern. It was embarrassing at first, particularly when Sal decided to entertain without giving advance notice. In time, it no longer mattered. Cal decided it was part of life's need for sex and went on with his normal routine, leaving Sal to his romantic pleasures.

Cal preferred fishing. If a friend joined him on the boat he owned with his partner that was okay too. He had spent many nights there; some to give Sal privacy, others, to enjoy a quiet outing. But Cal was not always alone on the boat. Ann Oakley, an abrasive woman in her late sixties, ran a local hotel with her sister and brother-in-law, Gladys and Henry Grant, and the woman enjoyed some of her leisure time fishing with Cal. Neither talked much. She brought the food: he supplied the beer. They were perfect together: both needed an escape from the tourists.

He watched his partner eat another candy snack. The man was gifted, particularly with his experience in food preparation. When the winter food supplies fell short, Sal was always able to whip up something wonderful and wholesome to suit their bar clientele. If the man wore an apron, he would be considered a featured chef. As it was, even with their limited menu, their patrons seemed to like eating there.

Still, for as long as they knew each other, as friends and business partners, Sal could be a pain in the ass. Likeable as always, he was cocky as hell…like now. Cal's thoughts were brought up short by the clicking sound of Sal's snapping fingers.

"Hello!" Sal chortled. "Stop with the daydreams. I need your help." A wrinkled frown furrowed his forehead as he unfolded a sheet of paper from its envelope. After reading the note aloud he tossed it on the bar. "I really don't need this shit."

"What are you worried about? You're looking at February." Cal scanned the letter. "The ice fishermen sure as hell don't need your help. Liquor maybe, but they can get that elsewhere. But why mention the engagement party now, when it's six months away? And why is he inviting you anyway? That's my question."

"There must have been a falling-out over us, and he's fortifying the family of my coming. They may not be happy he's inviting me. It will be our first meeting since we left. The letter doesn't mention my mother, so I guess she's not invited. But why would Raymond exclude his aunt? That makes no sense."

"Maybe with the death of your father in June, they felt she…," he paused. "But the family was never close to Rosario, if I recall correctly…"

"They made their presence felt at the funeral, I'm told, but I smell Segis' hand excluding her." Sal smiled inwardly, thinking of his own plan. "I want you to come with me," he said quietly. "I think it will be at

Raymond's house, not some swanky hotel." He pointed to the Buffalo address. "Segis will be there to honor his granddaughter. That's a given."

"Are you're asking me to crash the party, or am I supposed to be your date for the evening?" Cal wiped the right corner of his mouth, a trait of his that went back to childhood. "Either way, the answer is no thanks." The last person he wanted to see was Sal's cousin, Raymond, the man whose life they saved some twenty-six years earlier. Nor was he interested in reliving the noble act that ruined their lives. But most of all, Cal did not want to shake hands with the man who crossed their palms with a lot of money and insisted they start over…somewhere far away from Pittsburgh.

"If you don't go, I can't either!" Sal's anger surprised him. He seldom got angry over little things. This was something different. Attending the engagement party was obviously important to him. "Instead of doing something about the situation, you've kept yourself locked-up." He heard Sal roar. "All because she took the kids and left you hanging. You should have told her to go to hell and checked on the girls yourself. Give the fucking halo a rest!" he bellowed. "It's time we even the score and I can't go alone."

"What do you mean you can't go alone?" Cal shouted back with a rage of his own. "You don't need my support. I've given more than my fair share. The bastard took the best years of my life. Everything I had. I've got nothing left." His voice trailed off slowly. He was remembering a different time, another place. He had the girls. They were a family. He never felt alone then.

"My point exactly," Sal fumed. "I go alone, it's nothing. But together, we remind them of the past. It's what we gave up, so their dynasty could continue."

"What makes you think they care? That's ancient history to them."

"I know that," Sal insisted, "and we did get a pile of money. But this gives us a chance to rub their faces in it, when they're all together. To make it work, I need you to come with me."

"Do I hear a plan in the making?" Cal quizzed his partner. There was no way on Christ's green earth Sal would disclose even a seed of what was planted deep inside his head. Yet, Cal wondered if Sal was going to make a speech. If so, then Sal would be at the top of his game. He was a master with words. And knowing his partner as he did, a toast from Sal at the family engagement party would be priceless, pointed and very punitive.

"And ruin everything," Sal replied, watching his partner rub a hardened food spot on the counter with a bar cloth. "You know me better than that."

"That's what I was afraid of." Cal walked outside the long bar to straighten the sixteen stools that abutted the counter, ten of which faced Sal and the three others that sat on each end. Then he retraced his steps, faced his partner and growled. "I don't care how fancy this shindig is, I'm not wearing a monkey suit."

Sal studied his partner. They were both in their fifties, yet Cal looked younger, somehow. He would have looked good in a tux. Tall, slender, and handsome, he'd look good in anything. Granted his golden locks were a truer color years back, but they still retained their former sheen and a few of them strayed to the one side of his oval face, framing the laughing blue eyes that often went with his notorious chuckle. Fortunately, it was not a formal affair. A tuxedo was not required.

They were a good pair, Sal thought to himself. It might work even better than he thought. "You're sure?" Sal wanted confirmation. "I need to reply."

"Give me ten minutes and I'll get you a notarized statement," he answered sarcastically. "I said I'd come. But you owe me…big time. Just understand that."

"Right. I'll make you and old Annie a bag lunch next time you go fishing." Sal crinkled his candy paper, just in time to catch Cal's sailing bar cloth. He walked to the other end of the bar and dialed his cousin's number on his cell. "I plan to come," he said. "Thanks for the heads-up."

After ending the conversation, a wide grin crossed Sal's face. Raymond's daughter would never forget her engagement party: the girl would understand the meaning of sacrifice, and the way her grandfather treated the two people whose lives were altered for saving her dad.

Then he dialed another number and asked, "You sure about this?"

***

Later that evening when throngs of tourists crowded the bar, both men were focused on serving the busy weekend clientele, those at the bar, and the ones in the lounge whose drink orders were taken by the waitresses. Sal never attempted to lip-read at those times. It was too difficult servicing the crowded lounge and the mass of people crushed between the bar stools shouting drink orders. However, at one point that night, something deep inside him snapped when he began filling three cocktail orders. He studied a table of three women being served by the waitress and kept a watchful eye on them all evening long.

Somewhere near eleven, Sal watched the women pay their individual checks and prepare to leave the bar. He grabbed the waitress to scan their receipts and, dissatisfied that only cash payments had been made, threw a bar rag at Cal and immediately left the premises.

For some unknown reason, as Cal watched his partner sail out of the bar, a foreboding tremor ran through his body. This was not like Sal. Had he seen someone from his past? Cal became filled with apprehension. For the first time, in a very long time, he worried about his childhood friend.

Chapter 2
Recognition

Sal trailed behind the three women when they left his bar and watched them turn into a side street. Chatting and laughing in their approach to the hotel, they were totally unaware of the big-framed man following them.

Of the three, it was the small-figured woman who interested him the most. Since the back of her chair faced the bar, her dark hair and silhouette were the only features he could see clearly. However, it was her drink order that made him suspicious. It made him think she might be the one he had searched for, the woman he had left behind in anger, years earlier. Although Sal expected failure, he had to follow his instincts. He had made this same mistake many times before: a mistaken face in the crowd or the wrong woman at a mall. Yet, as Sal continued watching the three of them, he noticed the smallest woman's sway as she walked, and a realization began to take hold in his mind. He could feel the rapid pounding of his heart. Could it really be? After twenty-six years? His thoughts raced as he watched them enter a hotel.

He slipped into the building alcove through a side door. He needed to hear the conversation, but more important, Sal needed another look. It was important, more important than anything else that had occurred in his life up to now. He had to know if it was real: that precious time period when he was younger, those years before his life had tanked. Maybe this was an illusion too. His mind had played tricks on him before. Was this just a repeat? Yet somehow, this felt different. It had to be real. This time…it just had to be real.

He was not in a good spot. Sal could hear the conversation vaguely, but he could not see well enough to read the women's lips. He had to wait until each woman went her separate way.

He watched them gather their room keys and heard tentative plans being made for breakfast. Then when the women parted, two of them walked down a first floor corridor, while the third, the one who held his interest, stepped into an elevator. As soon as the doors closed, Sal stepped out of the alcove.

"Henry." Sal rushed to the front desk and slipped him a Jackson. "The small brunette," he said, "I forgot her room number."

"I don't know how you young bucks do it." The old man slipped the twenty into his pocket. "She'll be waitin for you in room fourteen, but don't do nuthin on the front porch. We're respectable. At least, Gladys keeps tellin me that, the old hen."

Sal smiled, thinking of Henry's wife, the old woman who always carried a rag in the pocket of her house dress. Gladys went through life wiping dust.

Sal took the elevator hurriedly, walked down the hall and stopped at the entrance of door fourteen. What if he were wrong? What would he say? How foolish would he feel? Then, he composed himself and stood tall and determined. He was not wrong. Not this time, not now. This time he was certain. Sal knew deep in his heart he was not mistaken. And he had twenty-six years to plan his revenge if ever they met.

Painful memories flooded his mind. The woman he hunted long ago was behind the door facing him. And the memories of his search that night, not being home...the place she was supposed to be, flashed before him, and he pictured her making love with another man. He felt a fiery rage growing deep inside him...a hot surging anger rising upward...a fury that was hidden so long ago. Sal could feel the hard pounding of his heart as his anger mounted. She had lied to him...used him...betrayed their love with someone else. Now, it was his turn to even the score; and even the score he would, as only someone with his kind of animal strength could. He knocked softly and waited.

As the door opened partially, a small-statured woman, with piercing dark eyes, wearing what appeared to be a nightgown, peered around it and recognized the man immediately. "Sal." Her voice echoed the hallway, as she tried slamming the door on him. But it was too late. He had already pushed his way into the room and chased after the dark-haired woman, swinging her body around like a rag doll to face him.

"You bitch," he snarled creasing her cheek with his heavy hand. Then fuming with pent-up rage, he ripped-off the woman's night-gown, threw her on the hotel bed and, within seconds, the naked man was deep inside her: her hands pinned under her body, making it impossible for her to move under his big heavy frame. That she was forced and unwilling was of no consequence. He was too busy feeding his own psyche. In the broad spectrum of things, he had always planned to ravage the woman, should they ever meet again. He wanted her to feel the intense kind of pain he had been carrying for decades.

As he plunged deeper and deeper into her, he could feel the start of her hot fluid mixing with his. He listened to her uneven breathing and knew that as mad as she was, as angry as they both were, nothing could make either of them forget how great their lovemaking sessions had always been. He increased his rhythm, pumping her hard and fast. He knew she would come around.

"Oh, God, you're good." He rocked her back and forth, freeing her arms and hands for a last final thrust.

Feeling completely drained, Sal looked into the woman's dark eyes, as she lay quietly beneath him. When he moved to brush his lips with hers, he felt the hard slap of her hand on his back.

"Get off me, you big gorilla!" She tried rolling away from him.

"Where the hell do you think you're going?" He yanked her back roughly, and in remounting her again, covered her body completely.

"Let me go, you hairy ape," she hissed and rolled her naked body out from under his and stood facing him. "You're sticky shit's running down my leg. You couldn't wear a condom. No. Not you. Always skin to skin and I'm always left cleaning-up after your shit."

"Yeah, like it didn't suit you," he barked, sitting on the side of the bed. "You liked it that way when you were safe. You're probably still opening wide after I broke you in."

"What's the matter?" The naked woman looked down at him, her hands glued to her hips. "I'm not tight enough for you? Or are you only screwing virgins these days?" She glared at the huge naked figure, her hatred mounting. It was like yesterday. She remembered it all…the hurt, the pain, and the years of struggle.

Without a word of warning, he bolted suddenly and, creasing her cheek again, swept her nude body upward and shook her vigorously. "Don't you fuck with me!" he snarled. "You're the one who left my dick hanging in the wind."

"Your ass." She struggled to break his grasp. "I didn't leave; you did."

"That's bullshit and you know it." He barked at the raised figure. "I looked everywhere for you, searched for you. I came by."

"I came by." She mimicked him. "And yet, the Italian witch of East Liberty had no clue of your whereabouts."

"Stop!" he fumed, lowering her to the floor. "Your mouth's like a river constantly flowing shit. You're still shooting darts at my mother."

"And why wouldn't I?" she challenged. "She refused to see me. Talk to me about her precious son. That broom she uses to guard her door at night, the one to keep the *strega* witch away, it's nothing but a ruse. Every Italian at Sons of Columbus knows she really uses it to fly on. Teresa's always been one miserable bitch. So, go ahead, hit me again. Take your best shot." She raised her cheek, as if daring him, waiting for the force of his heavy slap.

Incensed by her derisive comments humiliating his mother and, not knowing exactly how to respond, Sal grabbed the naked woman by her armpits and forcefully began lifting her again. But before he could raise her high in the air, the woman wrapped her legs around his nude body and tightened her grip, then quickly locked her flailing arms around his neck. Sal tried shaking her loose by swinging their naked bodies around and around in circles, but he was afraid of pulling her away from him and risk hurting her. He stopped spinning suddenly and yelled, "Get down, for Christ sake. I don't want to hurt you."

As the woman slowly inched down his hairy body, she could feel his readiness, and the memories of their being together years earlier flooded her brain. The hungry want of the man began growing deep inside her, and soon, she was experiencing an awakening rush that pulsated through the lower part of her body. Yes, she wanted him. And she wanted him now. As she pressed up against him, she signaled her desire and tilted her face upward.

Lifting her gently, Sal whispered, "Gwennie." He brushed her lips with his tongue, before his mouth enveloped hers completely. "My Gwennie." He cradled her in his arms, his lips pressing hers, and carried her toward the bed. He felt the excitement of years earlier with this woman. That was his sweetest memory of taking her, loving her as he had in their youth, blending gently into each other, while vowing a life together. "I never got enough of you," he whispered. "I still remember taking you on Floric." He reminisced about the small dead-end street they discovered for making uninterrupted love. "How scared you were. How good it's always been. I remember everything about us."

"Sal." She opened herself to him and touched his body lovingly. Then wrapping her legs around his back, she joined the frenzied two-hundred-twenty-pound gorilla giving her his all. The only thing she heard when they exploded together was his voice moaning hoarsely, "Gwennie, my Gwennie."

"Oh, Sal," she whimpered, still feeling the emotion between them.

"Gwennie." He lay drained on her, his body covering hers almost completely. He kissed her lips then moved down to her breasts.

"That's a first." She watched him mouth her nipples. "You were never a breast man."

"You never had much to nibble on." He stopped momentarily. "Still don't."

"Too bad Rosario didn't agree with you."

"Again, with my family," he bellowed. "What is it with you? You can't even leave the dead alone."

"I'm sorry." She apologized, "I didn't know. But your father was a lech."

"He was harmless."

"Did you know he tried to cup my breasts at Terry's reception, just to see if I was filling in?" Gwennie referred to an Italian neighbor's wedding years earlier. "I was only fourteen!" She fumed at the studied face resting between her breasts. "I told that bicycle sniffer if he did it again, I'd kick him in the balls."

"I can't believe he'd do something like that."

"Your father was always banging someone," she corrected. "He's probably in hell doing some paisan right now. He wanted to get me too, but I could never figure out why. Rosario didn't know about you."

"At least we kept it in the family." He moved his hand. "Let's see if you filled in." Sal messaged her one breast.

"You're not scoring points with shit like that." She smacked him.

"It's not your tits I'm after. I want you, Gwennie. I always have."

He lay drained beside her. Neither spoke. There was no need. They were together: they were satisfied; yet emotionally, they were miles apart. He turned toward her and drummed his fingers across her smooth creamy body.

"You're so beautiful. You still look the same as I remembered you, twenty-six years ago."

"And you're the same Blue Whale I fell in love with. A little heavier, maybe, but the best part of you hasn't changed," she said, giggling. "How the hell did you recognize me anyhow?"

"Your back was to me but I remembered your drink."

"Crown Royal Manhattan."

"Then I got curious." He brushed a few stray hairs from her face. "I would have recognized you anywhere. Your face never left me." He studied the woman from his past. "Stay with me, Gwennie. I'll take good care of you. I own a lot of property here. We can make a fresh start."

"I can't." She reached over and kissed him. "Not now."

"You're married."

"No. There's never been anyone else, ever." She emphasized the last word.

"So, you never." His eyes widened. "Never?" His finger swayed back and forth.

"No. Only with you." There was a glimmer in her large brown eyes as she caught the sexual reference. For decades, she had been living the chaste life of a cloistered nun. It was time he knew the truth.

"Then why? I don't understand." Her refusal puzzled him. "There's a lot I don't understand. I tried to find you, months after I left. Nobody knew where you were. My source thought you went off and got married." He seemed annoyed that she would even think of marrying someone else.

"Just a damn minute," she interrupted sarcastically. She knew full well his source of information was Buddy Haskins, the good friend who taught him lip-reading. "I didn't know what happened when you left either. I asked, but no one knew. I even used John's absence as an excuse to find out about you. You both left at the same time. But your mother wouldn't talk to me when she got back from Italy. She hates my mother. Well, they hate each other. The rift goes right through both families, all because of church gifts. How stupid, but you already knew that. My family would have thrown your ass on the street, if they ever caught us together. That's why Floric was so great. But I think John knew we were having sex. I wonder if he ever regretted introducing us. I know he never told Josephine we were going together. Her thoughts wouldn't have been so disgusting, if he had."

"The first time he saw us together, you were working at Sears. John knew everything after that and covered my ass with the family sometimes. The worst part was missing you the night we left and listening to the heartbreak of his crumbling marriage." Then Sal gave her a total accounting, from the events that triggered their disappearance to the present day circumstances.

"So that's why everything was so hushed up. It was all about your cousin, Raymond. Did you ever find out?"

"I don't follow."

"Was the guy killed in the fall?"

"We were told he was. It was the oldest Kinney boy, Edward. I think that was his name. It was all hushed up somehow. We never knew what happened to his body. We were told it wasn't safe to come back. Then after finding this place, we just stayed."

"Who told you?" She read the puzzled look on his face. "Who said that you couldn't come home?"

"Nate," he answered, "Yablonski. He was our contact in Youngstown."

"How does he fit in with Segismondo Del Grosso?"

"You don't have to be Italian to be connected. But I knew they were tight. And you don't cross Segis. We had to stay low. We were given a lot of money and told to find some place safe until things cleared. Each time we asked to come home, Nate would tell us to wait a little longer. John was unhappy, losing his kids. He did send Josephine money, but your sister wanted no part of him. She made it impossible for him to see the kids. And then, when my contact couldn't find you, I was really pissed. A lot went through my mind. When we came here, the months just grew into years and we stopped asking. We gave up trying to go back. The realization had already set in. It was too late."

"And your mother? Did she know? How close is the big ape to Teresa?"

"She knew I was alright. My uncle made sure of that…" His voice fell flat with a disappointing pause. He left the subject of his uncle drop quietly. "I couldn't contact her until later, after we moved here, just to let her know I was alive. She cried when she heard my voice the first time. We talk. But she doesn't know the whole story to this day. So she wasn't lying to you, Gwennie. She didn't know where I was. She was very hurt by my leaving."

Gwennie's eyes narrowed. There had to be more to the story than a bridge death…if there really was one. Was Sal told the truth, or was he deliberately kept in the dark, for some reason known only to his crooked uncle? Segis had always been a two-faced son-of-a-bitch. Playing the odds kept the family in line. His bodyguards saw to that. Of course, they were also two-faced. It was inherent in their genes; it ran in the family. But then too, Segis' sister, Teresa, was something unto herself. Once considered the family beauty, her cold attitude toward her brother, his criminal dealings, and those of the family who did his bidding, was generally observed at most social functions. Still, the reasons for her hostility toward all of them, and for Segis in particular, were unknown. She kept that a private matter, privy to no one. With that kind of hate relationship, so obvious to all the neighborhood paisans, Gwennie wondered how Teresa could believe Segis' story concerning Sal's safety. But even more important, did the woman know the truth? Did she know that her brother was responsible for separating Teresa from her son?

Suddenly, she became angry. In the big picture of life, Segis robbed her too. He took twenty-six years away from her…years she could have shared with Sal. Segis was solely responsible for ruining the lives of four people…hers, Sal's, John's and Teresa's. Her sister, Josephine, didn't count. She screwed up on her own…she didn't need help.

"Let me get this straight," Gwennie said pointedly, "you never checked to see if Edward Kinney actually died in the fall?"

"Why would my uncle lie about that? What would be the point? He was trying to protect me. That's why he had us leave town."

In her own mind, Gwennie felt Segis had lied to his nephew, but she couldn't understand the man's reason for it. All she knew for certain was that the uncle could not be trusted. She'd have to check on the Kinney story herself.

"Let me get up," she said quietly. The small woman walked into the bathroom for a quick shower and towel wrap, before retracing her steps back to the bedroom. She grabbed her handbag from the desk and sat down on the bed beside Sal. The woman ruffled through a swath of pictures inside her wallet and stopped at a laminated copy of a young dark-eyed man with black curly hair. From his sitting position, he looked rather large and muscular, yet his facial features looked very familiar.

Sal caught her steady stare. "How old is he?"

"How long have you been gone?"

"You're serious." He watched her expression. "Does he know?"

"I've always been straight with Daniel. I had to. It wasn't easy growing up. He hates his grandparents, although he's never met any of them. He's not too fond of you either. But I did name him after your paternal grandfather." She gazed at the picture lovingly before fixing her eyes back on Sal.

"I want to meet him." Sal interrupted her thoughts.

"That's not possible. He's in school," she explained. "Studying for his PhD."

"Then when?" His expression changed. "If he's my son, I want him in my life."

His skepticism set her off immediately. "There is no if!" She spat loudly. "And I'm not asking shit from you!"

"I didn't mean anything by that, Gwennie." He tried to calm her. "For Christ sake, I just found you after all these years, and now I learn I have a son? That's a lot to digest."

"I had to tell you." She shook her head. "If you found out after seeing me, you'd hate me even more."

"Hate you? I just asked you to stay with me. Be with me. When you really love someone, it never goes away. That feeling is always with you…it's always there. That's how I feel about you. I always have."

A quizzical expression crossed her face. "When did you start slapping women around, or is it just me that riles your silly ass?"

"It's you. You're the only woman I ever slapped. I had so much pent-up anger thinking you went with someone else. I couldn't stand the thought of having someone else touch you. After all those years …and now you're here," his voice trailed off. "That won't happen again. But you are not leaving me, even if I have to tie you up and keep you on our boat."

"Our?" Her face fell. "John's still here, with you?" She stopped speaking. "Or are you married?" She hadn't thought about her last question until now.

"He goes by Cal now. He was working the bar with me. You didn't notice? We're partners. And no, I never married, but I haven't been celibate either. Not with all the transient women that come here."

"Obviously." She eyed him. She could understand women 'putting out' at Put-in-Bay. Both sexes wanted a good time on vacation. However, her own philosophy was different. "I don't share," she said defiantly. It was necessary he understood her guidelines, if they were to continue the relationship.

"That won't be a problem."

"Good. Then you won't be peeing through your nose."

"And I actually want to live with that mouth." He rolled his eyes.

"But you get the rest of me too." Her laugh was contagious. "Think positively," she said. "But now, I think you should leave."

"Not a chance. I want to know about you and Daniel. Get in bed and we'll talk."

"We're just going to talk," she agreed, confirming his ground rules while slipping under the covers.

"Well, maybe a little body-rub before we go to sleep. But first, I want to know everything that happened after I left. How did you get pregnant?"

"Well…A bright and shining star came out of the East." Gwennie slowly raised her hands upward to draw a picture.

"Cut the crap, Mary," Sal fussed. "I take off and you're pregnant. How did you manage?"

Gwennie pulled away from him, and began to relate the tragic events that transpired after his disappearance. Once her parents became aware of her pregnancy and refusal to identify the father, they threw her out of their house and disowned her completely. Disgrace was the ultimate sin in the Italian family years earlier. She contacted her old friend, Rosemarie, a former co-worker at Sears, and left the area. Then without notifying anyone, she moved in with a shunned great aunt who lived in Albion and had their baby, Daniel. Later, with her great aunt's help, she got a job at the nearby college in the admissions department. There had never been any communication with her parents. To them, she was still the *puttana* who disgraced the family name. In their view, Gwennie no longer existed. She expounded further after Sal raised more questions.

He felt saddened by the account she had given him. Although he had been unaware of her pregnancy, Sal was to blame for her misfortune, both with the family disowning her and her lack of financial support. He became ridden with guilt. "I want you with me, Gwennie. Marry me. I know it's a screwed up mess, but Daniel will see how much I love you, always loved you." They lay silent under the covers, when Sal turned and kissed her. "I'm getting saluted."

"Tell me something new, you big gorilla. It's time your glue-gun went to sleep."

After Sal turned off the night lamp, he drew her velvet body to him and, edging her lips with his tongue, whispered, "Who is Rosemarie?"

"Screw Rosemarie," Gwennie murmured.

"I'd rather do you," he said before changing the subject. "I'm glad I pushed my way in tonight," he said, wanting more information. "Why did you try to close the door on me?"

"Same reason you continued to slap me. I was angry. I felt betrayed because you left me when I was pregnant and my family turned against me. I went through a very bad time. If it hadn't been for Rosemarie and my great aunt, I could not have survived." Then Gwennie gave Sal a more detailed history…from the time of her banishment to her unpredicted meeting on South Bass Island with the man she had always loved.

"I want to hear about you and Daniel."

Satisfied by her answers to his intermittent questions, Sal kissed her gently. "I may not be a practicing Catholic, but I believe God brought you back to me because He knew we belonged together."

"I love you, Sal." Gwennie lay comfortably cradled in his arms.

"You will always be my Gwennie." Sal closed his eyes.

Comforted by the turn of events, Gwennie Damico listened to the hum of Sal's breathing and soon fell asleep.

Chapter 3
Past History

John Calvin Burkett sat on his usual bar stool reading the morning paper, while enjoying his morning coffee. It was not unusual for only one of them to open the tavern for the slow morning trade. There was no real need for both men to be there, when one of their more experienced waitresses could easily help tend bar, if business picked-up. Today, however, was different. Although Sal was scheduled to open, Cal couldn't chance it. In fact, Cal wasn't sure where Sal's thoughts were focused, after leaving the bar so hurriedly the previous night.

"Hey, Romeo!" Cal greeted his partner who suddenly breezed through the front door, wearing the grin of a very happy camper. "When you didn't come back last night, I thought you might have gotten lucky with one them. Your shit-eating grin tells me you scored."

He watched Sal walk behind the bar, place both hands on the counter and face him directly. For some strange reason the sudden change in his partner's expression bothered him. He had the feeling that this was not about one of Sal's one-night stands. This was not his usual, out at night, back by morning and check for clap. No. Somehow, this was very different. He could feel it.

"Is something wrong? Has something happened?" His friend's strange demeanor was very disconcerting.

"I found her, Cal," Sal said in earnest. "I found Gwennie. She was here last night, but I didn't see her. Her drink order made me take a second look." He caught Cal's puzzled expression. "Crown Royal Manhattans. I remember her ordering those at a watering hole in Pittsburgh. So I had to make sure."

"Oh, Christ." Cal's face fell, as he sat frozen on his bar stool. "What have you done, Sal? You didn't…"

"No. No." Sal reassured him. "I stayed with her. It was like being on Floric all over again…even better."

"That's a relief." He no longer felt drained. "I thought you…" Cal left the thought unfinished.

"I know. I know," Sal echoed. "I was really pissed when I found her. I didn't know whether to kiss or kill her, so we made love instead. Being with her took me back, Cal." He was almost wistful, pondering what his life could have been. "It left me with a big hole that should have been filled a long time ago. Made me realize how much I missed."

"Tell me about it," Cal answered sarcastically.

He studied the big man who now realized what Cal had been preaching for years. How much they had missed. How much they had given up by being Good Samaritans. When they could have gone back, it was too late. Too much time had passed. It was too late to pick-up the pieces of long frayed relationships. The lives of everyone connected to that memorable night had changed. However, the rage that was felt by Josephine continued to linger, particularly when Cal tried contacting her. After several futile attempts, he finally surrendered and gave her want she wanted: a large final payment and no further communication. Now, the daughters were grown and gone forever. Their youthful memories of a father who loved them would never be remembered. Instead they would be replaced by a dad who abandoned them early in life. He had tried to explain that to Sal so many times. What they lost could never be recaptured. Still, against all odds, Sal did find Gwennie. How was that even possible? Had his partner been given a second chance at having a normal life?

He studied the big man standing on the other side of the bar. For some reason, the picture of King Kong, the gorilla, and skinny Jessica Lange came into his mind. He remembered Guenale Damico as a frail, little girl with a very sassy mouth, when Josephine first introduced them. However, Gwennie was a little more rounded when she met Sal, yet she still retained her signature qualities: small in stature, pleasantly thin and effusively salty in conversation.

"Gwennie said, 'I was still her Blue Whale.'" He brought Cal out of his reverie. "I can't believe she remembered calling me that."

Picturing the whale's massive organ, Cal exploded with laughter. "I want a heads-up, when your ten-foot dick pole vaults the bar," he said. "I'll need to clear the lounge."

"Yeah, yeah, yeah." Sal moved his hand downward to the contents of his fly. "This ten-footer not only hit bottom, it put a happy smile on her face."

"So when do I see Mona Lisa?"

It took Sal less than a second to decipher the meaning of his partner's question.

"You don't, at least not now, but I know she's coming back. I asked her to marry me. We have a son, Cal. His name's Daniel."

Cal froze once again, riveted by the news. "Are you sure? ....How?" None of it made sense. That Sal fathered a child years ago and learned of it just now made him suspicious.

"I'm sure. I reacted the same way you did, after she told me. In fact, her Roman nose was snorting fire when she told me to piss off. She didn't need any help or my money, thank you very much. She's fixed financially."

"I don't get it." Cal expressed doubt.

"She didn't either." Sal laughed. "At least, not until last night. But I did give her a bit of the Blue Whale for breakfast. So, I know she was in a good mood this morning."

"What happened after we left? Did she mention Josephine?"

"She gave me the whole story concerning the pregnancy and how Josephine put the screws to her."

Then Sal detailed the events that occurred after he and Cal left for Youngstown, leaving their loved ones behind, and the tragic years that followed.

"There were a lot of consequences after our departure," Sal began. "If you remember, the night before we left, you and Josephine had an argument that left you fuming. When she threw a glass pitcher at you, and the shards hit Peggy instead, you spent most of the night in the emergency room getting the kid stitches. But, while you were at the hospital, I was banging Gwennie. I didn't have any rubbers with me that night. I remember. I took her twice. But I thought we were safe."

"You dumb shit." Cal's thought slipped from his mouth.

"I know. I know. But I always wanted Gwennie. I intended to marry her after we saved enough money. We figured neither family could stop us, if we could pay our own way. But everything changed when we were forced to leave town and I couldn't find her."

"I know all that," Cal said.

"Yeah, but you didn't know Gwennie had to make her own way. The family kicked her out of the house after they learned she was pregnant. She wouldn't identify me, so there was no forced marriage. Of course, Josephine added her two-cents to stir the fire. She accused you of being the father. Josephine told her parents she suspected you two were having an affair. That's because Gwennie was always at the house. Forget the fact that Josephine was constantly after her to babysit the kids."

"Damn," Cal hissed. "So when Josephine couldn't get to me, to make me suffer even more with losing the girls, she did it through her sister. What a bitch. I'm sorry, Sal. Obviously, Gwennie never did identify you. As far as I know, the family never knew you even existed. I never told Josephine about you and Gwennie."

"I was so pissed when I couldn't find her the night we left. All sorts of things crossed my mind. She knew we were golfing, so she went to play bingo at the church with her mother. Then they stopped for cannoli with her mother's friends. Gwennie told her sister when she missed her period, because they had always been close. Gwennie thought her sister would keep the secret until she could work something out, but Josephine reported the pregnancy to their parents. That's when Josephine told them she suspected you of being the father. That completely severed the sister relationship. Gwennie never thought Josephine would turn on her."

"That explains her rage the night she threw the pitcher at me. I didn't see it coming. Josephine must have thought I had been shagging Gwennie instead of her. What a suspicious bitch. That's why she wouldn't let me say goodbye to the girls. I tried contacting her twice and sent her letters and money," he mused. "And to think I might have stayed in that miserable marriage for the sake of our daughters. I'm glad I paid the settlement she asked for. What a spiteful bitch."

"Now it comes out. After all these years, we've both lost family." Sal complained. "I don't know if I'm madder at Josephine for the misery she caused Gwennie or at Segis for keeping us in exile."

"You're sure, about Daniel being yours?"

"Absolutely. I broke her in." He gave John a knowing look. "Although you never said anything, you knew we were making it together. I'd pick her up after work, go for a drink and then make out. Don't look at me like that. I love the woman. Always have."

"Where is she living now? Is Daniel with her?"

"Gwennie explained that last night," Sal interrupted, wanting to fill the missing gaps after their departure. "Gwennie got help from an older friend who worked with her at Sears. She lived with this woman, Rosemarie, for awhile, and then her great aunt contacted her. Gwennie moved to Albion without telling anybody. Of course, Rosemarie knew, but she was always very secretive. I think the great aunt was somewhat of a free spirit, who was scorned and shunned as the family nut." Sal glanced at Cal and then continued his explanation.

"I can understand the Damico mentality." He referred to Gwennie's Italian family. "They never fully accepted you. You were not Italian or Catholic, but you did marry their knocked-up daughter, Josephine. Great aunt, Ida, on the other hand, was an independent cuss in her own right. She ignored the Italian mentality and did the unforgivable. She fell in love with a Jew and moved in with him. No Italian, no Catholic and no marriage. She had disgraced the family and they wanted no part of her. So there was never communication with any of them. So how did great aunt Ida come to know about Gwennie? Rosemarie tracked her down without telling Gwennie. The woman had heard an accounting of the great aunt's history years earlier. When the great aunt learned what the family had done, she came after Gwennie immediately. She helped Gwennie with the baby and got her a job at a nearby college, where she took courses part-time. Apparently, the woman was very fixed financially. Gwennie inherited her entire estate."

"And Daniel?"

"Spitting image, Cal. He's the picture of me when I was young." His eyes widened. "He's working on his PhD at Carnegie Mellon right now. Daniel knows I abandoned his mother. Gwennie always told him the truth. Now she wants to give him a full accounting of our meeting."

Cal closed his eyes and envisioned his younger daughter. "Daniel and Megan must be close in age. He's younger by two or three years, I would guess."

"I'm sorry." Sal felt uncomfortable dredging up memories of Cal's daughters. "Here I am spewing with hope and…"

"No. Don't feel that way. You can't change the truth. So how did you leave it?" Cal's eyes shifted toward a couple entering the bar.

"She's back in two weeks," Sal shouted as his partner approached the twosome sitting at one of the tables. He watched his partner repeat their drink order and began placing their cocktails on a bar tray.

"Give it a rest." Cal told his lip-reading partner when he returned with an empty bar tray.

"I can't." Sal smiled. "This Blue Whale needs stimulation."

"Maybe Henry will lend you Gladys." Cal eyed him sideways and waved to the incoming waitresses before leaving the bar.

Sal watched his partner exit the place and laughed to himself. The last thing he wanted was "a little gathering of dust" with Gladys. He had just been given a second chance at life with the woman he loved. He was starting over and wanted to spread the news. He checked his cell phone and quickly dialed a number.

"Mom," he said, when the woman answered. "I'd like you to fly up here in two weeks. I'll buy the tickets. I want you to meet the woman I plan to marry and your grandson, Daniel. It's a long story," he added, and then listened to her question. "He looks exactly like me when I was his age. Why?" he asked.

Chapter 4
The Accident

Amherst, New York – Christmas Night

Miles away from Put-in-Bay, a pudgy middle-aged man hadn't been home long enough to enjoy his single malt scotch, when a phone call summoned him to an address in Wellington Woods, a prestigious residential area of town. The only information given him was that a woman had fallen down the stairs of her home and was declared dead.

Although no name was attached to the given address, none was necessary. Ben Burrows, a twenty-five year detective for the tony town of Amherst, New York, knew better. He had been following a related case that went back six months earlier, one that included kidnapping and murder. Alice Beck's fall to her death was no accident. He predicted it would happen. He didn't know the how or the when, but only the fact that it would. Now, the frog-eyed detective had to prove John Beck murdered his wife.

The man was extremely smart. There was no trace of his handiwork anywhere when his first murderous plan failed. His wife had been the real target but Peggy Roberts was abducted by mistake. So John had to find another way to get rid of his wife. But the men he hired for the kidnapping plot had to be eliminated first.

Judd Thorne, the man who actually abducted the wrong woman, was murdered almost immediately by John's front-man, Mel Travers. However, the fatality did not go unnoticed. Seth Stone witnessed the shooting death of his half-brother and reported it to Ben. Yet somehow, Mel Travers managed to disappear and was never found. Now that Alice was dead, the only one that remained standing was the murderer himself, John Beck.

What a helleva way to end Christmas, Ben thought as he slid into his cold car. He was glad the vehicle had four-wheel drive, with all the snow that had accumulated since four o'clock that afternoon. That was the exact time Peggy Roberts arrived with a shopping bag of presents for Clarisa and Poag. Having been to the Clarence motel before, Peggy was familiar with their living quarters behind the office. Ben's sister, Clarisa, greeted her warmly and Poag Fowler, his brother-in law, had prepared a succulent prime rib meal for the five of them. Five. He couldn't forget Seth Stone, his fishing friend, who had planned on staying at the motel overnight. With the hazard driving conditions, Ben suggested Peggy sleep there also. Now he wondered if the two friends had resolved their differences. They had been testy with each other before the Christmas meal and silent during it. And although Clarisa and Poag were completely oblivious of their petty exchange, Ben could sense the chemistry growing between them and knew sooner or later their physical needs would explode.

Ben's mind wandered back six months earlier…when Peggy Roberts was first reported missing and Seth Stone answered his half-brother's terrified cry for help.

Seth had driven to a house in Clarence Center, after his mentally challenged half-brother phoned him. A "job," Judd had taken inadvertently, was actually part of a kidnapping plot, and he had abducted the wrong woman. In a fit of anger over Judd's stupidity, his partner, Mel, flashed Seth a picture of the intended victim, a dark-haired, dark-eyed woman. Blonde, blue-eyed Peggy Roberts did not fit that description.

Then Mel initiated a devious plan to save himself. He threatened to kill Judd, if Seth refused to dispose of Peggy Roberts and return later to report. However, after witnessing Judd's murder accidentally, Seth quickly realized Mel's intentions. The man had devised a perfect plan to leave no witnesses alive. With this in mind Seth quickly escaped with the kidnapped woman.

Seth and Peggy believed someone, other than Mel, had planned the kidnapping and later identified John Beck as the man who wanted his wife killed. That same night, Peggy uncovered an assignation between her husband and Alice Beck at one of the local motels in the area. Infidelity, betrayal and revenge were the motivating factors that set John Beck's murderous plan into motion.

Peggy Roberts had been totally unaware of her cheating husband. John Beck, on the other hand, was aware of everything... except being seen with Mel Travers by Seth and Peggy who reported the man's murderous intentions to Ben.

Still, the detective had no real evidence against him. So the man moved freely toward the next stage of eliminating his wife.

But did it have to be on Christmas night?

Ben's thoughts turned to the investigation as he pulled into the curved driveway of the house and parked beside the coroner's van. Before stepping from his car, he reached inside his glove compartment for a small digital camera and a pair of latex gloves. He stuffed them into his heavy jacket pocket, along with a plastic bag that he pulled from the well of his car door. His years of experience taught him to have these things on hand, just in case he needed them. And some inner voice told him to be prepared when he met John Beck. Ben knew deep-down in his gut, regardless of what the evidence showed, John Beck had murdered his wife. He slid out of the car and onto the hardened snow, a solitary figure walking toward a large showy house. He sidestepped the police car that blocked the house entrance somewhat, passed a lone woman watching the operation and scaled the two steps to the front door and entered.

Ben approached the dead body lying at the bottom of the stairs very carefully. It was important to make a mental assessment of everything he saw. He would put it together later. But for now he had to capture every visual detail, hoping it could lead to more concrete evidence. He studied the scene of the fallen woman with some speculation. He pulled out his camera and took several pictures of what he knew was a crime scene; but for now, it was the scene of an accident. What he needed was evidence and his mind began to encapsulate every detail of the scene before him.

In celebrating the Christmas holiday, the woman had been neatly attired before the fall. Now, she was a lifeless victim, whose long-sleeved red dress lay in rumpled folds, her two arms stretched out and upward, amid a scattering of pearls from a broken multi-strand necklace decorating her throat. A red shoe, broken at the heel, lay nearby the foot of one leg. The natural assumption was that her heel broke during her descent, causing a fall, and subsequently, her death.

Ben wasn't sure of that evaluation. Yet, there was nothing he could say to the coroner. He had no evidence against John Beck, but he knew the man had murdered his wife. He just had to prove it. The detective nodded to the coroner and the aide, who also took pictures, signaling he was done with his part of the examination. They could remove the body and everything connected to the fall. He watched the gloved aide gather the small pearl beads into one evidence bag and the red shoe, into another.

Ben approached a tall dark-haired man who was engaged in a conversation with Danny Boyle, one of the first policemen called to the scene and a monthly poker player at Ben's house. The seasoned policeman had worked cases with him before. He read the detective's nuances well.

After introducing himself, Ben shook John Beck's hand and offered his condolences. As he spoke, Ben kept thinking of the similarity between this man and Jeff Roberts, Peggy's ex husband. They were the same relative height, and both had dark hair and eyes. But perhaps, John Beck was a little older, late thirties maybe. The man was not as handsome as Jeff and somewhat heavier. But there the similarity ended. John Beck was one smart son-of-a-bitch, a lot smarter than Jeff Roberts. He must have been aware of their affair almost immediately. He was, no doubt, fixated by it, and the passing glances between Jeff and Alice had not escaped his notice.

"I know this is a trying time, but I need to know the circumstances surrounding your wife's fall," Ben said.

"I was in the dining room. We were just going to have dessert, when Alice ran upstairs for a gift she forgot to give me. I waited. Then I heard a scream. I couldn't get to her in time." The man's voice was crisp; his words, measured.

"What was it?" The detective questioned.

"What?"

"The gift."

"Oh. A pair of beautiful cufflinks. An old family heirloom complete with a scratches. Alice's family," he added.

"May I see them?" Ben followed John Beck to the dining room table. Dessert plates centered two individual place settings. Above them a cutting knife sat beside a large apple pie. An opened box lay near one place setting. Inside sat two onyx cufflinks, each with a small central diamond.

"They are quite beautiful." Ben agreed with the man's assessment. "But I don't quite understand how they got to the dining room table."

"The box was on the stairs," John Beck explained hurriedly. "I thought it would be dangerous to leave them there. Someone else could trip."

"That may be true, but you removed evidence that could help explain the direction of your wife's fall." Ben chastised the man openly. However, Danny Boyle looked away and remained silent. He knew from past experience, no one interrupted the detective during an investigation. Reaching into his pocket again, Ben took out his camera and snapped several pictures of the entire table. Then he reached into his pocket again for the evidence bag.

Inwardly, Ben was angry. Someone less experienced in law enforcement would think this was the action of a distraught husband. But the detective knew better. John Beck wanted to corrupt any piece of evidence pointing to murder. Nevertheless, Ben remained composed and continued to play the cunning man's game.

"I'll need to take the cufflinks with me," Ben said simply. He took a clean folded handkerchief from his trouser pocket. "Don't worry. These will be returned when I complete my report." Ben noticed a small black smudge on his index finger when the handkerchief encompassed the box, but quickly forgot about it. His thoughts were on the box, which he gingerly placed into the evidence bag and quickly tagged.

"I don't understand." The man strongly objected to their removal. There was no reason for it. His wife had died of an accident.

"It's standard procedure. By law, we have to look at everything involved in your wife's accident. Right now, I need to check the stairs. Where did you find the box? Which step?"

The detective trailed John Beck up the stairs to the fourth step from the top of the landing. The man stopped suddenly. A frown crossed his face. "Now I'm not sure where I found them. It could have been the third step or maybe the fifth."

"Was the box intact or opened and scattered?"

"The lid was on a different step, at least I think it was."

The detective retraced his steps down the staircase and up again, checking the wall and each step carefully as he climbed. At the top of the stairs, the seam binding between the stairs and hall carpet was loose and baggy.

"Where does this go?" Ben pointed left.

"My office," he said, obviously annoyed with the detective and trailing policeman for lingering too long.

Ben noticed a black smudge on the office door frame then thought of his index finger. After taking several pictures of the door frame and stairway, he turned around and walked down the hall, followed by both men.

"This must be the bedroom area." He continued to lead.

"Our bedroom's straight ahead. What are you looking for?"

"Shoes."

The detective entered a large bedroom decorated totally in white. The only contrasts, those blatantly obvious, were the black handles of the dresser drawers and the assorted black pillows thrown carelessly on the large king-size bed and corner divan. Every piece of bedroom furniture rested on an expensive wall-to-wall white plush carpet.

He scanned the room quietly before opening a closet door. A colorful array of women's shoes sat neatly arranged on a two-tiered rack. Some appeared more casual than others. Ben focused on three pairs of high-heeled shoes, similar to the ones Alice Beck wore when she fell. He took the pair of latex gloves stuffed inside his jacket pocket and quickly slipped his hands into them. Taking one pair of high-heeled shoes in hand, he walked down the hall to the top of the stairs and slipped one of the shoes along the loose binding. The caught heel caused an untoward downward motion. That alone could account for the woman's loss of balance and thereby, precipitating her fall. Upon removing the shoe from the binding, Ben noticed a darker and more noticeable smudge on his index finger, but said nothing.

"How long has the binding been loose?" Ben addressed the dead woman's husband.

"A few weeks," he replied. "Alice contacted the builder two weeks ago."

"Why wasn't it fixed?"

"The men were coming after the holidays. Alice agreed to their schedule. It's on the calendar in the kitchen."

The detective retraced his steps to the bedroom, still holding the pair of shoes. "I need a bag for these and those." He pointed to the other high-heeled shoes resting on the two-tiered rack. Ben watched the man's expression. Something wasn't right. He could feel it. "That is, if you don't mind."

The man opened the bathroom vanity for a box of waste basket liners and watched the detective drop three pairs of high-heeled shoes into one of them.

"All I need now is the phone number of your builder and we're finished," Ben said. "I want to thank you for your co-operation. I know this is not easy for you."

"I just can't believe she's gone," the husband said sadly. "We just moved into the house Alice always wanted." He pulled the builder's card from his wallet. "I have another one in my office."

The three men crossed the loose carpet seam carefully and descended the stairs in single file. After saying goodbye to the grief-stricken husband, the two men, one empty-handed and the other, holding bags with shoes and cufflinks, approached the detective's parked car. The coroner's van had long since disappeared.

Using the remote, Ben unlocked his car and placed both bags on the back seat. Their eyes met briefly.

"Helleva way to spend Christmas," Danny hissed.

"Particularly for her. She's dead."

"You aren't buying." The young policeman understood.

"Not the shit he's selling."

"Thing is. He's cocky smart."

"You got that right, Boyle. You certainly got that right."

Ben backed out of the driveway and headed toward the police station. It was going to be a long night. Proving this was murder would be tough, if not impossible. John Beck was so convincing with his attitude of pretended care: a real mask for a cunning man.

Chapter 5
Motel Guests

Streaks of dawn filtered into the motel room through an opening between the drapery panels. It was that in-between hour, when night fades slowly over the horizon and gives way to the increasing light that heralds the coming of dawn.

Peggy Roberts and Seth Stone were fast asleep during that gray-like hour, and the only reverberating noise came from Gabriel, Seth's large German shepherd, whose intermittent snores pierced the slumbering silence, as he lay curled in the corner of the room.

When Peggy shifted to a new and more comfortable position, she inadvertently rolled into Seth who was awakened suddenly by her movement. He extended his arms immediately and pulled her to him. Brushing her lips lightly, his eyes scrutinized the facial silhouette studying him in the dim morning light.

"Hi," he whispered. "Sleep well?"

"Hmm," Peggy responded, curling in closer to the man who had rescued her from a kidnapping and been supportive when her marriage fell apart. But all that happened months ago, and the detective, still working the abduction case, needed more evidence to arrest the man who planned it.

Her world seemed different now. She and Seth had made love the previous night, their first time together, and those physical emotions, ones so deeply hidden within her, seemed to have fully emerged with his caring tenderness. She tilted her face toward him and finding his mouth, edged her tongue along his lips. She could feel his readiness as she pressed against him, and the sudden want of the man surged through her body demanding release.

Peggy parted her lips slightly, inviting entry and signaled her need by opening herself to him. Seth inched his hand slowly down the curves of her body and, feeling her readiness, plunged deep inside her. He listened to her soft gasps with each undulating motion and increased the speed of their rhythm.

Peggy began moaning when a series of prickles flooded her entire body and sent signals to her brain. She knew with exact certainty that her moment had come.

"Seth," she moaned: her mouth, parched; her message, clear.

They clung together as one, never wanting to let go of the moment: that euphoric moment of heightened pleasure, before the ebbing begins.

A few minutes later, Seth kissed her gently and half-smiling whispered, "Feel better now that you're nourished?"

"For now, but I have a very healthy appetite."

"Then you're in for a great buffet." He moved away from her and sat on the side of the bed. He knew Gabriel was waiting by the motel door for his early morning release and walked over to let him out. As soon as Gabriel leaped outside, Seth slipped back into bed.

"Are you still sleepy?"

"Not really, but I don't want to get up just yet."

Seth pulled up the bedcovers as they cuddled facing each other.

"Are you sorry?" Peggy asked. "I mean about last night and now?"

"Why would I be? We can't deny our feelings or the chemistry between us. Why do you ask?" He studied the silhouette of her face.

Although she agreed with his statement, Peggy wondered where the relationship was headed. She had to know his real interest in her.

"We're good together, Seth, but I need to know about Helen. Do you still love her?"

"I will always have feelings for Helen," he said wistfully. "But she's gone. It took years to accept the fact that she was never coming back. Since I didn't want to suffer that kind of pain again, I never looked for another relationship. But we had issues that precluded any legal union."

The statement left her confused. "I thought you were planning to be married. That was my assumption when I spoke to Ben about you."

"Then it was a wrong assumption. Yes, Helen and I loved each other, but we never planned to marry. Poag and Clarisa probably thought we would and waited for an announcement. But it never came."

"I don't understand. If you loved each other, why not marry? That makes no sense."

"Is that what happened with you and Jeff?" His tone changed abruptly. "You went together, fell in love, and then married. So where is the happily ever after? Where did the relationship go sour initially, before he started cheating? And why does your sister hate him so much?"

His words had a stinging effect on her. "Why are you saying these things? Have I offended you in some way?" She raised her body to a sitting position against the headboard of the bed. "I would never have asked about Helen, if I knew it would upset you."

"You have no idea what I mean." He ignored her comment. "What do you really know about a person without exploring his thinking and sexuality?"

Peggy glared at him and wondered what the hell he was talking about. Was he going to translate his thoughts into something she could understand or just leave her hanging in mid-air? Peggy felt like she was back in philosophy 101 in college. Those professors never made any sense to her. They seemed to have had their own form of communication: a language no one else understood and they wanted to keep it that way. That she should explore Jeff's mind and body, before marrying him, almost brought a smile to her face. She pictured a machine with all sorts of cords attached to Jeff's head, ones similar to those used in a Frankenstein movie, while she asked him a barrage of questions. Life in a dystopian world: a match by machine... perfect.

"I don't like your idea," Peggy said. "I'd rather take my chances on loving someone I think I know, without some scientific formula."

"What the hell are you talking about?"

"You!" she hissed. "You seem to be insisting on some kind of mind exploration…"

Seth exploded with laughter. "I have no idea what planet you're on." He opened the door for Gabriel and watched him trot to a corner of the room to thaw out from the freezing snow. Then he sat on the edge of the bed and faced her.

Peggy ignored the comment and demanded an explanation. "I want to know what you mean and how it relates to Helen. It started with your marriage or the lack of it."

"It's very simple. People just don't communicate with each other. If couples did, there would be fewer problems in their marriage. Most often, they marry and establish a routine, day in and day out. It becomes mechanical. When kids come, they're simply incorporated into the lives of a programmed family. Where is the conversational flow, the necessary exchange of ideas, or the sexual excitement of two bodies merging into one? Or has the latter also become routine? In the beginning a person can be too much in love to realize the error of the relationship. It might start with a strong physical attraction, then ebb and die, because there was never any real communication between them initially. Think of living with someone who provided great sex but had nothing but air between his ears."

She found his explanation unbelievable. "Communication is one thing, but you can't expect some sort of excitement every day of your life. Setting the bar too high can be problematic and a very lonely place."

"So a person should just settle for marriage, because another offer may not come her way? Is that what you're saying? Is that what you did? Settle for Jeff?"

"No!" Peggy objected. "I loved him. He was everything I could have ever wanted in a husband. Yes, he broke my heart, but no matter how many conversations we could have had, I would not have known him any better. I could never have determined he would betray our marriage with other women or have a vasectomy."

"And how did that dysfunctional relationship leave you? Did that make you more fearful of getting into another one?" The silence was almost deafening as he waited for an answer. Her response would be a defining moment for both of them. It would give a sense of direction, if they were to continue their relationship.

Peggy paused momentarily, her eyes never wavering from the dark-haired man staring back at her. They had been apart for months, yet Seth filled her thoughts daily. Still, the thought of being attached again frightened her. Peggy was afraid to admit the truth, even to herself, in the weakest of moments, when the sight of him left her limp. Peggy knew deep within her being that she was in love with this man, yet she was fearful of entering another relationship. She was afraid that someone else would break her heart. "Yes, it did." She acknowledged his question.

"You just established the whole point of this conversation." Then Seth caught her puzzled expression. "Think about it this way. Wouldn't it be wonderful to love someone unconditionally, knowing you are on the same page: mentally, emotionally and sexually. Betrayal or guile would never enter into the equation."

"If that's what you had with Helen, why didn't you marry?"

"I never said I had this with her. I thought I clarified that point earlier. There were several shortcomings in our relationship and neither was willing to compromise. That she was much older than I was a big stumbling block for her. She refused to have marriage on the table. Of course, I was more concerned with issues like dominance, insecurity and the physical side of our relationship."

"How much older?" Peggy questioned, somewhat shocked by the revelation. His loving an older woman was something she had not expected.

"It doesn't matter now, she's dead." He refused to be specific.

"Was she a demanding person?" Peggy remembered his first objection.

"Not in the broad sense. But my traveling bothered her. Helen wanted me to stay in town more often and for longer periods of time. That, of course, was impossible. I had to become established as an artist and make my work known. She may have felt insecure about our relationship, but I never gave her cause. That annoyed me. However, I found the woman magnificent intellectually. She had a brilliant mind.

Her qualities, her beauty and generous nature overshadowed any of the shortcomings that I mentioned. In the big picture of life, she was the woman I wanted in mine."

Peggy listened closely to his running commentary. He never fully touched on the third aspect that troubled him: their physical relationship. Since there was no euphemistic way of approaching that issue, Peggy went in another direction.

"If these things bothered you so much, how could you have fallen in love with her?"

"Shortcomings are a part of everyone's humanity," he replied quickly, making it a cogent point. Seth wanted her to understand the broad brush of loving someone. "You diminish those shortcomings when other qualities, ones much more admirable, overshadow them. Aside from being trustworthy and beautiful, she was the most stimulating woman I had ever known. Helen read everything imaginable, but more important, she digested it and offered very intelligent opinions, whether they be political, social or religious. She was an amazing human being. I have never met anyone her equal and I don't suppose I ever will."

His comments made Peggy feel insignificant. She had always thought of herself as being a reasonably smart woman, not a mental giant perhaps, but not intellectually deficient either. But in this particular arena, she was out of her element. Seth had remarkable intellect, was very articulate and obviously needed Mensa type people around him for stimulation. Peggy did not fit that category, so it was best to end their relationship now, before it started. She turned her face away, hiding the tear that trickled down her face, but Seth pulled her back to face him.

"Don't turn away from me, Peggy. Why are you crying? If I said something to hurt you, I'm sorry." He cradled her body, combing her long blonde hair with his fingers. "We've been through so much together. I don't ever want to hurt you. Now tell me what's wrong? We could always talk to each other."

"I don't fit in, Seth. I'm not smart like Helen."

"Neither am I," he said. "I don't read every piece of written material that comes my way."

"What if I don't satisfy you?" she asked, thinking of the third shortcoming mentioned. From his reaction, Peggy knew she had struck a nerve.

"I want a complete kind of love, Margaret." Upon hearing her proper name, Peggy knew he was addressing an issue of consequence...something that could ultimately affect their relationship. She sensed his careful choice of words. "I lacked that with Helen." He paused for a moment, trying to find the right words to convey his meaning. "How can I phrase it? She was not adventurous... and although we loved each other, we understood that particular divide."

Then he explained another matter that made no sense to him. "I could never understand why I had to stay in town, when we wouldn't see each other for weeks. There was no physical contact, not even a quick lunch together. We'd talk on the phone, but that was the extent of it. There was never a concern for my loneliness or unwanted celibacy. That's how wrapped-up she was with her literary group." He fell silent again, then said, "Intellectual mind-speak is not what I want in life. It may be stimulating to one's thoughts, but it is cold comfort to a body in need of warmth and stimulation. Now, you know why I chose to be alone."

"Do you have feelings for me, Seth?" Her unexpected question surprised him.

"You already know the answer to that question. Why do you ask?"

"Did you ever want me, the way I want you?"

"You must have had some inkling the night Jeff betrayed you with Alice. When you cried in my arms, I wanted you so badly, my body ached; but taking you then, when you were so vulnerable, would have ruined our relationship. Can you understand that?"

"But we're beyond that now. If we were compatible...if I satisfied you...on certain issues, would you be faithful to me?"

"What you are saying?" Being faithful was never a consideration. What he wanted was deep mutual love that fulfilled the wants and needs of both parties. He wanted total love.

"I think you know."

Peggy had already deciphered the negative aspect of his relationship with Helen, the one that was paramount. For an intelligent woman who continually sat on an intellectual perch, Helen had to be stupid when it came to the stark realities of life. The man needed the love of an intelligent woman who could satisfy his physical demands…all of them.

"We're good together, Seth. Your traveling presents no problem to me. I have a gift shop to run. As for a more adventurous kind of love, I think the woman in me can certainly provide that." She studied his expression as the light inching between the draperies fell across his face.

"Are you sure you fully understand my meaning?" A major commitment was in the making and he wanted to give her a second chance to change her mind.

"I understand your needs." She drew him to her slowly, their prone bodies facing each other. "I want you in my life, Seth, and I want to be the only woman in yours. Nothing else matters." As her hand began trolling down the smooth hairline center of his body, she listened to his uneven breathing, so eager with the anticipation of her touch and being joined again.

"You are going to be a very, loved woman," Seth whispered afterward, looking down into her beautiful face. "I want you to stay with me tonight." He kissed her gently and moved his body slowly away from hers. "Take your shower, now. We're having breakfast with Clarisa and Poag."

Seth watched the naked woman walk toward the bathroom. Peggy's breasts sat high on a slim curvaceous frame that held a tiny waist and flat abdomen. Seeing her naked body fully for the first time sent shivers through his body in expectation of their second night together.

While the tall and handsome Seth was taking inventory of her body, Peggy was hatching a plan of her very own. If the muscular dark-eyed man wanted an adventurous romp, she would make it memorable.

Chapter 6
Breakfast

Seth and Peggy knocked on the motel office door and walked in unannounced, knowing they were expected that morning for breakfast.

"He's going with the grits again." Clarisa Fowler greeted them, referring to her husband, Poag, who was firing-up all four stove burners. Pouring each of them a cup of coffee at the kitchen table, the dark-haired woman continued her rant. "You're also getting bacon, sausage and eggs in a hole. Now tell me how you handle cholesterol and heart problems with that kind of breakfast? That's what I'm going to be faced with. His diet never seems to change."

"Quit your bitchin, girl, and take me to room five. I'll show you how healthy I am." Her smiling husband shot back.

"Yeah, yeah, yeah," his toothy wife moaned. "One Jacuzzi splash and you're off to sleep."

"And this from the woman who humped me last night," Poag laughingly interrupted..

The man, who was cooking breakfast had a weather-beaten face, and was somewhere in his fifties. Tall, thin, and gray, Poag was always ready with some verbal quip, humorous or sarcastic. Together, he and his large breasted wife, Clarisa, enjoyed playing the seduction game. Clarisa would pretend to be married to someone else, while he tried convincing her of his prowess by inviting her to room five, the one with a Jacuzzi and king-size bed. This, of course, was the same room that hosted Seth and Peggy's two morning romps and one the previous night.

"Oh, hush," Clarisa hissed. "That's more than they want to know."

"All four of us shared some sort of Christmas nectar last night, so who are we kidding?" Poag brought his angular-shaped wife up short.

"Poor, Ben." Clarisa changed the subject as she watched Poag set platters of food on the table. "I talked with him this morning. He was called out on a case involving you and Peggy." Her dark eyes fixed on Seth. "Remember John Beck, the man behind Peggy's kidnapping and essentially Judd's murder? Yes, I know Mel killed your half-brother, but it was John Beck who planned the whole thing."

"Pass the food, Clarisa," Poag instructed, totally disinterested in re-hashing the long drawn-out phone conversation with her detective brother again.

"Clarisa scrunched her face at Poag, passed every food platter, and then, continued her accounting. "Well, after Ben left here last night, he was called to the scene of an accident. It was none other than John Beck's house. His wife, Alice, had fallen down the steps of her new home. When Ben found her body at the bottom of the stairs, she was dead."

"Oh, my God, Seth!" Peggy panicked. "You were right, all along. You said, 'He'd think of another way to get rid of her.' If Mel's involved, you could be at risk. He showed you her picture and might think you can make a connection. Fortunately, he didn't see you at the window when he shot Judd."

After listening to Peggy's outburst, Seth moved his attention from her to Clarisa. "Did Ben find any evidence of murder?"

"Nobody knows right now." Poag answered Seth's question. "You know how methodical Ben is. He won't divulge anything until he can wrap it up. Right now, I think he's fishing. I just hope he's using the right lure."

Seth caught Poag's meaning instantly. "Knowing Ben, he'll make the right call when he has enough evidence to make the arrest stick."

"Speaking of calls, Megan phoned this morning." Clarisa turned her attention to Peggy. "She called your home first and then your cell. She was worried that something happened again. Then, she remembered you were spending Christmas with us. I told her we insisted you stay the night because driving was too dangerous. She wants you to call her."

"That wasn't the only call," Poag addressed Seth. "Barthalemew's partner phoned. You must have told him you'd be here. Anyhow, his restaurant's open today and he's expecting you for dinner. He just wants confirmation."

"I must have turned off my cell phone," Seth explained.

"We both did," Peggy added. "It was a long day."

"But a better night," Poag said, winking across the table at Peggy. "Make your calls. I'll get more coffee."

Peggy disappeared into the living room, unaware that Seth was following her. He pulled her to him and kissed her. "Tell Megan we're stopping by around noon and not to fuss. If she wants to feed me a sandwich, I like prosciutto. But tell her no big meal. I am taking you to dinner, so I don't want a big lunch. Insist on it. Make her understand." Without further instructions, Seth left her for the more private motel office.

When Seth returned to the kitchen without Peggy, Poag grabbed his arm and spoke softly. "It's alright, Seth. Helen would have wanted you to find someone," Poag said, referring to his dead sister. "She's been gone over five years now. That's too much time to spend alone. You're still young. You have a life ahead of you." Clarisa listened quietly to her husband's words and nodded in agreement.

Although he met Poag's stare, Seth remained silent. He offered nothing. Poag interpreted the silence to mean his friend was still mourning the loss of his sister and sleeping with Peggy meant nothing more than a sexual release. "Whatever happens, just know I understand." Poag wanted Seth to be aware of his support.

There was nothing Seth could say. How could he respond? Yes, he took the woman and manipulated every inch of her body. And he enjoyed doing it. But, would he go further with her? Would all his wants be satisfied? That had to be determined. He would not settle for less. Not anymore. How could he tell the dead woman's brother, that his sister hadn't met his expectations? True, he loved Helen deeply. But he wanted more in a relationship now. He ached for more understanding of his needs. His celibate days were over. He wanted all of his appetites satisfied.

"It's ok." Poag interrupted his thoughts. Seth had been his steadfast friend for at least eight years. In fact, they had been friends long before Seth met Helen. When she dropped by unexpectedly, they seemed to click immediately and started dating. Clarisa and Poag thought they would marry eventually, but the hit and run driver ended any dreams they may have had. Now with all the years that had passed, Seth was still alone.

"We'll see," Seth said. "I'm in no hurry." His eyes swept past his middle-aged friends to an open doorway.

"No hurry for what?" Peggy entered the room.

"More food," Seth answered. "I'm stuffed and we have a dinner reservation for five-thirty."

"Are you really taking me to dinner?" She caught Seth's nod. "I'd like that." She was pleased Seth wanted to be with her. Peggy refilled her coffee cup and continued to stare at Seth. "Megan will be home all day. She's so excited we're visiting them. Knowing my sister, she'll probably call every hour until we're there."

Without any warning, Gabriel walked up to Seth and stared at his master. Knowing his wishes, Seth crossed the kitchen and opened the back door. Gabriel raced outside and was quickly joined by Poag's dog, Reese. The two German shepherds raced around in the snow and stopped occasionally to irrigate the trees surrounding the property.

"I fed them," Clarisa said. "They ate everything."

Seth understood Clarisa's cryptic remark to mean their meal included more than dog food. He wondered if their meal contained prime rib or apple pie. In either case the dogs certainly enjoyed a Christmas left-over breakfast.

When Poag rose to clear the table, Peggy jumped from her chair to help him.

"No." Poag insisted. "It would be better if you cleared the motel rooms, in case they're needed."

"Right." Peggy agreed. "I wasn't thinking."

Within minutes, Seth and Peggy shrugged into their outer clothes and headed for their respective rooms. Seth went to room three for his suitcase and shaving bag which he quickly used and left the room immaculately clean. Peggy, on the other hand, folded the used wet towels and set them on the counter. She set an opened cake of soap on top of them, along with the small empty bottle of shampoo. Then crossing the bedroom, Peggy stripped the bed and folded the blanket, spread, and used sheets. She placed the blanket and spread into one pile and the used sheets into another. She was taking inventory of her effort when Seth knocked on the door and entered the room. He took a quick check of the bathroom and complimented her.

"I just might hire you." He placed five twenties on the desk, took her arm and locked the motel door. "We have to return your key and say goodbye to Clarisa and Poag. Then, I'm following you to your house."

"Why? I don't understand." Peggy was truly puzzled.

"It will become clearer as the day progresses." His hand inched up her skirt.

"Oh." The exclamation may have escaped her lips, but her mind was on *clarifying* his plans for later.

Having said their goodbyes to Poag and Clarisa, they entered their respective cars and journeyed toward Amherst. It was not long before Peggy was able to realize Seth plans for later. It was a time of surprises…all the way around.

Chapter 7
The Visit

Seth followed Peggy to her Amherst home and parked his car on the driveway beside hers, leaving Gabriel stretched out on the back seat. He followed her inside the two-story home and watched her take a cursory inventory of the first floor.

"Everything, ok?" Seth broke the silence, causing her to smile.

"So far," she answered, turning toward the staircase leading to the second floor bedrooms. "Are we really going to be together tonight?" Peggy asked, still unsure of their plans as she took the stairs, knowing Seth was trailing behind her.

He sat on an easy chair in Peggy's bedroom and watched her study him. "Casual dress?" She caught his nod. Without a further thought, Peggy sailed into her walk-in closet and, pulling-out a hanger holding a black dress, checked a small jewelry box for two gold necklaces which she used to accessorize the outfit. "What do you think?" She watched his reaction.

"It's perfect," he said, a feeling of pride sweeping through him. "You'll also need something for work, unless I can talk you into a day of bed rest."

"Dream on, sweet prince. I have to open tomorrow. But I'm available later." Her blue eyes sparkled with meaning. "What is that?" She pointed to a slit of paper protruding from the drawer of a tall chest. "That was Jeff's." She crossed the room and pulled open the drawer. The paper seemed sandwiched between the drawer bottom and the wood underneath. "What the...?" She identified a postcard and turned it over.

"What is it?" Seth took the postcard from her.

"Niagara on the Lake. Now I know why he was so concerned about Alice's mail being delivered here, and why he questioned me the night of our anniversary party. I guess it was one of their rendez-vous signals." She took the card back from him, tore it to pieces and tossed it in the wastebasket. "It doesn't matter anymore."

In less than an hour, Seth watched the woman pack a suitcase with clothing, accessories and sundries, totally confident that nothing had been overlooked. Finally, Peggy took a ledger that sat on the front hall table and slipped it into one of the suitcase pockets.

"Where am I going?" She rolled her suitcase to the front door. "Should I take my car?"

"You'll need it for work tomorrow unless I can change your mind," he said wickedly. "Follow me to North Forest Road. We'll leave the car at my uncle's house on our way to Megan's."

"Blarney Stone? The house you inherited?" Suddenly, Peggy realized her error. She had spoken too quickly. "Clarisa told me...at Judd's memorial," she faltered.

"It was the name of his restaurant. Clarisa and Poag call it Blarney Stone two, or just Two for clarification. You can call it Blarney Stone. I live there part-time. The third floor is so much bigger and lighter than my house in Lockport. It has a lot of windows. It's really perfect for me. I've always loved the old rambling place: the massive furniture, the heirlooms, and in particular, the big king-size bed." After the brief explanation, he walked Peggy to her car and stowed her suitcase in the trunk.

***

Within the hour, Seth and Peggy had parked their cars at the North Forest address and refreshed themselves inside the old brick house. Then much to Peggy's surprise, Seth entered one of the garages and unveiled another car which he drove to Brad Croft's home on Los Robles.

"Who owns the BMW?" Megan rushed out to greet them. "It's a beauty."

"It was a garage surprise of Seth's," Peggy explained. "He only uses it when Gabriel's not with him." She caught her sister's puzzled look. "His dog." Peggy reminded her. "Seth brought him to the shop last October." From Megan's renewed expression, the reminder jogged her memory.

"What a beautiful car." Brad Croft said, after introducing himself to Seth. "Come inside, Megan made lunch."

As they gathered around the table filled with food platters, Megan began scolding her sister for not answering her mother-in-law's party invitation.

"I have no idea what you're talking about." Peggy rolled her eyes. "Maybe you misunderstood. I have never been invited to any of her parties."

"Misunderstood. Fat chance!" Megan bristled and continued her petulant discourse. "You've been invited to Barbara's annual New Year's Day party. She sent you an invitation but you never answered it."

"That's because I didn't get it," Peggy snapped back.

"Maybe you threw it away with your Christmas cards." Megan continued to be annoyed.

"No. My cards are still on the family room mantle. I had problems with the post office months ago, but those issues have long been resolved. So I don't know what happened to Barbara's invitation."

"Why worry about it, now?" Brad refereed the two angry sisters. "Peggy can phone mother with her answer later. I really don't foresee a problem."

"You are coming, aren't you?" Megan capitalized on Brad's comments. "Ben will be there and you can take Seth as your date. Barbara will be so excited, if you tell her you're bringing Seth. She's always been a patron of the arts."

Seth remained silent throughout their whole conversation, observing each participant, although, he focused, most often, on Brad Croft. However, he was taken by the striking resemblance between the two sisters at first. Both had shoulder-length blonde hair and sparking blue eyes, reminiscent of sapphires, but there the similarities ended. Megan was shorter, somewhat thinner, and had high cheekbones. Seth remembered their meeting in October. Even then, she seemed more comparatively extroverted, almost to the point of being volatile at times with her outrageous opinions. Her sister, Peggy, was entirely different. Having spent time with her, in their search for answers after the kidnapping, he knew Peggy to be more inward emotionally and much more even-tempered than Megan, although she, too, had her moments of rage. His thoughts went back to the night at the motel, when Peggy caught her husband with Alice Beck and banged on their door with the pizza delivery routine. He laughed inwardly at the thought.

The tall hazel-eyed Brad Croft intrigued him completely. The man had to be somewhere in his early thirties. His dark-brown hair with its auburn highlights bordered a fair-complexioned face of high cheekbones and a full mouth. When the man smiled, he could have been the poster boy for every dentist in the United States. Brad Croft had very white teeth and a seemingly perfect bite. By every count, he was quite handsome, and although unknown to Seth personally, Brad Croft seemed like an even-tempered man with an engaging personality.

"Well, Peggy, what do you think?" Megan's question brought Seth's thoughts back to their conversation. "I know you're available. I'd rather see you come to the party than stay home, twiddling your thumbs."

"I don't know." A puzzled Peggy turned to Seth.

"Hey," Megan interrupted, staring at the couple. "Is something going on between the two of you, something we don't know about?"

"Megan, you just told me to invite Seth!" Peggy hissed. She felt embarrassed with Seth sitting there, watching her and listening to their fiery conversation. Then continuing her position on the subject, added, "I have no idea what his plans are for the holiday. I can't pre-sume anything. You're not being fair to either of us, and you're making me feel very uncomfortable about an invitation I did not receive."

"Your sister's right. We should not interfere." Brad was the perfect arbitrator. His wife had put her sister in a very uncomfortable position. Perhaps the woman wanted to go to the party with someone else, or maybe, not at all. Of course, there was always the possibility that Peggy had not received the invitation.

"Of course, you're right." Megan agreed with her husband's assessment. Then, in her own unique way of rushing things, she addressed her sister again. "Peggy, I'd like you to come to the New Year's Day party at Barbara and Franklin's house. If you decide to come, would you please ask Seth to come as your date, if he's available?"

Seth started to snicker. He found Megan's manner of solving the New Year's Day issue hilarious. The sister would not take indecision or a firm no, for any kind of answer.

"Peggy." Seth took control. "I would gladly consider being your escort to the New Year's party, if you would reciprocate by being my date for an affair my uncle's partner is hosting. You will meet him later…at dinner."

Megan clapped her hands. "Yes! Yes! I am so happy. Let's call Barbara right now."

Peggy spoke with Barbara Croft briefly to explain the postal issue regarding the invitation, and then, after accepting her kind offer, told the woman she was bringing Seth Stone as her date. Although Barbara Croft was very polite on the phone, her voice turned cold with Peggy's acceptance. For some reason, the whole tenor of the conversation made Peggy feel uneasy. Had she made the right decision by accepting the invitation? Perhaps, the woman was angry because Peggy was late in answering it. She knew Barbara was very strict with rules of etiquette. Still, it left her wondering if it was propriety that bothered Barbara, or Peggy, in general. She had real misgivings about accepting the invitation.

"You look like someone whose hand got caught in the cookie jar," Megan scolded. "What's wrong?"

"Barbara sounded strange when I accepted the invitation."

"Don't let that throw you." Brad reassured her. "She always gets crazy this time of year. Mother's up to her hip-boots planning the party and she is driving the help nuts. We try not to go there before New Years, if possible."

"Brad's right, Barbara's a nut case before the affair. Everything has to be perfect. Why am I telling you this? You were with us at Thanksgiving. Granted, Barbara enjoyed herself, probably for the first time in a long while, but you saw her checking the table settings, the food and everything that went with it."

"That's a bit harsh," Seth offered. "I heard she was ecstatic with her praise for you. In fact, I was given to believe that your Thanksgiving dinner was their best holiday outing ever."

"Really." Megan blushed. "Who told you that?" Then, she stiffened. "It was Peggy."

"No, Megan. This came from Ben. And you know he's not one to make-up things. Apparently, he was talking to your father-in-law."

"See. I told you." Brad reaffirmed the position he long held. "I knew they enjoyed themselves. My parents would never tell Junior or Rosalie our Thanksgiving was better than theirs. They couldn't. If they did, there would be hell to pay. Rosalie can be a real bitch."

"Interesting family," Seth mused.

"As long as I know their true feelings, I don't care if they never say anything," Megan answered, her face glowing. "I'm really glad you told us, Seth."

"It's always good to feel appreciated. It's even better when it's acknowledged. So I thought I'd pass it on. Ben enjoyed the holiday as well. But you already knew that." Then Seth asked Megan directly. "Can you tell me why you disliked Jeff Roberts so much?"

"What?" Megan didn't know what to say. His question came as a surprise.

"I don't want to make the same mistake," Seth replied simply. "I am taking your sister to the New Year's party, remember?"

"Escorting Peggy to the party should be no problem. I don't know why I distrusted Jeff. There was just something about him that wasn't right. I felt it from the very beginning. Maybe it was the tomatoes." She laughed at the thought.

"What are you talking about?" Peggy groused.

"The tomatoes. He knocked the bag out of my hand, remember?" She turned to Peggy. "They squashed all over the dirty floor in

Pennsylvania Macaroni at the Strip in Pittsburgh. Jeff sent me to get a new bag, but he never paid for it."

Seth began to chuckle. He knew exactly where Megan was coming from. Skinning it to the bone, her philosophy was simple: if you say you're going to do something, mean it; otherwise, take your bullshit somewhere else. "I'll have to remember that."

Megan knew Seth understood her meaning. She only hoped her sister would be smart enough to appreciate him. He was a keeper.

Seth checked his watch and turned to Peggy, indicating that it was time to leave. Seth thanked Megan and Brad for lunch, as they walked them to their car. Megan embraced her sister, and kissing her cheek, whispered, "You are one dumb ass, if you don't nail him."

They watched the car pull out of the driveway and disappear down the street.

"What do you think?" Megan spoke first. "He seems like a nice guy,"

"Yeah, I wish she would have married him." Brad was quick to respond. Megan nodded and agreed with his assessment.

***

"You didn't tell them it was my uncle's car." Although his face showed no expression as he drove, there was a hint of surprise in his voice. "Why?"

"That's not my place, nor my business, Seth. Or anyone else's for that matter. What you want told is your prerogative, not mine."

"I like that. I like the way you think. However, you may find it more difficult to be silent on other matters as well. But then, you will come to understand why I feel it necessary."

Peggy was extremely reluctant to question him further. She felt a foreboding, almost a warning, to be cautious about saying anything related to Seth's personal life. It was almost like seeing another facet of him, a man she thought she knew. A chill ran through her. Was she stepping into another relationship, one much more dangerous than infidelity? It couldn't be. This man saved her…but for what?

"Where are we headed?" She watched him turn into the intersection on Main Street. "If we pass a supermarket or drugstore, I would like to stop."

She watched him pull into the parking lot of a large supermarket. "Do you want me to come in with you?"

Peggy shook her head. His company was the last thing she wanted. "I won't be long." She rushed out of the car and into the store.

"Like I haven't heard that before," Seth said to himself, as he watched her step inside the building. It wasn't surprising that she wanted to stop. No doubt, it had something to do with the dinner invitation. She wanted to make a good impression on his dead uncle's partner, the one who was now the sole owner.

"Okay, we are good to go." Peggy placed a small bag inside her purse.

"Do I get to know what you bought?" Seth drove up North Forest Road.

"Eventually," Peggy said. "But first, I think you should tell me what we are doing now."

"We are going home to get ready for dinner, young lady. No funny stuff. So don't try to seduce me. I have a very low threshold when it comes to you."

"You're no fun." Peggy scolded laughingly. "Do I get a promise for tonight, or do I sleep on the couch?"

"I'll have to think about it." He parked beside the rambling brick house, took Peggy's hand and greeted Gabriel inside.

***

On Peggy's first visit to red-brick Blarney Stone, it was merely to freshen up in the first-floor lavatory. Now, while Seth was outside with Gabriel, Peggy decided on a brief tour of the uncle's house to get a feel of the family stronghold.

Most impressive of all were the room sizes. She took a cursory look at the huge living room with its massive leather furniture, and then went on to view the library, where hundreds of books lined the shelves along one side of the room, while the family portraits, so neatly hung, guarded those rare treasures from a wall directly opposite them. She inspected the large dining room with its rectangular table nesting eight chairs and a huge china closet that faced a server on the opposite side of the room. Finally, Peggy found her way to the kitchen, which to her, was a culinary dream.

"C'mon, young lady." Seth appeared in the doorway with Gabriel trailing him. He took her hand and leading her to the front hall, grabbed the suitcases, along with his toiletry bag, and took her upstairs to the master bedroom.

"Oh, my God," she gasped. A huge four-poster king-size bed, framed by two night stands and a large ceiling mirror overhead, centered one entire wall of the bedroom. A chaise lounge and foot stool sat idly by a picture window, while a long dresser of nine drawers, three in each set, and two chests, each with four drawers filled the other surrounding walls. A small dressing table and chair sat in an alcove near a huge walk-in closet. As Peggy stepped into the room, she spied an open door that lead to an enormous bathroom complete with Jacuzzi, separate shower, two sink cabinets and a linen closet. In an adjacent room sat a toilet and a bidet. Along the same wall, a sink centered two towel racks.

"You like it?" Seth's question ran the gamut of expectations.

"Overwhelmed." Peggy lacked suitable words to describe her feelings. The mirror reflecting the bed would scare the crap out of her, if she had to get up to pee at night. Still…she could see the possibilities of a mirrored romp with him. She would definitely be buying sexy nightwear…something extremely sheer…something he could easily remove…or tear.

"You don't like it." His face stiffened.

"Get real!" Her blue eyes sparkled. "A mirrored bed invites visual play, and I hope to have a very good performance record. But you told me to behave. So which is it?"

"Go take your shower. We have a dinner reservation." He reminded her. Secretly, Seth was relieved that he had been mistaken by her initial reaction to the room.

"Just one minute!" Peggy halted him with her hand. As he stood facing her, somewhat confused by the sharp tone of her voice, she quickly unzipped his fly, felt inside his pants, and said, "Okay, we're still on for tonight."

Peggy could still hear Seth laughing as she gathered a few of her things and walked toward the bathroom. Before entering, she caught his attention. "I'm going to be awhile. I just don't want you to worry about me."

Seth thought Peggy had to relieve herself, and promptly gave her reassurance.

"We have time. Even if we're a little late, it won't matter." He watched the door close quickly, and without another thought, Seth took a robe from the closet, grabbed his toiletry bag and, strolling down the hall to another bathroom, stepped into the shower stall.

***

It was after nine when they arrived back at Blarney Stone. Gabriel stood guarding the front door and greeted Seth by rushing past him toward the large expanse of trees that bordered the property. Seth watched the German shepherd make circles in the snow, spraying each tree graciously. While Seth and Gabriel were busy outdoors, Peggy took the opportunity to further inspect the living room with its plethora of statutes, jade carvings and wooden bowls. She moved slowly around the room and noticed a family picture sitting on the fireplace mantle. Her eyes studied the two men standing in a yard fronting an old house. Judging by their clothing, the photograph had to be quite old, and the two young men pictured appeared to be somewhere in their early twenties. Yet, what struck her was the family resemblance of both men. Their combined features reminded her of Seth, and yet, one of them struck another familiar chord inside her head. Peggy had the feeling she knew him, had met him somewhere. She shrugged off the notion. Everybody had some characteristic reminiscent of someone else, she thought to herself. Still, somewhere deep inside her brain, she couldn't dismiss her thoughts about the pictured face.

"You coming?" She heard Seth's voice, before noticing him at the bottom of the stairs waiting for her. "Would you like something to drink?" he asked, coming toward her.

"I'd rather…" She left the sentence unfinished as he pulled her to him. "Tell me you want to play in my big bed."

"You have no idea…" Her reply was almost inaudible.

Peggy felt the strength of his hand leading her to the bedroom. It was only after they undressed hurriedly, and Peggy stood naked facing him in the dimness of the nightstand lamps, that she saw the look of shock cross his face.

"Margaret!" His eyes were glued to the lower portion of her body as he moved slowly toward her.

Peggy silenced him with a soft muted whisper. "I thought I'd do a complete bikini fix." She moved his hand slowly down the center of her body and inched his fingers along her soft smooth folds, knowing the silkiness of her flesh would arouse his deepest desires.

Flushed with so much emotion, Seth quickly cradled Peggy's body and placed her on the massive bed. "Margaret. I can't believe you did this!" He smothered her with kisses as he positioned her.

Although the mirrored reflection showed a woman with outstretched hands grasping a bed sheet and the back of a man moving slowly down her body with kisses, it never captured the loud rapturous moans that filled the room.

When her dreamlike state ended, Peggy lay contented and fulfilled. At that moment there was nothing else she needed in life. The handsome man she wanted lay holding her. He had awakened sensations within her that she had never felt before, quivering and vibrating ones that coursed through her body and sent her floating into the atmosphere. This was the kind of love Seth wanted. He wanted a total love, both mind and body. Now, she fully understood his meaning at the motel.

"I still can't believe you did that for me." Seth broke the silence.

"I'm a good listener," Peggy whispered.

"I see that."

"Come to me." She moved away from him.

"Are you sure?"

"Now," Peggy demanded. She looked up at the ceiling mirror, before taking a new position. Unfortunately, Peggy knew she would not be able to witness this reflection. She would be too busy.

Later, as they lay with the covers around them, a contented Seth pulled Peggy closer to him. "At some point, we'll have to talk about our future."

"In what way?"

"You want four children," he said.

"Don't you think we could do that? You're as virile as a rabbit."

The remark caused Seth to laugh. "I'm not so sure about that, Peggy."

"Did you have a vasectomy?"

"No. But I'll be forty-one and you'll be thirty-four. That's all I meant."

"Then, I'll take whatever we can hatch together."

"You are going to be a trip to live with."

"That's what I'm counting on." She kissed him and curled into his body before closing her eyes. She knew a little wax would go a long way.

Chapter 8
New Year's Day

Barbara Croft sat on the edge of a large upholstered chair, staring through the diamond-shaped window panes at the expanse of her yard. The tall, stately trees with their outstretched branches lay stark and laden with snow. Although her eyes focused on their natural beauty, her thoughts were centered elsewhere. Today was their big day, hers and Franklin's. This was the afternoon when their wealthy and powerful friends gathered to schmooze and trade favors with each other. They came in groups; they came in pairs; and some came alone, but all of them came to attend the annual New Year's cocktail party to see and be seen. It was a perfect winter's day for a party: sunny, brisk and cold. An omen, perhaps a good one, hopefully, of better things to come from this New Year's Day gathering, as opposed to Megan's volatile performance the previous year. She only hoped Brad could keep his wife in check and restrain her from assaulting some other invited guest. Granted, Winifred Pitts was a bit of an ass, tossing ice cubes down Megan's dress, but who would have expected her to haul off and knock him to the floor. To add to his humiliation, she demanded he leave the house; this, amid the applause of women Winifred previously abused with his cruel jokes. It was beyond belief: a daughter-in-law requesting one of her guests leave the house. Indeed! The woman had unbelievable nerve.

A maid interrupted her reverie with a service request. It was time for Mrs. Croft to check the dining room table for the hors d'oeuvres arrangement.

The tall slender woman with the beautifully coiffed hair had an elegant demeanor about her, as she walked gracefully into the large dining room and checked the enormous rectangular table for the placement of silver, service china and candelabra, so in keeping with the festive gala that would begin within the hour. After giving her nod of approval, the woman walked up the curved wooden staircase to her room. It was time to get ready. Within sixty minutes, she would be meeting her very important guests.

***

A short time after the cocktail party started, the crowd seemed to flow from one enormous living room into another. A few steps from the second large living room sat a small conservatory. There in the atrium, away from the few gathered groups, Megan spotted Ben Burrows and greeted him in a very demanding way. "What are you doing hiding in here?"

"I am not hiding," he hissed. "I need a breather from your... friends."

"They found you." She giggled, referring to the smorgasbord of available middle-aged women who frothed for companionship.

"Not funny, Megan." Brad cautioned and turned his attention to Ben. "Are you talking about someone in particular?"

"I think her name is Victoria. If you look in the next room, she's standing by the piano."

"She's a very good friend." Megan emphasized the last word of her sentence.

"Yes. I know. She told me of last year's performance. They're waiting to see if you're going to do a repeat. I understand he's been invited."

"No," Brad corrected. "Winifred Pitts is here. I passed him on the way in. He was being greeted by my parents."

"I didn't see him," Megan interrupted. "Wonder why."

"He's probably hiding from you." Brad joked. "I know I would."

"Tell me you aren't planning a repeat." Ben grew serious, knowing the twenty-eight year old woman's volatility.

"It depends. I think the law calls it, probable cause," she answered quickly. "If he does an ice cube, I'll do my fist."

Ben glanced at Megan sideways. He would have loved to have seen her take down this Winifred Pitts person. From Victoria Reynolds' description, it must have been one helleva scene the previous year: Megan decking the man after he threw ice cubes down her dress. Then adding to his further humiliation, she tossed those same ice cubes right back at his face and threw him out of the house. Her cheering section, a group of women, who loudly applauded her gesture, had been the butt of the man's cruel jokes for many years.

His animated condition suddenly changed when Charlene Winter, another female guest, tapped Brad's shoulder for an introduction.

"You look familiar. Have we met before?" Ben asked the homely middle-aged woman whose noticeably gray hair was streaked with black strands. While he spoke, her dark beady eyes, hidden behind very thick glasses, seemed to be studying him. Her heavy make-up seemed to enhance, rather than hide the lines of her face, and the frumpiness of her frame only added another dimension to her ugliness.

"You are amazing." She complimented him. "We met a week ago, Christmas night to be exact. You're the detective investigating Alice Beck's accident. I saw you briefly when I was standing outside her house. She was my next door neighbor, a very lovely woman."

"How well did you know her?" Ben asked evenly. "I thought they just moved into the neighborhood."

"Excuse us," Megan took Brad's arm, interrupting their conversation. "Jennifer's over there and we need to see your sister."

"What was that all about?" Brad demanded as they walked away.

"Damned if I know, but when those frog-like eyes of his get even bigger, Ben's in detective mode. So it's best if we leave them to talk privately."

***

Barbara and Franklin Croft stood elegantly dressed in the huge main living room, greeting their guests and making small talk as one group followed another in the quasi-reception line. Peggy and Seth were among the last guests to arrive, and Barbara made a special point of greeting the couple with lingering interest.

"Barbara and Franklin Croft," Peggy began, "I want you to meet my escort, Seth Stone." The men immediately shook hands in a friendly gesture, while Barbara merely smiled. However, her eyes remained fixed on Peggy's date.

"You must be the artist Brad and Megan talk about so often. I believe they have a print of yours on the wall of their living room."

"Yes." He agreed with her statement. "Brad was kind enough to show it to me when we visited."

"Perhaps I should attend one of your exhibits." She continued to study him, but soon turned her attention to another late arrival.

As they approached the bar at the far end of the room, Peggy felt someone touch the sleeve of her dress.

"Peggy?" The man questioned, uncertain of the recognition.

"Do I know you?"

"Franklin, Junior. We've never been formally introduced, although we must have met somewhere along the line."

What could she say? Yes, and I've tried very hard to forget it. She was thankful the restaurant outing, where they bumped into each other, was brief and impersonal…after Megan's wedding.

"This is Seth Stone." She drew his attention to her escort.

"Seth Stone, the artist?" He caught Seth's acknowledgement and snickered. "You're the one who went with Helen Fowler, if I recall correctly." He made a devious smacking sound with his lips and smiled knowingly. "Helen was the ideal woman: she had beauty, intelligence and a very hot body to match."

At his insinuation, Peggy knew Seth wanted to deck the man, but she quickly intervened. "Yes, and it's too bad you couldn't get any. Rumor has it you have a very small penis and can't dress it left."

She took Seth's arm and steered him toward the buffet table.

At some point, the dingbat would remember she was the sister of a very acerbic Megan. However, the sharp tongue was a family trait that Peggy seldom used. Tonight was different: she was a lioness protecting her cub.

"God you're brutal…fast thinking, but brutal." Seth shivered. "I don't know where you come up with this stuff, but I'm glad you're on my side." As he fed her an appetizer, he spotted Megan and Brad coming toward them.

"Hey, what's up?" Megan approached her sister. "Are you having fun?"

"I think your brother-in-law's an asshole," Peggy offered.

"Honey, he's part of a matched set with Rosalie. What would you expect?"

"Not a helleva lot."

"Did Franklin say something offensive?" Brad asked Seth, thinking it best if the men handled the problem. "He thinks he's being cute, but his comments always come back to haunt my father."

"No. Peggy took care of it," he answered quietly, his eyes sweeping the room. "Has anyone seen Ben?" His answer came when Megan lead them to the atrium to find the beleaguered detective surrounded by four women.

When Ben saw them, he immediately excused himself and, grabbing Megan by the arm, walked her to a private spot in the hall.

"What the hell have you gotten me into?" he growled.

"What do you mean?" She voiced surprise.

"I got five name cards in my pocket and an offer for a night cap. I can't do this." The man was totally out of his comfort zone.

Megan exploded with laughter. "When we made the bet last Thanksgiving, didn't I say this party would be like a smorgasbord, with every woman wanting a piece of you? I told you then, everyone would love my Frog Prince."

Ben Burrows studied her in silence and wondered what the hell a fairy tale had to do with his predicament. But he dispelled the thought immediately. "Are you going to leave me hanging or are you going to help me? I didn't bring a gun to kill myself!"

"What do you want me to do?"

"Don't leave me alone with these women. Stay with me."

"Okay, Romeo. I'll play your Juliet." She took his hand. On the way back to the atrium, she noticed Seth and Barbara holding a private conversation to the exclusion of the other guests. Across the living room, Franklin Senior and Peggy were also actively engaged.

Megan thought the intensity of their conversations was rather strange.

***

Later that night when Barbara Croft was getting ready to retire, she had a brief exchange with her gray-haired, distinguished-looking husband, who was sitting on the side of the bed, removing his slippers. "I think this had to be our best cocktail party to date. Everything went off as planned."

"You mean Megan behaved for a change." Franklin corrected her.

"Well, we all know how unpredictable she is."

"Get a life, Barbara. How would you have reacted if Winifred did the ice cube toss on you?"

"He wouldn't have," she groused.

"That's only because of our standing in the community. He wouldn't do anything to jeopardize that relationship. It would cost him money and be dropped from everyone's guest list. He couldn't risk that."

"I suppose you're right."

"That's no supposition. He picks on the less fortunate women in our group, widows and spinsters, like Victoria Reynolds. Frankly, he had it coming. I noticed he stayed away from our Megan."

"I didn't notice," Barbara replied absent mindedly. She had much more on her mind that evening. She didn't need to watch Winifred Pitts make an ass of himself again.

"I made it a point to observe Ben Burrows tonight. I noticed a flurry of women around him in the atrium. I like the man but would not consider him especially handsome," Franklin said, pleased with his observation. Most women in their social group considered Franklin a rather handsome and physically fit man. That he was in his sixties made no difference. He had that sexual elegance women loved.

"He's interesting and entertaining at the same time. That's Ben's appeal."

"Then what's so appealing about Seth Stone?" His dark eyes widened. "The two of you talked for a very long time."

"I guess we did," she answered quickly. "He's very serious about his work. I may just take a look at some of his paintings."

Barbara Croft ended the conversation by slipping under the covers and snapping off the bed lamp. She wanted no more questions about Seth Stone, particularly from Franklin.

***

Peggy was getting ready for bed at Blarney Stone when her cell phone rang. "It's Megan." She told Seth who was sitting on the other side of the bed.

"What?" Peggy repeated, "When? You tell your brother-in-law he's an insensitive asshole, and he's asking for trouble if he continues to bother me. He's screwing with the wrong woman." She listened to Megan's conversation.

"No. Don't get Brad or his father involved. I have another avenue to pursue if Junior persists."

Peggy continued to listen to Megan rant. "No," Peggy said firmly. "Just pass on the message, if he gets back to you, otherwise forget it." She pressed the end button. There would be hell to pay if Junior's wife, Rosalie, learned her husband had been chasing other women during their marriage. Peggy knew how to "unwittingly" drop the bomb, if it came to that, and she played the scenario in her mind.

"Junior called her, didn't he?" Seth questioned. "You must have really pulled his chain." He drew her to him. "I want you to stay with me."

"I am with you."

"Look up." He pointed to the ceiling mirror.

She saw their reflection as they lay facing each other. "God, I look fat."

"No. You have a great body." He disagreed, cupping her breasts playfully.

They continued to watch their reflection, when Peggy noticed Seth's growing readiness and crossed her leg over his thigh.

"You're my kinda girl." He raised his body, while she slid her other leg under him, inviting entry. With Peggy's legs clasped tightly around him, Seth rolled over on her and forced himself deep inside her small cavity, causing her to gasp. He moved swiftly with an undulating motion until he heard her sighs of pleasure and knew she was near peak. He moved deep inside her once more, knowing their precious moment had come.

Still locked together, Seth edged his tongue along Peggy's mouth before meeting her lips in a lingering kiss. He rolled over and lay prone facing her.

"Did you like my going deep?"

"I like everything you do to me." She cuddled closer to him and grew serious. "You excite me, Seth. I can't explain it. But when I think of you, I get these stirrings deep inside me and I want to take you to bed. Maybe I'm becoming a nympho."

The remark caused Seth to laugh. "If you are, then you're my nympho." He slid his hand toward her thigh.

"Don't start anything you can't finish," Peggy warned.

"Try me." He leaped suddenly and silenced her completely.

Later, before going to sleep, Seth made a terse statement. "I think we're really good together." He said nothing further and closed his eyes.

Chapter 9
Disclosure

A week later, Barbara Croft sat in a food court mall, idly sipping a cup of coffee. Several small packages lay on a nearby chair.

"I see you took my advice and went shopping."

"You wanted the meeting to look accidental."

"How long have you been waiting?"

"Not long," she said, looking at the younger man who slid into a chair opposite her. His clear brown eyes studied her as if she were some specimen under a microscope.

"You're making me feel uncomfortable." She lowered her dark eyes.

"That was not the intention of this meeting." Seth wanted to clear the air.

"Then, what was? You obviously knew about us. I could see it in your eyes at the New Year's party. You think I'm a slut."

"Barbara, this is no time for games. This may be our only meeting, so let's get on with it. I loved him as much as you did."

"He was the only man I ever loved. God forgive me." Her eyes brimmed with tears. "It had been all arranged; the marriage, I mean. Money always marries money. Don't let anyone tell you otherwise."

"Was it before, or after? It's important I know the circumstances."

"We met years ago. I was already married to Franklin then and had Junior and Jennifer when we met. But I fell hopelessly in love with Barthalemew the first time I saw him. When our bridge group went to his restaurant for lunch, there he was...so tall, so handsome and so charming. I felt the chemistry between us immediately. We both did. I went back alone the next day and he took me right on the spot, in his back office. I had never experienced love like his. What I had with Franklin was more mechanical, like having sex with a robot. Her eyes fixed on him. "You know, don't you?"

"Do you really care what I think?" Seth challenged, ignoring her question deliberately.

"Yes, I care. I have to. You've put me in this position," she answered quickly.

"I think you did that to yourself. But I am not the enemy. You must understand that. He told me everything, years ago. So, yes, I know."

"I loved him. We loved each other for years. The mirror in his bedroom is no accident. He wanted a reminder of …us."

Seth remained silent. He wanted to hear her version of the story. He had already heard his uncle's.

"It's ironic that we met in the mall today. He would meet me here and take me to his house. He never wanted my car parked there. When he pulled into his long driveway and then his garage, I always wore a hat, so no one would recognize me. We met at least three times a week. He had signals on his mail box."

"Red tape, yes; and black, no." My uncle told me.

"There were other times he was just so desperate to be with me. And I felt that same raw sexual need. I was a lovely young woman then and he was the handsome lusty man I adored. Think what you want, Seth. I am not ashamed. I loved your uncle."

"How could you have continued such a long relationship? Weren't you afraid Franklin would learn of your betrayal?"

"Franklin's had flings of his own over the years. He thought I was too stupid to notice. But, once again, it was a matter of money, position and family. As long as it didn't become public record, he was free to continue his lecherous pursuits at the Sovereign Club. My only love was Barthalemew and I'm sure I was his. I only wish we could have been together as man and wife. In a way we were. We were together for nearly nine years."

"Then things started to happen. Too many questions were being asked. Was that the case?" Seth felt he already knew the answers to his questions. Ending a relationship in that kind of situation seemed obvious, even to him.

"Barth was becoming afraid…of being caught…but not by Franklin."

Catching her drift, Seth finished her thought. "Brad was getting older. He was beginning to look more like my uncle: high cheekbones, hazel eyes. Better to have a closet ancestor with those genes than a live lover. That was a glitch you could live with."

"You make it sound so cheap."

"No. The reality was protection. Uncle Barthalemew told me it broke his heart when the two of you decided to separate. As much as he loved you, and he did, his concern was protecting Brad. He was part of the family, your family and that's where he belonged. My uncle couldn't give him anything without raising suspicion, but he was able to secure Brad's teaching position and get him published. He crossed a lot of palms with cash. That was the only way he could provide for his son."

"When I told Barth I was pregnant, he was so happy. There would be a legacy between us. He would have liked having his son carry his name, but of course, that would mean scandal, and he never wanted the boy tainted. So as years passed, we both accepted what was best for Brad. He attended his graduations, pretending to be there for someone else's child. It broke my heart."

"And now, almost two years after my uncle's death, I appear with your daughter-in-law's sister. Fearing I may reveal the truth worries you. I can see it in your eyes. I can read it on your face. But let me allay any concern you may have. Brad enjoys a wonderful reputation at the university. You should be proud of him. Biologically, we may be related, but for all concerned, if I marry Peggy, he will be my brother-in-law. A blood relationship will never surface."

"Does Peggy know?"

"No. Nor will she. My family secrets are mine to keep. I offer no skeleton key."

"How can you be sure?"

"Because she knows I am an honorable man. Her love for me is as deep as my uncle's was for you. There was never another woman in his life. Even though you were apart, he was faithful to you. Strange, isn't it? You were sleeping with another man while he was sleeping alone."

Seth reached into his jacket pocket for an envelope. "He wrote this letter to you when he became ill. I was to give it to you at an appropriate time. That's what he said, "an appropriate time." After our conversation today, I believe this time would fit that request. I don't know its contents, but I am certain you would not want anyone else to read it. Burn it or return it, but don't keep it. That would not be wise."

"Thank you so much…Seth." Her words faltered. She became so overcome with emotion, a tear trickled down her cheek as she fingered the letter. "How can I see you again?" Her cracked voice questioned.

He moved to her chair, took his handkerchief and wiped her tears. "You were the only woman in his life. He loved you. You must always remember that." Seth felt somewhat sorry for the woman. It was probably the only time in her life that a tear-stained Barbara Croft looked so pathetic. "One of us should leave now. I think it would be better if you sat here a few minutes longer. I understand you are a patron of the arts. That would be a good excuse for a meeting, should you need me." He gave her a business card with his cell number and left the food court.

***

It was only ten-thirty when Seth left Barbara Croft and sat in his car, deep in thought. He felt totally depressed and was glad Peggy wouldn't be back until six. Early that morning, she was bubbling with excitement over Janice's fitting for Amy's June wedding. The mother-of-the-bride found the perfect long dress for the occasion, but, of course, it had to be altered. Apparently, the wedding was to be a big affair with hundreds of people. Peggy's happy mood, however, had not transferred to his. Seth had made the appointment previously with Barbara Croft for that very morning. He had strict instructions from his uncle; promises he made before the man's death, to carry out at the appropriate time. After their New Year's Day conversation, Seth felt it was the perfect time to deliver his uncle's letter to her. He wanted their meeting to take place as soon as possible. Now, instead of feeling "task accomplished," the meeting only brought back memories, ones of continued involvement.

As he sat in the mall parking lot, he began to wonder if the actions of his uncle, and even those of his own father, were part of an extra-marital genetic pattern. His uncle's great love was Barbara; his father's, Iris. He hadn't thought about the generational situation for a long time. No. This would not happen to him. Were they younger than his forty years, when they met their soul mates? He only knew they were two lusty men, each searching for an ideal woman who could share his dreams, fulfill his needs and listen attentively to his concerns in life.

On the other hand, Seth felt certain he had met his own soul mate. He wanted to spend the rest of his life with Peggy. This was the woman who would forever cling to him, fulfilling his dreams and giving him all the love and affection he desired. In return, he would plant his seed deep within her, giving her the gift of children and family she so desperately wanted. Now, in the beginning stage of their relationship, Seth took her because she wanted his body penetrating hers, expressing her deepest desire. He, on the other hand, couldn't get enough of the woman, or the intensity of those desires, as he watched the mirrored reflection of her stroking his body parts and making love to him.

His mind wandered back years earlier, ones filled with bitterness. He thought of the balancing act between his Buffalo home and the seven week sojourn with his father, and ultimately, Iris. If it came to a preference, Seth could understand his father's desire to be with the beautiful flaxen-haired artist, instead of the cold inflexible Sarah, he called his wife.

It came to him suddenly…as he sat thinking of the women in his father's life. Was his father's selection of women a parallel of his own… the man's preference of a loving Iris, over a cold Sarah; or Seth's own exciting Peggy, over an unadventurous Helen? A frown crossed his face. How could he not think of the comparison? A difference, however, assuaged those thoughts. Seth had never married. But an inner voice reminded him of his verbal commitment to Helen.

Seth felt tormented. How could he possibly condone his father's extramarital relationship, be indifferent to his uncle's, and then vehemently condemn Jeff Roberts'? How could he reconcile this in his own mind? How could it be right for two men to enter an adulterous relationship and wrong for a third? Granted, a difference existed: the first two men remained faithful to their soul mates, while the third moved from one affair to another. Still, that did not excuse the men from ignoring their marital status or give them absolution. Seth felt like he was going through an ablutionary phase of his life and wanted to wash his hands of the whole aggravating situation.

What saddened him most was the disinterest his mother displayed when his father began to sell his paintings. He wanted to quit teaching but Sarah wouldn't hear of it. She wanted the security of a regular salary. Her insistence caused a real divide between them. It was at that point the polarization of their marriage began. Then one day his father told a young Seth he had made arrangements to live elsewhere; but he assured the boy they would be together during his summer vacation. Yet, it seemed like only a short time had passed before Silas Thorne moved in and Seth's half-brother was born.

His mother never discussed their differences or explained his father's reason for leaving. So Seth remained silent during those years, never challenging and never disclosing. And despite her objections, Seth visited his father and Iris as often as he could. Yet, regardless of past issues, Seth cared for his mother after Silas died.

The past transgressions mattered little now. His parents were dead. But there were three things Seth knew for certain: through connections, his father made his college entry possible; he chose to spend his summers with his father and Iris to master their artistic techniques; and the family secrets given to him would remain buried, unless a disclosure promise was made previously by the party involved.

Seth watched the flakes of snow continue to mount on his windshield. He was tired. More than that, he was weary of carrying secrets, those of the dead and others of the living. Yet, he was more fortunate than most to have had the instruction his father and Iris provided. The schools he attended merely added to his credentials, while Iris readily supplied an avenue of dealers and scheduled shows. She had been a well-known artist in her own right. Yes, Seth reflected, he was lucky and began to visualize Iris in her flowing caftan, and his father in Bermuda shorts. They would take him into the studio after breakfast and begin teaching him the basic art principles they had learned many years earlier. Minutes later his reverie ended. Seth started the car and, turning the windshield wipers on high, pulled out of the parking lot.

He thought about his earlier conversation with Barbara Croft. His uncle must have been one helleva lover, he mused, thinking about the mirrored ceiling. And although Seth thought about it, he refused to frame a picture of the twosome.

It was only when he got home and sat on the couch with Gabriel, that Seth realized one important thing. Through all the morning turmoil, he had not eaten. "What do you say, shall we check the refrigerator?" Seth may have asked the question, but Gabriel got there first.

***

Later that same night, while Seth was sitting in the huge Blarney Stone living room, he watched Peggy approach the fireplace mantle and study the picture of a youthful Barthalemew and Andrew Stone.

"I can see the family resemblance...the hair and facial features. Did both of them have hazel eyes?" Peggy never heard Seth's response, but she could feel his eyes piercing her back.

Seth watched her index finger trace the faces of the two men in the photograph, knowing her attention was chiefly centered on the face of his uncle. Nevertheless, her curiosity did not surprise him. He almost expected it, given her intellectual prowess. However, he remained silent, wondering when she would raise questions about the man and his possible progeny.

"Janice saw you at the mall today," Peggy said, aware of Seth's interest in her finger tracings. "She went shopping after the fitting. I told her we needed some things for a party we're going to." Peggy wanted Seth to have that information, should Janice mention seeing him. However, she never referred to his food court companion, Barbara Croft.

"I think we should go to bed." She turned to face him.

Seth continued to sit on the couch in silence. He was waiting for her to say something…perhaps ask questions…ones that could open old wounds and betray family secrets of things that happened years earlier… past events that had precluded her and now affected her directly.

Peggy remained silent and met his stare. She understood his mindset completely and felt it was time to clear the air with the man she loved.

"Sometimes suspicion can cloud a relationship," she began. "That's not going to happen with us. I'm interested in sharing your life, not your secrets. Those, you carry alone."

Peggy watched the expression of relief edge across Seth's face and asked laughingly, "So…am I sleeping with you tonight or do I hump Gabriel?" She took Seth's hand and led him slowly upstairs.

Seth knew Peggy had suspicions…but he also knew she would never question or verbalize them…to anyone.

Chapter 10
Charlene

By the second week of January, Ben Burrows was more than anxious to get on with the investigation of John Beck. He didn't need evidence to know the man murdered his wife. He tried to kill her once before, but the plan collapsed when the wrong woman was taken. Nevertheless, the man felt he could live without the fear of arrest, since there was nothing to connect him to the death of his wife. That fact really upset Ben.

He had been anxious to get the test results back from the lab, but no one moved fast right after the holidays. Now he would have to piece together the evidence he had and add the lab results later, hoping they would strengthen his case. If only he could find Mel Travers and question him, then Ben could prove John Beck's murderous intention months earlier…when the whole abduction scheme failed.

He examined the clutter on his desk. One basket overflowed with case files, while small note pads, placed in a semi-circular pattern along the top portion of his desk, seemed to indicate some kind of code related to the case he was currently investigating. In the center sat a calendar and a larger tablet containing the notes he had written over a week ago.

Ben grew restless. He was anxious to have the test results, and too weary to do anything with them. He leaned back in his chair, placed his hands behind his head and swept his small scarred office with his eyes. A bag of sorts, sitting on one of his two worn guest chairs, caused him to bolt from his office to the bullpen.

"Who put the bag in my office?" He addressed no one in particular.

Danny Boyle caught the detective's attention immediately. "Some young woman came by two days ago. She said that you knew her. Megan. Her name was Megan."

Ben thanked the young policeman, entered his office and tore open the gift. Inside the bag sat a box that held a 1.5 liter of 2010 Clos du Val Cabernet Sauvignon and a note.

Roses may be red
But violets are not blue
The way that I feel
Is special for you

Merry Christmas.
Love,
Megan

Ben hadn't felt so touched in a long, long time. He knew the young woman cared for him…and it was reciprocal. He would help her in any way he could…and she knew it.

A smile crossed his face. She was his young Juliet at the New Year's Day party, leading the short, pudgy detective away from a smorgasbord of women littering around him like the clutter on his desk.

"The hell with it," Ben sighed. He pulled the jacket hugging the chair arms, tucked the wine box under his arm and grabbed the large tablet off his desk. "I'm going home," he yelled loudly, walking toward the exit door…as if anyone really cared.

Ben felt like getting drunk but knew he would save the expensive wine for a special occasion…like I have so many, he thought.

***

Ben sat at his kitchen table scanning the tablet to refresh his memory. He had done some leg work, but it was problematic trying to talk to salespeople, with the huge crowds rushing to exchange their Christmas mistakes before the return period expired. Everybody had frazzled nerves and needed distemper shots.

Ben was getting nowhere with his investigation. He found an overflow of onyx cufflinks at the department stores, but they were not like John Beck's. Then too, he had the box they came in, complete with smudges, but as yet, no test results. Could he prove the smudges on the box matched the composition of the carpet binding seam? If so, they would probably match the smudge on the man's office door frame also. Would there be residue on the dead woman's shoes? Ben would have to wait for the lab results.

He went through his notes quickly and at the very end of a page, the name Charlene Winter was penned in. Then, Ben remembered. She was the woman at the New Year's party, the next door neighbor he saw on the night of Alice's accident, when she stood on the sidewalk, huddled in the cold. Although they had a conversation at the Croft party, the woman was clearly more interested in things unrelated to his investigation. So questioning her was futile. Fortunately for him, and yet not so providential, several ladies came by to meet and engage him in even more romantic endeavors. It was only through Megan's intervention that escape seemed possible.

"Crap," he said aloud. "One way or another, I have to do it." He reached for his cell and searched for a phone number. He heard the phone ring three times before Charlene Winter answered.

"Yes, Ben Burrows." The detective identified himself, before asking to interview her at the station the following morning. But by the time the conversation ended, they unilaterally agreed to meet for a lunch date at Sessions, a local nearby restaurant. However, being a quick thinker, Ben had to find a satisfactory way to get rid of the ugly woman and concoct a plausible story. After checking his daily schedule, he told the unattractive woman that he was only available between the hours of eleven-thirty and one o'clock. That would be enough time to ask a set of questions over a quick lunch. That was his story and he was sticking to it. However, it was the "Toodle-loo," that kept ringing in his ears when she ended their conversation.

"Toodle-loo, my ass," he said, thinking of the gray-haired woman with the black streaks running through it. She wasn't the ugliest woman he had ever seen, but she came damn close. Her lined face looked like a wrinkled road map, and her beady little eyes behind those bottle-like lenses could easily have served as gas station icons.

Yet he had to meet her to get some sorely needed information. He was sure she could tell him things that would help move his investigation along. But Ben wasn't sure how to get rid of the woman politely. He didn't mind taking her to lunch. He just didn't want to take her anywhere else. Ben had never been in a situation like that before… where he was surrounded and wanted by a group of ladies looking for …whatever the hell it was, women that age wanted. He felt like the Bachelor series on television, only this reality was an old fart surrounded by a bunch of middle-aged women. Over the years, Ben had women give him that 'fisheye' look. But ignoring something like that was easy. He would look the other way and move on to another case. This was different: there were too many women…all at once.

He looked at his ring finger. He could tell her he was married, but a woman like Charlene would know his wife had died. It would be better to tell her the truth: he was already in a relationship. *With whom?* A voice in his head questioned. "I'm not worried about that." He cast the thought aside. "I can lie like the best of them. I'm a detective."

He underlined Charlene Winter's name in his tablet. He knew exactly what information he wanted to extract from her. It was the kind of thing all women talked about. She would know if Alice planned to give the cufflinks or something else as a Christmas present to her husband. But if the cufflinks were purchased, that meant they were not a family heirloom, and then Ben would canvass more stores. If John Beck purchased the cufflinks, and not his wife, Alice, he would be caught in a lie. That would be damaging evidence against him.

Ben needed the lab results, not only for the cufflinks and smudges, he needed the shoes to be thoroughly examined and tested for cracks. He had already requested one for residue. His thoughts continued. Alice would have wanted her shoes to match the red dress. So John was fairly certain Alice would wear the red pair to complement her outfit. But suppose the heel or heels didn't break. Were the heels of her other shoes carefully manipulated to break and cause an accident somewhere else? Would John Beck have planned other places for Alice to die?

Ben was deep in thought when he received a phone call telling him the test results had arrived and were currently on his desk. It took less than five minutes for the detective to shrug into his coat and head for the station. His investigation was starting to gel. His next concern would be finishing a quick lunch with Charlene Winter. He pictured the lady with the strands of black hair slicing the gray ones. Maybe he should wear shades on his luncheon date. Her hair wouldn't be so odious then. No. He couldn't do something like that, something that dishonest. He'd have Danny Boyle call him at twelve-thirty on his cell and give him the MYA code. That would be the proper thing: the right thing, the Move Your Ass thing. Then he could apologize to the woman as he rushed out the door to his next appointment.

Ben made the station in record time, more anxious than ever to get to work. He wanted desperately to arrest John Beck for his wife's murder. He wanted it so bad he could taste it.

***

At eleven-thirty the next morning, a rather short, pudgy detective with bulging eyeballs, walked into Sessions Restaurant searching for a woman who had gray hair with black strands running through it and steady beady eyes that peered behind thick lenses.

"I think you're looking for me, Ben, I'm Charlene Winter," an attractive woman with coiffed mahogany-colored hair greeted him. Without the glasses, her clear brown eyes no longer looked beady, and she appeared to be a much younger woman than the one he remembered at the Croft party. "Are we still on the same page? You wanted to see me."

"I did…er…I do," he said, his eyes fixed on hers. "You look different." He stopped speaking, not wanting to explain.

"I should."

"Meaning?"

"I was in character for a private function and didn't have time to change. I'm an actress. I was playing the part of old Aunt Agnes, and took it much further than I should have by hitting on you. God, were you out of your element! I never saw a man squirm so much by a gathering of ladies. You need to get out more."

"You certainly are talented." Ben ignored her last remark. "I needed to talk with you about your neighbor, Alice Beck."

"I gathered that." She told him. "The cocktail party was not the place for that kind of discussion. Many of John's clients were there. I think Victoria Reynolds is one of them, so if I seemed perverse or a bit Looney, that was the reason."

"And you feel we can speak frankly, here, in this restaurant?" He opened the menu.

"Unless you want to go into the back alley and pretend a little hanky-panky," she answered laughingly. "What's on your mind?" she asked, after the waitress took their food order.

"What can you tell me about Alice and John Beck?" He made it a point to watch her body language closely as she began to speak.

"I can't give you much. It's just a feeling you get when you meet people." She prefaced her observation. "This is going to sound stupid, but they didn't feel married to me. It seemed more like they were going through the motions of marriage without the love. But I only observed them at a neighborhood Christmas party...stupid, huh?" Her thoughts suddenly turned in a different direction. "Is this the kind of thing you do in accidental deaths?"

"We have to investigate everything before we can close a case. The state requires it. And you know how that goes," he said. "Your tax dollars at work."

"I don't have anything concrete to add." She tasted her club sandwich.

"Did you ever have a conversation with Alice regarding her move to Wellington Woods or things she had to do?"

"I knew she was a nurse at the hospital. She seemed very organized for being busy all the time. We talked before they moved in, when she came to clean."

"I don't know what you mean." Ben pushed for more information.

"Well, there are times when my house looks like a train wreck, especially when I am rehearsing a part. But with Alice, everything had to be in its proper place, at the proper time…all the time. Whether it was cleaning, food shopping or buying Christmas presents, she was always ahead of the game."

"She did sound organized," he said evenly. "Do you know what presents they exchanged at Christmas?"

"Haven't a clue. I saw the briefcase she bought for him. But what he got her, I don't know."

"Do you know anything about a pair of onyx cufflinks?"

"Do they have diamonds in the middle and a slight scratch on the back of one?" She caught his nod. "That little bitch! Alice probably felt safe because she knew I was moving to Alden. I did report them stolen," Charlene said, and then, taking a totally different posture, demanded an answer. "Why do you have them? I know," she answered her own question, speculating, "Alice had them in her pocket or in her hands when she fell. Do I get them back?"

"You will in time." Ben reassured her, just as his phone rang with the MYA code, but he was more intrigued with the direction of their conversation. "I'm going to have to leave soon." He tapped his phone. "But am I to understand that Alice stole the cufflinks from your home?"

"It couldn't have been John. He was never alone in my house. Alice watered my plants when I did a play in Dayton before Christmas. She had a key. No. John would not have stolen the cufflinks," she said, then hissed loudly, "I am too damn trusting. That's the problem with being a free spirit."

The waitress took the check and money before Ben stood up to leave.

"I'll check your report on the stolen cufflinks," he said. "Can you tell me the cost and at what store they were purchased? Do you remember?"

"Edgar's," she answered quickly. "I paid somewhere around two hundred, but that was a long time ago…right before my husband's death."

"I appreciate your help, Charlene, really I do."

"Come see me some time. Bring a date or something. I usually perform at the Lancaster Opera House."

Ben took a long look at the woman and laughed. "You'd probably shit if I did."

"Probably, but not on stage." Her resonant voice rang out.

Ben left the restaurant exploding with laughter. It didn't happen often, but Charlene pulled it off. The woman bested him!

***

Ben slid into his car and headed for the station. He had a lot of work ahead of him, work he would enjoy doing. Hours later, Ben was still writing furiously in his notebook, putting it all together in a summary: pictures, observations, lab results and the conversation with Charlene.

"So, are you going to get him?" Danny Boyle stood in his office doorway.

"A little more to go and we're done, hopefully."

"Knew you could do it," he said, walking back to the bullpen.

Ben watched the man leave. Yes, he had a lot of incriminating evidence, but not enough for an arrest. He needed something to nail his case against John Beck. According to the lab report, the shoe residue matched the soot-like stair-tape and the smudges on the cufflink box. They probably were a match to John Beck's office door-frame too. And the builder confirmed Alice Beck's phone call that scheduled the carpet repair after the holidays. The incriminating evidence he had was not enough to convict.

Any lawyer would tell a jury, "The woman caught her shoe in the loose carpeting and fell. And naturally, there would be soot residue on her shoe. In such an emotional state, after calling the police for help, her husband retrieved the cufflinks and box from the stairs to avoid another accident. And, of course, anyone in that state would want to check the loose carpeting. That would account for the transference of black smudges on the box."

Ben had witnessed high-powered, moneyed-lawyers before. The attorney would tell everyone in the courtroom that it was after all, an unfortunate accident. Although the door frame smudge was never mentioned, Ben felt certain the attorney would have a story for that too.

According to the lab report again, the heel of one red shoe appeared to have cracked during the fall; the other remained intact. There was nothing in the report to indicate foul play. But Ben was not convinced. John Beck must have been certain of her apparel. He may have even suggested she wear it. Somehow, someway, Ben knew the carpet binding and heel were connected to her murder. He just couldn't prove it. Now, however, Ben had another avenue to pursue. He grabbed his jacket and left the station hurriedly.

An hour later, Ben entered a jewelry store with a photograph of the cufflinks taken in evidence. The older watchmaker at Edgar's remembered the cufflink scratch and also Charlene Winter who bought them for her husband. He always took care of the nice woman's watch repairs. Ben found the information depressing. So, other than the smudge on the box, the cufflinks had no relevance to the case. However, Ben wanted to witness John Beck's expression when he told him his wife was a thief. What Ben really needed was the one person who could tie it all together. Over six months had passed and he still couldn't find Mel Travers.

Chapter 11
Engagement

When Cal entered the bar on a cold February morning, two weeks before they were to leave town for the engagement party, he found Sal studying a month old invitation over a cup of hot coffee.

"I need an ice cube," he said, reaching into the freezer bin under the counter.

"You're going to need more than ice cubes the way you're going," Cal complained. "You should think about scrapping the plan before it's too late."

"Plan? What plan?" He feigned ignorance.

"The plan you concocted before Gwennie appeared on the scene, the one with Buddy Haskins. The man's not worth killing."

"What are you talking about?" Sal stared at his partner.

"Doing the wrong thing. In four months, Gwennie retires to live here permanently, and you've got a chance to start over. Now you want to throw it all away because the man screwed you. I wish to God I had your opportunity...," his voice cracked. "I'd give anything to see my girls again."

"I'm not planning on doing something stupid." Sal reassured him.

"Then don't bring a gun. I don't want to be caught with a firearm by the police."

"It is registered." Sal reminded him.

"Yeah…here, but not in New York State. They're liberal about everything but concealed weapons. Your ass will be jail bait."

"I don't need to bring a gun." His partner pushed. "I have something that will hurt Segis even more than death."

"Are we sharing?" His eyes grew wide. Although he was relieved that shooting was not in Sal's plans, Cal never knew what to expect from his friend of many talents. He watched Sal pop a Kit Kat into his mouth. Whatever he was planning, Cal was certain it had to do with Segis' presence at the engagement party.

His thoughts went back a quarter of a century…long before Gwennie reappeared…to the night when they were forced to leave town. Sal made it his business to stay in touch with Buddy Haskins, his impaired friend, when he couldn't find Gwennie after his search. He reached out to him for help; he reached out for news; and he reached out because the one person who made his life so bearable had disappeared. There was no trace of her anywhere. Gwennie's arrival at Put-in-Bay, fluke that it was, changed everything. Sal worked less and traveled more. Where he went remained a mystery at times. But on other occasions, he was quite open. Cal knew Gwennie would be living at Put-in-Bay by the end of May. Whether or not there would be a wedding was never discussed; however, Sal made it clear that he and Gwennie would occupy one of his rentals and not live above the bar. And apparently, Sal and his son, Daniel, bonded almost immediately after the young man heard the whole story of his parents' separation, and learned that neither of them ever married. To him, that indicated a deep love his parents had for each other. Still, Cal felt uncomfortable. Something was going on: something he was not privy to. He could feel it. Sal was going to the engagement party with a purpose: he had a plan to execute. It had to be something devious, something that could hurt his uncle, just as easily as a bullet from a fired gun.

Cal watched his partner unwrap another Kit Kat snack. "I don't understand how your teeth can be so white, between your caffeine intake and the amount of candy you eat."

"That's easy. I use mouthwash."

"I know. I've seen you with Jack Daniels. Only you're not supposed to swallow the stuff when you rinse." Cal caught the colorful envelope Sal slid down the bar. "Should I open it?" He caught Sal's nod and read the new invitation. "Sounds fancy. Are you sure you still want me there?" Cal wasn't sure he wanted to witness Sal's plan at the elaborate affair.

"You're coming. I already told you that. You're the added reminder of what he took from us."

"Are you going to…?" Sal silenced him before he could ask about his plan.

"Il nostro momento di sangue prevarra," Sal said, promising his moment of blood would prevail: meaning his day with the family would be unforgettable.

"I hate it when you don't speak English," Cal groused, before turning to one of their regulars coming through the door. "Hey, Jake. You gotta be freezing your ass off." He watched the ice fisherman perch a stool. "Catch anything?" He poured the man his usual shot of whiskey.

"Where's your brother?" Sal slid a cup of coffee in front of him. "God, you look cold. I'll heat-up some homemade soup if you're interested."

"Make it a kettle. Herman's coming in with three other guys. Not a good day for fishing. I can't remember it being so wet, cold, and windy."

"Old age gets everybody sooner or later," Sal replied.

"That hurt." Jake winced, and then grew sober. "I want to know if it's true. Are you leaving town?"

The two owners looked at each other, bewildered by the man's statement. Cal slid on a bar stool beside Jake while Sal leered at him from across the counter.

"Where did you get the idea we were leaving?" Sal watched Jake sip his coffee.

"Herman heard you talking on the phone about leaving."

Sal started to snicker. "I was talking to my cousin, Raymond. We're invited to his daughter's engagement party. We're closed Valentine's Day weekend."

"Hey, asshole," Jake greeted his brother lumbering in with three other men. "You can't fish worth a damn and you can't hear worth a shit. Get it right. They're off for a Valentine party, not a permanent stay."

"It's not that your whiskey's better," Jake told Cal. "You've taken care of us for so long, I think we'd miss the couch."

Cal eyed the couch against the long wall. During their first ice fishing season, Cal and Sal bought a 96 inch couch after one of the men passed out. Over the years, a few did need help, but most of the men sat on the couch with drinks and invited others to draw-up chairs nearby to join their conversations. So it was not unusual to see a noisy grouping of filled chairs around the couched fishermen. That was the beauty of it. They came to renew friendships at a time when South Bass Island was not overrun with throngs of tourists, and they had their favorite watering hole to themselves.

When they came into the bar, the men were cold and some were weary, but all of them were in need of whiskey to "take off the chill." As more and more fishermen ventured into their bar, Sal made soups and stews which he served with fresh bread. The two owners enjoyed a reputation of running a fun-friendly place at reasonable prices. The only thing that changed was the couch. They removed it during the tourist season, only to replace it months later, when their ice fishing friends returned. Regardless of what anyone said, the couch held many memories of those forged friendships: it was that memorable time when they came to gather around drinking and joking after a day of ice fishing. The bar was a warm place, a friendly place, a reminder of home.

***

When the time came for their Friday trip to Buffalo, Cal was not at all surprised with Sal's hotel selection. He had seen the reservation two weeks earlier. Still he questioned staying in the suburb of Amherst, after learning there were other large hotels much closer to Nottingham Terrace, the address of the engagement party and home of Sal's cousin, Raymond.

"We've stayed there before, Gwennie and me," Sal said, referring to the hotel. "And it's just down the street from the best chicken wings in the city. I think they're better than the ones right in town. You'll see. Don't look at me like that," he groused. "When you go to Buffalo, you eat chicken wings and beef on weck or you're missing out on their signature dishes. Besides, I want to have dinner at Alexia's." He ended the conversation on that note.

Hours later, Cal pulled into a hotel portico on Millersport Highway, unloaded the car and gave the valet his car keys. As the two men walked into the lounge area adjacent the reception desk, three people ran to greet them, shouting in unison. Cal stood motionless, in shock liked some clueless robot. Standing there before him was Sal's mother. Where Teresa went, fireworks followed, and Cal wondered if this was part of Sal's plan for meeting Segis. He had, after all, been responsible for keeping them apart. So Segis thought.

"You don't need to register." Gwennie addressed Sal. "You're staying with me. Daniel and Teresa have rooms of their own. They're all next to each other, but we don't have adjoining rooms. Cal, you have to sign in." She watched him walk toward the reception desk.

"So, you went to the airport to get your grandmother?" Sal asked his son.

"It went like clockwork. The plane was on time, we checked into the hotel and had a long leisurely lunch," Daniel said. "Mom told Nonna all about the bridge thing and how Segis made you leave after saving his son. She also told Nonna about the family throwing her out when she was pregnant with me. Nonna didn't know the details and was very angry when she heard the true story. Now she knows everything and she and mom are close."

He hugged the smiling older woman whose body swelled with pride.

Sal met his mother's smile. Not only would Segis meet Cal again, he'd also see a reunification of Sal with his mother, Gwennie, the woman he loved and had to leave behind, and the son they bore together. And knowing his mother's temper, Sal predicted an explosive evening with the family. He couldn't wait to see his plan unfold.

"Okay." Cal returned to the group. "I'm checked in. What's on tap, chief?" He waited for Sal's lead.

"We freshen up and meet here in thirty minutes. We can have a drink, eat dinner or go to the Lancaster Opera House. I think they're performing a family comedy. We'll do a dry run to Raymond's tomorrow."

He led the group into the elevator. They were in total agreement. The night was theirs to enjoy. Tomorrow was a different story.

***

The following evening, in another part of town, a conversation concerning proper attire was taking place.

"Well, do I pass?" She modeled the new outfit she had purchased days earlier. Peggy stood facing Seth in a revealing cocktail dress that matched the sapphire blue of her eyes. "I'm a little nervous." She moved toward him. "I want to look nice for you."

Seth quickly embraced her. "You always look beautiful." He told her. "You would stand-out in any crowd, and it's not just the artist in me that sees how beautiful you really are. I am so proud of you." He kissed the tip of her nose.

"I needed to hear you say that, Seth. I feel more secure when I'm with you…when we're together." Peggy studied his face and tried to make him understand her feelings. "I don't want to be alone anymore."

"I'll always be here for you," Seth answered, then turned the conversation in a different direction. "We need to get going." He slipped into his sport jacket and took her arm, steering her downstairs.

"You're sure?" Peggy buttoned her winter coat as she watched him slide into his.

"No gifts. That was his request. My uncle's partner never stood on ceremony with me," he said, ushering her to the car.

***

The inside of the eight bedroom house was as large as the exterior, according to Teresa's friends at Sons of Columbus who seemed to know everything. Sal's mother had given them a brief history of the place earlier that day, so they knew the interior would be totally updated with the most modern appliances and accouterments, belying the 1930's exterior. Teresa also told them that the houses in the area were worth close to a million. That number, she found somewhat disgusting. She also voiced two observations about the eight bedrooms: either Raymond had the habit of a rabbit or he was taking in boarders.

Expressions of surprise crossed his face when Raymond answered the front door to greet his guests. He had expected his cousin, Sal, but the arrival of Aunt Teresa and three others was a total surprise. Recovering his composure, he invited them into a huge living room and exchanged introductions. Although he recognized Cal from years earlier, Raymond feigned ignorance and continued the pretense. He presented them to various small groups of relatives, friends, and business associates mingling about the room, and then directed them to the long buffet table in the adjacent dining room where he left them.

Having a secret agenda of her own, Teresa moved away from the buffet table, taking it upon herself to explore the house for a room offering complete privacy.

She returned a few minutes later and grabbed Sal by his coat sleeve and led him to a wrinkled old man whose girth seemed to fill the upholstered chair he sat on.

"Segis." Teresa voiced anger. "We talk in private now, or I make a family announcement when the engaged couple gets honored. I have nothing to lose. Rosario's dead and Sal's alive. Now!" she growled.

Then Teresa led both men into the private room she discovered and closed the door.

"You tell him!" She stormed immediately. "Explain why you sent him away thinking he killed someone, just to cover your own ass. You thought your Mafioso friends would begin to suspect incest with your mirror image around, and you couldn't have that kind of stigma. So the bridge episode provided the golden opportunity for exile. You bastard!" she snarled. "Tell him you're his father and how you made me your puttana."

Sal stood near his mother, completely in shock.

At first, he was unable to grasp the full meaning of her words. He understood what she had said: incest was the motivating factor for his removal. However, the reason why had escaped him.

"What's going on?" Raymond entered the room. "Why is the door closed?"

"Tell him," she challenged. "No?" She caught the look of fear in the man's eyes. "Then I'll explain the DNA tests I had done."

"Don't, Teresa. Don't ruin my family." Segis implored her.

"What about our family?" Sal suddenly interrupted.

He now understood what his uncle had done to him. "What about the years you took from us…from me? You lied. You made me think I killed someone and you were protecting me. Instead you were covering your own incestuous ass and sending me in limbo."

Sal continued to force the issue. "That never counted as long as you had Raymond and Jimmy. Your sons were always there for you, but you denied my mother that same luxury."

"What are they talking about, dad?" Raymond stood mystified.

"It was a long time ago…" He tried to explain.

"Not for me." Teresa silenced him, "Not the time, your frequent visits, or the birth of Sal. I lived it every day. You sent him away out of fear because he was your spitting image. You were so afraid someone would discover the incest, the continued rape and the marks you left on my body when I tried to defend myself. You took me because you enjoyed the sport. Fighting you off, turned you on."

"You raped my aunt?" Raymond leered at his father, shocked by the revelation. "Sal's my half-brother?"

"And Daniel's grandfather," Teresa added.

"Daniel?"

"Sal's son. He came with us tonight, with his mother, Gwennie."

"I don't understand." Raymond tried to clarify the situation in his own mind.

"It's not that complicated, Raymond. When Sal saved you from the beating some twenty-six years ago, your father led Sal to believe he killed the man and sent him away. What he really feared was someone comparing their physical likeness, and raising the possibility of incest between a brother and sister. However, that's not the end of the story. He got rid of you too." Her eyes continued to fix on his.

"You don't believe me? Who do you think arranged the partnership with Barthalemew Stone? A great deal of money was exchanged for that privilege."

She faced her nephew directly. "You were sent to Buffalo to cement the final portion of his plan. It was his last chance to erase the past. Although he couldn't escape it from me, his secret was safe as long as Rosario was alive. You were little when he brought bags of fresh corn to the house. Instead of staying in the car, you came into the parlor one day and found your father trying to rip-off my clothes. He always feared you'd say something or remember what he had done. That was always in the back of his mind. He told me that after an especially harsh treatment one day. Lying there, I could feel how much that dangerous incident excited him. Then when the beating episode happened, it was a perfect way to get rid of Sal and then, you. Now that Rosario's dead, I don't care who knows what kind of bastard Segis really is."

"What is it you want, Teresa. What more pain can you possibly inflict now?" The grizzled old man felt beaten. "Il reconoscimento di sangue e passato."

He implied the time of recognizing blood had passed, but his sister stood firm with conviction.

"Il reconoscimento di sangue non sara mai passato finche sono vivo." She answered vehemently.

Segis knew her vow to reveal the blood lines, while she still lived, was no idle threat. His wife and younger son would soon know he fathered a child with his sister.

Whatever the consequence, what did it matter now, at his late stage in life? And his mind wandered into a region unknown to her…a long time ago.

He had always kept his eyes on her and watched her blossom. Teresa, with her beautiful face and small tight body, would never know the animal she had unleashed within him during their youth. She would never know the full strength of his desire. Her long slender legs were meant to be opened, but only by him. He remembered crushing her screams at night and his continued use of force, but in the end, the fight had always been worth it.

Now, he just wanted her to go away. And yet, even in his old age, Teresa's looks and shapely body still stirred feelings deep within him. The brown-eyed woman's porcelain face seemed unchanged to him. And the slight streak of grey that crossed the mid-section of her dark hair seemed to add another dimension to her beauty.

How could anyone ever understand…how could he possibly explain? His feelings for her were never those of brotherly love. His sister was the only woman he had ever wanted. He needed to possess her in any way he could: fight her and force her down, so his body could lock with hers. Their parents were aware of his nocturnal visits, and although they opposed his actions, they ignored it by having their daughter marry Rosario. They thought that would encourage their son to find someone else. But while Rosario was at the bakery making bread, Segis was busy making Sal. Then it ended abruptly after his father threatened to expose him to Rosario and the priest. Now as his time on earth was getting shorter, Segis felt certain that the sins he had committed with Teresa would be paid for in another life.

"Raymond, you're ignoring your guests." His mother joined them. "I was wondering where you were, Segis."

"Hello, Gloria." Teresa greeted the heavy white-haired woman in her late seventies. "We were just going over old times."

"I'm glad we could get the family together. We should do it more often." She smiled, exposing a bad fit of false teeth.

"I think that's an excellent idea. I wanted Segis to have the opportunity to meet his grandson, Daniel. He's Sal's boy. We really should join the others." Teresa took Sal by the arm, but before leaving the room, she warned Segis. "Tell the family or I'll tell our paisans what a pig you are."

"Daniel's our grandson?" Gloria questioned Raymond. "How can that be?"

"Later, mom," he said. "I'll explain it later." He left the room in disgust. His father had lied to him. He told his son Aunt Teresa needed help with her buttons. Until tonight, Raymond knew nothing of the bridge fight consequences. He felt used and utterly betrayed by his own father.

***

Sal found Gwennie and Daniel sitting in a chair grouping, sipping wine and munching appetizers.

"How did it go?" Gwennie asked, offering Sal's mother a chair.

"I was magnificent." Teresa cleared her throat before becoming serious. "It's been bottled-up inside me for so long, I had to uncork it before I passed away. Segis didn't want me here. He was afraid of what I'd say, now that Rosario is dead. Otherwise, Raymond would have invited me."

"But what did we accomplish by confronting him?" Sal challenged. "It just made the family hate us more."

"What they feel toward us was not the objective: blood-line recognition was. It took some effort but I have the DNA tests to prove it. Segis is your biological father and Daniel's grandfather. That is an undeniable fact. They can accept or reject it in their own minds, but they can't erase the genetic markers or the betrayal. I suspect he will leave you a pittance in his will now. He wouldn't want it contested or have more adverse publicity connected to his family. This opened Raymond's eyes. He was shocked."

"How did you know about Segis starting Raymond's business in Buffalo?"

"Gloria told everybody about her son's new restaurant here. I got it at Sons of Columbus. Italians are always good with details. And I mean all of them. I wrote the man's name down and kept it. Barthalemew Stone."

Teresa fixated on Sal. "Don't think me ruthless for what I've done. I needed my revenge, for you, for Daniel and for my loveless marriage to Rosario. Now, they can suffer the wounds and humiliation we did." Then she continued.

"You don't think I would have married that lecher on my own, do you? His bakery business provided a great cover. While he may have been rolling dough, Rosario was really a practicing gynecologist, but my father wasn't aware of it. He would have never promoted the marriage otherwise. It was his way of stopping Segis or so he thought."

Her remark caused Gwennie to give Sal a swift elbow, with an "I told you so." hard thrust.

"Hey." He recoiled. He was about to reply with a smart-ass remark but changed his mind. "What have you been doing? Did you meet the rest of the family?"

"I was talking to that woman standing by the buffet table, the one in the blue dress." Gwennie pointed. "She's with the tall, handsome guy next to her. I thought she was a model. She's so gorgeous. But if I had her looks, I'd remove that scar with plastic surgery."

"Scar?" Sal questioned.

"The one on her arm."

A sudden bolt hit him. It couldn't be! He recalled the pitcher incident with Cal's daughter and the doctor's prognosis of scarring. "No. It couldn't be." He told himself again. That stuff only happened in movies...like Casablanca. Real shit happened just now, in the room with his parents. That was real life. Still to satisfy his own curiosity, he had to meet this woman.

"Have Daniel find Cal," Sal insisted. "And tell him to meet me at the buffet table. It's very important." He left Gwennie without saying another word.

***

"What looks good here," Sal addressed the lady in blue, "chicken salad or tuna?" He made a face, when he bit into a cracker topped with a smoked fish spread, causing the woman to laugh. "I'm Sal, the uncle from out-of-town." He reached out to shake hands with her.

"I'm Peggy, a guest from in-town, with Seth, another in-town guest." When she turned to introduce them, Sal pretended not to notice the diamond-shaped scar on her upper right arm.

"Where are you from?" She asked the big man.

"I'd like to hear that answer myself." A stranger moved into their circle. "I'm Cal Burkett, his sidekick."

"I'm Peggy and this is Seth." She turned to greet him. There was something so familiar about the man who approached their little group, yet she could not determine what it was. She kept staring at him, watching him shake Seth's hand, studying his every move. "I know this is going to sound crazy, but have we met before? You look so familiar."

"How'd you get the scar?" Sal took her arm. "It's important, Peggy."

Seth took her hand, and, as usual, during serious matters, used her formal name. "It's ok, Margaret. I'm here. I have a feeling there's a reason for Sal's question."

"My parents had a fight, a long time ago and I got caught in the middle..."

"By the shards of a broken glass pitcher," Cal continued the thread of her story, "that required fourteen stitches in the emergency room. You were only seven then."

He looked at her with the recognition only a suffering father would know. A tear edged his eye. "You're my Maggie Pie." It was the name he had given her when she was a little girl.

"Dad!" Peggy threw her arms around him and began to cry. "I never thought...."

Seth and Sal stood by silently until Peggy became somewhat composed. "Megan. We have to let her know."

"She's here? In town?" Tears streamed down his face. "I can't believe it...after all this time..." he choked. "Oh, Maggie Pie." He hugged her. "Not one day has gone by that I haven't missed my girls."

"I can attest to that." Sal raised his hand.

"You have to tell me everything," Cal said. "We have so much to catch-up on."

"I want you to know Seth, Dad." She moved away from him and brought Seth forward. "I'm in love with him."

Seth was shocked by her sudden burst of information. "This is definitely a night of firsts," he said, knowing the two men were suddenly studying him.

To which Sal replied, "You have no idea the truth in that statement." Then after catching Cal's attention, said, "I think we should rejoin the rest of our family. Gwennie's in for a shock."

"Aunt Gwennie? She's here?"

They rushed to the threesome who watched their every movement from their corner of the room.

"This is Peggy, my daughter." Cal introduced her to Gwennie first.

"I'll be damned." She embraced her beautiful niece. "I didn't recognize you. We have a lot to catch-up on." She hugged her again.

"We didn't recognize each other." Peggy laughed unabashedly.

"I know. You grew up and I grew old." Gwennie winked. "But you are gorgeous. Tell me about the hunk you're with."

While they were engaged in conversation, Cal continued to study the tall, handsome man his daughter loved. There was a quiet air of sincerity about him. When they spoke earlier, Seth's clear brown eyes never left his, nor did he try to change the subject when asked about his relationship with Peggy. And when the dark-haired man looked at his daughter, Cal witnessed the attentive tenderness of a man, so proud of the woman he loved.

***

That night when the two men were alone, Cal was filled with questions that took place during the family meeting.

"You okay with that." He referred to the conversation Sal witnessed between Teresa and Segis.

"No, I'm not ok. The bastard raped my mother and took away twenty-six years of a life I could have had with Gwennie. I'd like to see him rot in hell. But I can't live my life on what could have been. That would get me nowhere. I've lived those years over and over too many times."

"You're right," Cal mused. "Someone was looking out for us."

"Who would have thought," Sal said. "It's our time, now."

"Meaning what?"

"Going forward, seeing what's ahead now. Looking back is over for me. I've got Gwennie and Daniel. I'm concentrating on a new life. You should do the same."

"Maybe, but I'm not sure the other one will come around as easily. God knows I'll make the effort. She was always a stubborn snot-nosed kid screaming her lungs out at everybody."

"She could have changed. You can't just force fatherhood on her anyhow. Give her a chance to know you."

Sal's insight perceived something Cal had missed entirely. If his younger daughter didn't accept him as readily as the older one did, his only choice was to be patient. But he was anxious now. He wanted the family to bond and knit. He just wanted Megan to give him a chance when they met. "Maybe, I am jumping the gun." He understood his partner's message.

Sal agreed. "Just wait until you meet her before going into panic mode."

"You have something else on your mind." Cal read Sal's expression.

"Raymond grabbed me before we left the house. He is thoroughly pissed. By inviting me, he wanted to bring our families together. He never had the true facts of my leaving town or his father's real reason for excluding my mother to the party. Segis used Rosario's death as the excuse, telling Raymond she seldom went out these days. But tonight, Raymond learned the real reason we were both sent away. He has no use for Segis, and now, his mother's talking divorce."

"What did you tell him?"

"I just said, 'What did you expect? After what he did to my mother, his own sister, did you think that would stay buried forever?'"

Sal paused momentarily and attempted to explain the mentality of Italian women to Cal.

"Italian woman are notorious for total recall when they want revenge. You can't win with those forked tongues. It's inherent in their genes, right out of the hospital nursery. Only there's no '**warning label'** like '**Do Not Cross**' attached to their foreheads. My mother waited until Rosario was dead, then she let the shit hit the fan. She doesn't care anymore."

Cal listened patiently to Sal's detailed account, before changing the subject. "Something else is bothering you. I know you too well."

"My mother mentioned a Barthalemew Stone."

"So?"

"Isn't Seth's last name Stone? I wonder if Barthalemew was related to Peggy's boyfriend."

"He probably was. That's why Seth was invited to the party. But we're not going there. Do you understand? I want my family back, so don't kick-up any shit about relationships." Cal's voice was laced with anger.

Sal knew he had touched a nerve and regretted raising the issue. Questioning Seth would serve no real purpose anyhow. Barthalemew was dead. "You're right," Sal replied quickly. "We are not going there."

***

"You happy?" Seth kissed the side of Peggy's face. He studied the overhead mirror of them lying in bed. They looked good together. Better still, they understood and enjoyed each other. It seemed so simple. "You told your father, you loved me. When were you going to tell me?"

"I tried telling you that when I said, 'I don't want to be alone anymore.'"

"Then, it's necessary to explain my earlier reluctance. I didn't want to rush you into an unwanted relationship. I knew you would be afraid to trust anyone…after Jeff. But as time went on, I knew you wanted me. I felt the chemistry between us, but I had to wait until I knew you were sure."

"I am sure. I want to spend the rest of my life with you. I know it in my head; I feel it in my heart; and I recognize it in my soul. I love you, Seth."

"Then I don't want to wait. Marry me, Margaret. Let's get the license this week and get married as soon as possible."

"Well, okay…" She was struck by his absence of words. "You're supposed to tell me you love me back."

"Frumpy, I think I've loved you since those damn beads and sequins fell off your dirty dress in Judd's parking lot."

Peggy turned to kiss him. "Is this going to be a very unromantic marriage?"

"I don't think so. Look under your pillow."

Peggy reached under her pillow and pulled out a strange looking box. Inside, sat a ring with a large central diamond, clustered by smaller ones. He slipped it on her finger.

"Happy Valentine's Day, Margaret. I love you." He kissed her longingly. "It's generational from the Stone side of the family."

Peggy gazed at the heirloom on her finger. "I am a very contented woman," she whispered. "You've made me so happy. I love you so much."

"Just how much is that?" Seth wanted a verbal play.

Peggy looked up at the ceiling mirror and opened her arms as wide as possible.

"That much, huh," Seth replied, checking her reflection.

"Yep, that much."

"That's a lot." He nodded and cuddled her in his arms.

Chapter 12
Revelations

"I know it's Sunday, but I need to see you." Megan pleaded on the phone. "Please, Ben it's really important. Peggy met my father last night. My father! What are the chances of that really happening after all these years?"

"What are you really asking for, the truth or a check of his identity?"

"I need to be sure. I don't want to see Peggy hurt again. Things are just starting to settle with her, thanks to Seth. Can you come to the house around twelve o'clock? I invited him to lunch, rather Peggy arranged it."

Ben thought about Megan's invitation, knowing his presence was important to her. Although she called for verification, what she needed, without asking, was his support. She wanted his reassurance that regardless of outcome, he would be there for her. Megan was scared. He had been there before…when she needed him.

"Seth should come with Peggy. What about Brad? "

"He's home with me." Megan answered quickly.

"So there will be six of us."

"No. Eight. Dad's friend, Sal, and Aunt Gwennie are coming. I told you about Josephine's sister when you came to the house…when Peggy was kidnapped. Are you writing this down?"

"How did you know?"

"You always have that little pencil and notebook handy." She heard him chuckle. "Twelve noon Burrows." She heard the click of the receiver. Then she thought about him with his pencil and tablet, writing down the names of her luncheon guests. He couldn't start investigating the strangers before they came to her house. Of course not. That would come after the meeting, when they were gone, after he had their names, occupations and addresses. That would be more like it. She wouldn't expect anything less from a detective like him.

***

They all seemed to come at once. Seth and Peggy were the first to arrive. But before they could recap meeting Cal at the buffet table, he walked in with Sal and Aunt Gwennie. A few minutes later, Ben entered the room and went directly to the kitchen for a glass of water. Pretending thirst, he waited for Megan to meet him.

"Are you all right?" she said loudly, certain of being heard.

"Had something caught in my throat," he replied, and then whispered, "Follow my lead."

Ben walked into the living room, acknowledged the woman, shook hands with the two men and introduced himself. "I take it you have already met Megan's husband, Brad." He started the conversation. "I understand you met Peggy and Seth last night at a party. I assume you have also met your younger daughter, Megan." He stared directly at Cal.

"I have, just now."

"Megan asked me to find you. She wasn't sure you were still alive."

"You're the detective Peggy told us about."

"I am also a very close family friend." Ben corrected him. "I know you want to be a part of their lives," he said kindly, "but it would really help the girls if you told them why you left. That issue has been very hard for Megan to understand."

"You don't remember us, do you?" Gwennie asked her.

Megan shook her head. "No," she whispered. "I only remember my aunt was a lot of fun."

"I wonder if she was as kooky as the aunt in the play Friday night." Sal laughed, popping a Kit Kat candy into his mouth.

"You went to a play? Where was it?" Peggy questioned.

"Lancaster Opera House. The ugly aunt was hilarious. I offered Cal a hundred bucks to go out with her. I thought he could take her someplace dark, so he wouldn't have to look at her. The woman's got to be even uglier without her make-up." Sal continued mocking his partner, as he placed a twisted candy wrapper beside two others on the coffee table. Throughout the conversation Ben remained silent. He had been there, done that, with the attractive woman behind the made-up façade. Yet he wondered about the big man devouring so much candy.

"The table's ready." Brad ushered them into the dining room where plates of food sat on the table, along with several bottles of wine.

"I'm glad we're doing this." Cal focused on his two daughters. "This gives me a chance to tell you why we left town and what made us stay away so long. If I omit anything, Sal will add to it. You can ask me anything you want to: I will answer as honestly as I can. I say that because I may not have all the answers. I just hope Ben won't arrest me for any illegalities."

"That's not my intention. I am here as a family friend." He clarified his position, giving Cal the opportunity to speak freely.

After listening to her father's story, Megan asked the status of the man tossed over the bridge accidentally.

"I checked that out," Gwennie explained. "The assault actually took place near the end of the bridge. When Sal whirled him away from his cousin, he went over the railing and landed on a wide slope, like a landfill. Segis sent out his goons to see if he had been killed. Seems he left town a week later. Last I heard he had a job with a cable company in Oklahoma."

"That makes no sense." Megan's terse comment surprised them. "Two guys who save a relative get sent away, and the mugger gets a job in another state. I can make-up better stories than that. What aren't you telling us?"

"I'm to blame," Sal admitted. "Cal had to leave because of me. We had been playing golf and stopped for pizza, then all hell broke loose on the bridge. Afterward, we were led to believe we'd be facing a murder charge. Our only option was to disappear. But Cal never wanted to leave his daughters."

"Segis' orders," Gwennie added angrily.

"Seth and I met him before we left the party." Peggy remembered the fat man's resemblance to Sal when her father introduced them. "Is he some kind of gangster? That alone would be reason enough to follow his demands."

"Let's just say he knows a lot of people who provide services," Gwennie hedged.

Ben cleared his throat, drawing their attention to him. "I think Megan's question deals with motivation. We now know why you were sent away initially, but what kept you away and for so long a period?"

"You owe it to them." Gwennie turned to Sal.

Shame and humiliation flooded his face. "I can't tell you his real reason for keeping us away," Sal hesitated. "But he did. Unfortunately, I trusted him. In the beginning we kept asking to come home but were put-off. Then as years went by we stopped asking. It was too late to renew what we had back then. Too much time had passed. We knew we could never go back."

"I'm sorry, Megan, if this doesn't satisfy you. It's his story to tell, but I have one of my own," Gwennie intervened. "After Sal left, I learned I was pregnant but I wouldn't identify my lover. Josephine, my sweet sister, told our parents I was having an affair with your father and the baby was his. She must have dwelled on that idea months earlier, long before my pregnancy. I'm sure that's why she threw him out. You knew she made him leave, don't you?" Gwennie caught Megan's look of surprise. "I was disowned by my parents and had to make my own way. Sal and I found each other after I walked into his bar six months ago. We have always loved each other. I had no idea where he was or if he was still alive. Sal, of course, never knew what happened to me or that he had a son. So you see, Megan, you weren't the only one left behind."

"We met Daniel last night at the party," Seth interrupted. "He looks like you, Sal."

The statement made Sal smile. "I'm not trying to evade the issue." His eyes swept Seth first, and then fixed on Megan. "The bridge incident was used as an excuse to banish me, and I think that's the right word, on a permanent basis. Only I wasn't smart enough to realize it, until it was too late. I should have investigated it on my own years ago. Your father just happened to be collateral damage in our family war."

"But why the name change?" Peggy directed the question to her father.

"Actually, John Calvin Burkett is my real family name. I don't know how it got shortened to Burke. When we opened the bar at Put-in-Bay, we thought Sal and Cal were catchy names for business."

"And you're moving there?" Peggy asked Gwennie.

"I took the option of retiring at the end of May. We'll be living in one of Sal's rental properties. Come visit. We'll do all the touristy things. It's a fun place."

"Maybe we will," Seth answered. "We're applying for our marriage license tomorrow morning. As soon as Peggy sets the date, we're getting married. She has a very short window and plans a small wedding. I want to get married ASAP."

"Are you pregnant?" Gwennie asked Peggy without hesitation.

"No…" Peggy seemed reluctant to respond. "But I want four children."

"So you see, I have a lot of hard work ahead of me," Seth quipped, bringing uncontrollable laughter to the table.

"Would you stand for me, dad? My first aisle trip doesn't count."

"I would be honored, Maggie Pie. I didn't know you were divorced…," he said, surprised by the news.

"I think you should tell him about the kidnapping and the asshole you married." Megan told her sister. "Forget about Josephine in Florida, or wherever the hell she is living now. Start with the anniversary party and end at the motel. That's where Peggy found her ex with another woman."

After Peggy finished the tale of her abduction and Jeff's betrayal, her father shifted his attention to the detective.

"So that's how you became involved with my daughters."

"It may have started that way," Megan interrupted. "But Ben's been like a father to me. He's always been there when I needed help or was in trouble."

"Megan, I understand. I have no intention of changing your relationship." Cal caught her meaning. "I'd like to add to it, if possible. Accepting me will take time. I know that."

Megan ignored his remark and concentrated on her sister. "Peggy's the one in trouble here. We still don't know who was behind her kidnapping."

"But the evidence points to mistaken identity." Ben tried to ease the situation.

"The woman I saw pictured wasn't Peggy," Seth added. "I don't think she's in any danger. She will be staying with me and Gabriel anyhow."

"Gabriel's his dog, a very large German shepherd." Ben clarified the reference.

"Is there anything I can do?" Cal questioned the detective. "I want to help."

"Things have been relatively quiet, but I'll keep your offer in mind."

"We should go." Gwennie checked her watch. "We've got a long drive ahead of us."

"Are you going with Sal to Put-in-Bay?" Peggy asked.

"And Cal," Gwennie said. "Daniel took my car. He and Teresa are bonding in Albion. He talked her into staying with him instead of flying home. They have a lot to talk about."

The Put-in-Bay trio left first, followed by Peggy and Seth. But Ben stayed behind, knowing Megan needed to vent her feelings. Although Brad was her husband and a loving spouse, what Megan needed now was a father figure.

"I thought I would feel something when we met," she said. "I feel nothing for my biological father, Ben. Why is that?" She moved toward his outstretched arms and began to cry.

***

On the day of the wedding, approximately a month later, Peggy and Seth introduced the Put-in-Bay group to Clarisa and Poag Fowler and Janice and Fred Sommers, all of whom had been placed on a duty roster as wedding participants.

Of course, Ben had an idea of his own when Seth and Peggy were still hashing plans for their big day.

"You want what?" Peggy answered Ben's phone call. "I think you've been chasing dead bodies too long."

However, when the wedding day arrived, all unfolded as planned.

John Calvin Burkett, father of the bride, walked his daughter, Peggy, down the short aisle of the church, while Megan tended to her sister's bouquet as matron of honor, and Poag Fowler guarded the wedding rings as best man. Sal and Fred seated those in attendance and Janice, Clarisa, and Gwennie checked the bride's attire first and then the decorated pews.

Never had the guests seen a more radiant bride or a deliriously happy bridegroom.

After the wedding service, the guests gathered at Alexia's restaurant and were milling about, when Ben's "friend" arrived, an ugly woman with black-streaked gray hair and bottle-like glasses. Almost immediately, Ben took the woman to meet the father of the bride and his partner, Sal.

"I understand you wanted your friend to meet me." She moved closer to Sal's face to get a better look at him through her very thick lenses. Charlene Winter had already been schooled on her current role in the wedding production.

Cal moved away, ready to exit their group when Charlene grabbed his coat sleeve. "Not so fast, honey. I think you're supposed to be my date today. If nothing else, we can split the hundred Sal's paying you."

"Well? Cough up the money!" Her finger poked Sal's chest.

"Perfect!" Ben choked with laughter. "Go ahead." He ended her performance and watched the woman walk into the ladies room.

"What the hell's going on?" Sal bellowed.

"Watch," Ben said simply.

A few minutes later, an attractive woman with coiffed mahogany-colored hair greeted them. Without the glasses, her clear brown eyes no longer looked beady and she appeared much younger without the wrinkled made-up face.

"How'd I do?" she asked. "Think I'll make it as an actress?"

"Oh, God," Cal said, somewhat embarrassed. His eyes moved from Charlene to Ben. "I don't know how you pulled this off."

"We're old friends," he lied. "I thought we'd give old Sal here his comeuppance, or is that too old a word?"

"I think you should collect the hundred dollars." Charlene told Cal.

"The deal was a date. This is a meeting."

"I plan to fix that." Cal took her arm and walked away.

"Nice play, Ben." Sal groused, popping a Kit Kat snack into his mouth.

"If you'd stop eating the candy for a minute and think about it, they just might hit it off. You've got Gwennie, who does he have?"

"Who the hell do you have?" Sal hissed defiantly.

"Too damn many to count," Ben said, catching Sal by surprise. Ben thought of the women from the New Year's party who kept calling him and walked away from the big man.

Sometime later, Cal drew Ben aside for a serious conversation. "Peggy and Seth told me the whole story when we got in last night. I know about Mel Travers and John Beck. They also told me about Alice's accidental death and think John planned it because she cheated on him. Megan still doesn't know those details and Peggy doesn't want to worry her. If there is anything I can do to protect Peggy, please call me." He gave Ben his cell number. "I'm glad Megan has you. She was such a little thing when I was forced to leave. In time, she'll know the truth about my prolonged absence. Peggy pieced it together and understood how the threat of exposure would become problematic for Segis. So when the bridge mugging occurred, it was his golden opportunity to get rid of Sal." Cal shook Ben's hand. "Remember. Call me." Ben watched him join the other guests.

Ben knew Megan had been watching them closely, and it was only a matter of time before she would question him.

"Essentially, it was about you," he explained when she cornered him. "He was curious about our relationship. Cal knows you haven't accepted him as your father. I think he's disappointed about that. But he knows I'll help you in any way I can."

"I don't know who's tossing more bullshit, you or him!" She started walking toward her table when his phone rang.

"Ten minutes." She heard him tell the caller. "Megan," he shouted, as she scurried to follow him, away from the noise of the party. "Later, when the guests are leaving, tell Seth and Peggy I was called out. I don't want to ruin their day."

"Another accident?"

"Yes, but different circumstances."

"Wait!" She hugged him. "Be careful." She stood in the doorway and watched him leave.

"And where is my hug?" Brad stood behind her. He watched her arms stretch backwards in an attempt to clasp his body.

"Satisfied?"

"A little lower would have been better," he said laughingly and walked her back to their table.

***

"Did you tell them?"

"No. I decided to keep it a secret."

"They'd be laughing their heads off, if they knew."

"Most newlyweds do go to Niagara Falls for their honeymoon," Peggy protested, watching Seth stow the luggage in the car trunk.

"True, but they don't live in Buffalo."

***

Within twenty minutes, all three were crossing the Peace Bridge into Canada...Seth, Peggy and Gabriel.

From there it was only a very short drive to the Canadian side of Niagara Falls...the ideal place for a <u>honeymoon…</u>.

<u>and the usual day trip for guests visiting Buffalo….</u>

Chapter 13
Mel

Ben was surprised when he was summoned. He had been at his desk working the Beck case, his frustration mounting with each turned page of his notebook. There had to be something, some piece of evidence that would nail the man who murdered his wife. So when the phone call came, he wasted no time leaving his office to head south. Not much was offered at the time. A man's body had been found, and the detective, who was working the case, thought it could be of interest to Ben or related to his unsolved murder. Police and detectives shared information and cooperated when asked, but Ben was at a loss to explain the phone call. He had not asked for help. In fact, he was up to his ass with questions, not answers, with John Beck's murder of Alice. And he had hit a brick wall with Judd's killing. There was not a shred of real evidence. In short, he had nothing. So, if he had nothing, how could he possibly have asked for help?

The middle of March was cold. It had been cold for a wedding, and it would be just as cold standing out in the middle of a heavily wooded area along Route 79, nearly a half-mile from the site of Judd's dead body approximately eight months earlier. These thoughts ran through Ben's mind, as he tried fighting off the winter chill coursing through his body in his very cold car. He hoped the trip wouldn't be a waste of time; so many of them were. Nevertheless, he had to take advantage of every opportunity offered him.

He parked off the shoulder of the road and felt the crunch of snow beneath his shoes. His feet would be soaked after trudging through the woods in the mounted accumulation, some several inches deep. How anyone found a body in the tree clustered area surprised him. However, Ben did notice a highway truck and guessed some worker wandered into the woods to relieve himself. He probably went deeper into the treed area so he wouldn't be seen from the highway and discovered the body.

Ben arrived to find a section taped off and three men milling about, while a fourth man, kneeling and bent with intensity, was in the middle of examining a body. A tall, gray-haired man, approximately Ben's age, shouted commands and seemed to be in charge. Ben walked over and introduced himself to a man named Donald Murphy. Although he seemed friendly enough, the man was all business and got right to the point of Ben's being there.

"We've been waiting for you. Danny Boyle thought you could help identify him." He watched Ben study the body, and then detailed the murder scene.

"Somebody stood behind the victim and shot him twice in the head. Had to be someone he knew. Outside pockets were sacked, but the bugger had an inside one. It's probably a picture of his wife."

"Danny Boyle? He's one of our best," Ben said, concentrating on the victim's decomposed body.

"I'm doing the nephew a favor. He said that you were working a murder case and didn't know if there was a connection."

In his gloved hand the man held a picture of Alice Beck.

"Mel Travers." Ben identified the body. "We've been looking for him since June on a murder charge. When you finish processing, I'll need the photograph, complete with prints, and a copy of the file. Danny was right on target."

"Danny's smart alright, but he tells me you're king when it comes to murder."

The man's remark made Ben laugh. "That's flattering but Danny's pulling your chain. He's good though and very thorough." Ben shook Murphy's hand and left the scene.

***

When Ben returned to his office, he immediately opened the file on Mel Travers. He read Seth's report describing Judd's murder and felt defeated. They had spent months searching for the man, and now, he turned up dead. What little evidence Ben had, along with Seth's report, was no longer useful. No one could arrest a dead man for murder. Ben had hit another brick wall.

Ben outlined the facts on a new sheet in his notebook. Mel killed Judd for kidnapping the wrong woman and he did it to save his own life. Then he tried to get rid of Seth and Peggy, never realizing it would come full circle. There was no doubt in the detective's mind: John Beck killed Mel Travers, the last remaining witness of his plan to eliminate Alice. The only thing the detective questioned was the time frame. From the composition of Mel's body, Ben created a possible scenario after the murder of Judd Thorne.

After killing him, Mel hid the body in Judd's truck and needed John's help in dumping it before dispatching the truck to a dealer in body parts. They discussed the arrangements during a drive to Remmy's tavern the next afternoon, when Seth and Peggy spotted them and took pictures. Later, that night the two men went to the wooded area off Route 79 to dump Judd's body. At that time, John Beck shot Mel in the head, dragged his body farther away from Judd's and tried hiding it under a large fallen tree. Somewhere in the scenario John got rid of Judd's truck. But he did it after murdering Mel. He probably drove the truck to some prearranged place and drove away in his own previously parked car.

His scenario struck a more resonant chord when Ben recalled the interview with Mel's sister, Nancy. The woman remembered three things: meeting her brother at Remmy's Tavern, stopping at her house for something he forgot, and driving him to a restaurant on Transit Road. That was the last time she saw him.

After meeting at the restaurant, the two men must have finalized the arrangements for Judd's truck before burying him that night. Ben pictured Mel shoveling dirt over a shallow grave, unaware of John's plan to pop two bullets into his head. Now the man had eliminated the last possible thread of a botched-up kidnapping scheme.

The passing months encouraged John to go on to his next project: Alice's accidental death. He was clever with both the planning and execution. However, the unexpected happened: Mel's body was found. While John played the part of a grief stricken widower, Ben had to prove the cases were connected. How could he prove John Beck killed Mel first and then moved on to Alice? Ben knew in his own mind, he could not tie John Beck to the kidnapping of Peggy Roberts or convince anyone that Mel murdered Judd. But if he could find the gun in John's possession, the one that killed Mel, that would be evidence enough to arrest and convict the man. Alice's picture in Mel's possession would provide motive if the entire kidnapping case became public. But the case rested on finding the gun in John's possession. Ben knew that wouldn't happen. John was too smart to keep it.

Ben read Peggy's kidnapping report again. She saw no one during the kidnapping, other than Seth. So it would have to be Seth's testimony of Mel's involvement, but Mel, of course, was dead. Then there was the question of Alice's picture in Mel's possession? What would Mel be doing with Alice's picture?

Ben played the attorney scenario in his mind. "The kidnapping was a hoax. Married Peggy Roberts was meeting her now husband, Seth Stone, clandestinely. And although puppy-dog, Mel carried a torch for Alice, there was no reciprocation."

It was almost four when Ben leaned back in his chair and stretched his arms. He was tired. There was no way in hell he could tie the kidnapping plot to John Beck. The players were dead, both of them. Of course, they never found Judd's truck, and according to an old police report, Mel's car had been previously demolished in a three-way collision.

Ben had to approach the murder from the only angle he had left. He needed the gun that killed Mel. Would John have kept it after all these months, or would he have tossed it somewhere? If Ben could find it, he would try to connect the rest of the evidence and prove that Alice's death was part of a larger plan that failed by a kidnapping mistake.

"If... I'm so tired of that damn word," he said quietly, but was soon unnerved by a very familiar shout.

"Hey!" Megan rushed to greet him. "I need..."

"Who let you in here?" Ben interrupted, before she could say anything further.

"Oh, they all know me. I brought in a case of scotch at Christmas..." Her remark left the detective positively speechless.

"Okay, I surrender. What's on your mind?"

"You have to leave now and come with me," she said. "My father called. He's coming over with Charlene Winter, Sal and Aunt Gwennie. Charlene insists you be there or she refuses to come. Does she have a thing for you or my father?"

"I can only speak for myself. No. We're just friends. I didn't know they stayed over."

"Join the club. I think they spent time doing Sal's family stuff, but no one tells me anything. C'mon," she insisted. "Tell me what to buy. Don't look at me like that. I have to feed them something. Peggy's not here to help me, so you're elected. I told you I wanted you in my family. What part of that don't you understand?" She watched him slide into his jacket and then took his hand. "We're doing food. Brad's taking care of drinks. Should we buy buckets of chicken wings from Duffey's or lunch meat from the supermarket? Maybe we should have both. What do you think, you're the detective?"

The group of police officers waved as they passed by. They were becoming accustomed to seeing that little blonde girl with the detective. Someone observing them together would think Ben was her father.

***

When they gathered around the table, Brad began pouring wine, while Megan brought in platters of lunch meat and cheese. Ben trailed her with a heaping bowl of chicken wings and a bottle of blue cheese dressing. Megan rushed back to the kitchen and re-emerged with celery, potato salad and rolls.

"See?" Sal pointed to the chicken wings and roast beef, but his eyes focused on Cal. "I told you. When you're in Buffalo, you eat chicken wings or beef on weck."

"I put the other condiments on the table," Megan said. "I didn't know if you used horseradish or mustard with your beef on weck."

"This looks delicious." Her father placed a portion of chicken wings followed by a celery rib and blue cheese onto his plate. "I didn't want you to go out of your way for us. I just wanted to spend a little time with you before we left tomorrow morning. I wanted to visit. That's why we didn't go to a restaurant."

Megan felt somewhat disappointed with the news of his departure but didn't know why. "So, you're going back tomorrow. When are you planning on visiting us again?"

"Season starts Memorial Day, actually shoulder season's two weeks earlier." Sal interrupted, before her father could answer. "It would have to be before that."

"Memorial Day." Charlene Winter brightened. "On June seventh, I have a week's play date in Sandusky. Rehearsals for 'The Mikado' start a week earlier, but I've done the role before. I seem to go from drama to musicals. Go figure."

"You're playing there? Cedar Point's only a boat ride from us." Gwennie caught the woman's attention. "Maybe we can get together."

"You must travel a lot," Sal offered. "You're everywhere."

"Yeah, in my business, the horseshit parable still stands. Some strict grammarian would call it a simile, I suppose, but when it happens so often, it should be considered a parable."

"What role will you be playing?" Cal asked the actress.

"Tell them, Ben."

"The daughter-in-law elect," he answered dryly, causing the whole table to snicker. "That's how it is. You can turn a beauty into a hag, but you can't reverse the process." The added comment had them rolling with laughter.

"How do you two know each other?" Cal expressed real interest. He wondered about the relationship between the detective and the actress. Was something of a serious nature developing between them? He couldn't picture the short pudgy man with such enormous eyes attracting a beautiful woman like Charlene Winter.

"My next door neighbor, Alice Beck, fell down the stairs and died. Although it was an accident, Ben needed to question the neighbors about the couple. I couldn't offer much. She was a nurse. He's a stockbroker and obviously, a creature of habit. Alice told me John and his office cronies would have drinks every Thursday night at Ballentines. It's a bar in town, near his office building. If he wasn't doing business out of town, he was home."

"How did you know about his Thursday schedule?" Ben was curious. This was a piece of information she had not shared with him.

"She came over the Thursday night before Christmas. She needed vanilla for cookies. I'm serious, Ben. She wanted vanilla! The ironic part of the story is that I actually had a small bottle. Baking cookies? I never cook, if I can order out."

"Then you really have to taste Sal's cuisine. He's very creative."

"Hey, I've never had one drunk complain to me." Sal challenged his partner. "My Put-in-Bay soup has everything put in it, including the Bay." The remark caused the group to laugh at the banter between them.

The lively conversation kept going at a rapid pace, when Cal suddenly became serious and addressed Megan directly, turning the room silent. They knew something important was on his mind.

"I wanted to answer your question about my next visit. I would like to spend Easter with you." He waited in silence for her response.

At the mention of Easter, Megan's face fell. A Croft holiday! How could she explain their schedule to her father? A frown crossed her face and she could feel the resentment growing inside her.

Ben caught her pained expression and eyeing Brad, offered a suggestion. "Cal could spend the day with Peggy and Seth. You could see him later that night."

"That would work." Brad agreed, seeing Megan's relief.

"Okay, what's the real problem here?" Gwennie pushed for an answer.

"My parents." Brad began. "Mother has this schedule. My sister-in-law, Rosalie, hosts Thanksgiving; my sister, Jennifer, does Easter; and mother has Christmas. She is a stickler about our attending."

"Don't forget Barbara and Franklin's big "do" at New Years." Charlene added to the schedule.

"We are expected to attend these holiday dinners or be damned sick," Brad explained the problem briefly. "If you have Easter dinner with Peggy and Seth, we can swing by afterward. Surely, you will be here for a few days."

"I'm thinking Friday through Wednesday or Thursday." Cal answered Brad's question, and then directed one of his own to Ben. "Will you be at Peggy's?"

"No. I'm having Easter dinner with my sister, Clarisa. You met her and Poag at the wedding."

"What are we doing, Sal?" Gwennie asked. "Daniel's busy."

"We'll come here and bug Cal. We could probably stay at Peggy's house. Why not bunk there?" He caught Gwennie's look. "It's vacant. Maybe I'll even cook the Easter meal."

"That's settled. We'll get together during your Easter stay." Brad ended the discussion.

"Where will you be?" Cal asked his actress friend.

"As I said before, the horseshit parable still stands."

Chapter 14
Easter

After Peggy returned from her honeymoon, Megan strolled into the gift shop and told her of their father's plan to use her vacant house during his Easter visit. She also mentioned Sal's offer to cook the holiday meal.

Although the news appeared to please Peggy, Megan could not understand her sister's reasoning. The fact that Peggy had moved into Blarney Stone, and now considered it her permanent address, was irrelevant.

"You don't really know these people." Megan referred to Sal and their Aunt Gwennie. "And how can you be so trusting of a man you hardly know, a man who claims to be our father? The story he gave was crap. Even I could come up with a better scenario for a twenty-six year absence."

"The fact that dad couldn't tell us everything, only means he's honoring Sal's silence. Dad said, 'It was up to Sal to disclose the whole story.' If you haven't figured it out, I'm surprised. Well, no. That's not true. You weren't at the engagement party. Sal is the spitting image of his uncle, Segismondo Del Grosso. His sister, Teresa, is Sal's mother."

"So what?" She shrugged.

"So nothing," Peggy replied.

"What are you telling me? Are you saying the brother shagged his sister? Christ, you are sick."

"Sometimes, sick is true." Her comment slipped out, before Peggy realized what she had said. "I'm not saying it is. But it would explain his uncle's reason for sending him away. Of course, dad would have been collateral damage and had to go with him. Remember, Sal used the word 'banished' when he gave us a quasi-explanation of their absence."

"Even if it were true, that kind of thing would be ridiculous… sending someone away. That's not the kind of thing people do these days. Why didn't he just have Sal snuffed out? Didn't Aunt Gwennie say the uncle was into illegal stuff?"

"I don't think she put it that way exactly. I got the impression he was some kind of Mafioso or something like that. In that position, he wouldn't want his associates to think he shagged someone in his own family. I mean how low can you get? And you're forgetting his sister, Sal's mother. He couldn't have her spilling her guts either. There must have been some reason she kept silent." Peggy sighed in resignation. "This is all speculation and I really don't know what I'm talking about."

"But it makes a helleva story."

"Regardless of the true story, I want them to enjoy the house. I can't keep the place indefinitely and I don't want to rent it. Seth's leaving the decision up to me. He's keeping the chalet on the escarpment. It's an escape and we like the view. Anyhow, Lockport isn't that far away. But my plan now is to get the house ready for dad and I want your help."

"You expect me to clean?" Her eyes nearly popped out of her head.

"No. I expect you to help me with a grocery list. I want food, drinks and snacks in the house for them. As soon as dad gives us a date, we'll go shopping. I'll have everything else done ahead of time."

"He mentioned coming the Friday before Easter and leaving the following Wednesday or Thursday."

"I'm not doing anything until he confirms his plans. I'm sure he'll call."

"Either way, let me know what we're doing," she said and hurriedly left the shop.

"I thought I saw Megan's car pulling out of the driveway," Janice remarked, as she stepped through the shop's back door with two cups of coffee.

"She came to tell me of father's Easter visit. He's going to stay at my place. Would you pop in to see if he needs anything? Megan and I just talked about stocking food in the house before he arrives."

"I'm glad for you, Peggy. I'm glad you found each other." Only Janice, in her uniquely genteel way could make Peggy feel such happiness in finding her lost father. "I want to unpack those perfume boxes before you leave."

"We're seeing Ben at four."

"I hope it's good news. Don't even think of coming back to the shop. I'll close."

Peggy already knew the reason for their meeting with Ben. He had already called Seth about finding Mel's dead body.

***

After leaving the gift shop, Megan raced into Ben's office to find him pouring over his notes. There was nothing new and nothing more that could be done. He had made his report, but his superiors felt there was not enough evidence for an arrest; one that would stand, once John Beck had his moneyed lawyers defend him. If he could find the gun that killed Mel with John's fingerprints on it, he could do something about the murder. And with Alice's death, Ben couldn't find one loophole. The lab tests came in but proved nothing. The position of the woman's body indicated she fell accidentally, according to the coroner's report. There was a plausible explanation for everything. He kept going over John's statement the night of her death. And later, when he went back to the house for a second look, he came up with nothing. Had John Beck committed the perfect crime? More important, would he get away with it? Would the man be smart enough to have one crime relegated to a cold case and the other, an accidental death? However, his thoughts were brought up sharply, by the clicking of high heels.

"What are you doing here?" He looked up to face Megan.

"I want to know about incest," she said, noticing his look of shock.

Ben cleared his throat. What the hell was she thinking now? With Megan, he never knew what clutter was going through her mind.

"I don't want a definition," she added. "I know what it is, although I can't picture that kind of shit going on, particularly in a family. I want to know if you've had cases or experience with it."

"I have, but we don't publicize it. It's not something you want aired. It's not only humiliating to the person who was abused, but it lingers in that person's memory…essentially, forever. Why?"

"Do you think it's possible for a brother to impregnate his sister and later banish his son for twenty-six years to avoid suspicion because they look alike? I mean it sounds like something in a movie."

"You're referring to someone we met recently, and yes, I got the impression something of that nature occurred. But I think it best if we dwell on the present, Megan. The past can only bring back hurtful memories. Think of your father's involvement. He was in the wrong place at the wrong time. He suffered the loss of watching you blossom into a beautiful young lady. The same is true with Peggy. I think your best option is to move on. Enjoy your father while you can."

"You see things so differently. You make everything sound so sensible. It drives me nuts sometime, but that's why I love you," she hugged and kissed him on the forehead. "I'll see you at the house."

"What are you talking about?"

"I want you with me when they come for Easter. Maybe we should ask Charlene too."

"If that's your sneaky way of asking, 'Am I dating her?' The answer is no. And I am not dating Victoria Reynolds either, although she did call me."

"Don't you ever get tired of sleeping alone?"

"Who said I sleep alone?"

"Touche! Burrows!" She thundered loud enough to get the attention of the police officers. "Watch out! He's razor sharp today," she shouted, passing them by.

Ben was amused as he watched her race out of his office.

He hadn't lied about not sleeping alone. He always had his gun with him. The wide smile faded when Danny Boyle popped into his office with a slip of paper.

"She called twice, but I didn't want to interrupt your conversation with Megan."

"Megan?"

"Your daughter," he answered. "She said you adopted her last year." He went on, unable to understand why Ben started coughing and choking so suddenly. He wondered if the man needed some water. "Anyhow, I took these messages for you," he said before leaving Ben's office.

Ben read both messages. They were exactly the same. Victoria Reynolds wanted him to call her. At that moment, Ben felt like strangling his 'adopted daughter' and her smorgasbord ideas. Instead, he threw the phone messages into his waste basket.

***

Later that afternoon, when they walked into Ben's office, Seth asked, "Are we too early?"

"No, you're good." He closed his office door. "I didn't want to have this conversation in a social setting. Here, we have privacy with no interruptions."

"You made our meeting sound ominous." Seth could not begin to imagine the importance of Ben's information. He wondered if something else had developed.

Ben picked up a thick file on his desk.

"I wanted to talk about Peggy's kidnapping and Judd's murder. We found Mel's body somewhere near Judd's. I told you on the phone his body turned up, but I wanted to bring you up to speed on the case."

The detective paused momentarily, thinking how best to begin. Once their conversation terminated, Ben knew they would be disappointed with the outcome.

"Judging from the decomposition of the body, the coroner's report indicates death occurred within a year or less. So, I think my scenario is right on target," Ben said pointedly and began to describe John Beck's premeditated murder of Mel after burying Judd. "He left no witnesses alive…or so he thinks. He doesn't know Seth witnessed Judd's murder, or that both of you knew he was behind the whole scheme to get rid of Alice."

"That means you're at a dead-end with Judd's murder." Seth understood the whole scenario too well. "With Mel dead, Judd's no longer an issue. You can't prosecute a dead man."

"We never did find the gun that killed Judd either. I think I misled you before. It was a Ruger that killed him. Someone filed the wrong information, so I went back to the lab for a recheck." Ben thought of detective Grassley with disgust. Drinking would be the man's downfall. Ben was certain of it. "We do know that a different caliber gun was used to kill Mel." Ben continued to vent his frustration. "I feel terrible, but have nowhere to go with this. I thought I could make a case against John Beck for killing Mel, but we found no gun. I have no probable cause for a warrant to search his house, although I doubt the gun's there. And the powers that be tell me I have no case with Alice. It's ruled accidental death. I know you are disappointed and frankly, I'm pissed. I am so frustrated with this whole case."

"Isn't there anything you can do?" Peggy asked.

"Not unless I can find the gun with his fingerprints." Although the detective answered Peggy's question, his thoughts focused on Seth.

"I've let you down," he said, "first, with Helen; and now, with Judd. A slap on the wrist was all the politician's son got for the hit and run fatality. And now, with Judd, no wrist slap, no case before a judge… nothing. I've failed you miserably."

"You've done everything you could to keep us in the loop. The man who killed my half-brother is dead. You didn't kill him; John Beck did. I know you're looking for the gun that killed Mel, but I don't think it's in his house either. He probably got rid of it months ago. He's covered his tracks all the way around, with both Mel and Alice."

"Frankly, Seth, I have no avenue to pursue. Judd's dead, Mel's dead, the lab results on Alice indicate accidental death and John Beck's home free."

"You can't keep beating a dead horse," Peggy offered. "You've done everything for us, Ben. If the evidence isn't there, there's nothing more you can do."

"I just wish it turned out differently, but I wanted to be honest with you."

Seth stood up from his chair and shook Ben's hand. "You've done everything you could," Seth said. "Just keep us in the loop."

***

When Cal Burkett called Peggy to confirm his Easter visit, she told him about the discovery of Mel's body and the accidental death ruling in the case of Alice Beck. There was nothing more to be done. For all intents and purposes, that case was closed. The other one, dealing with the discovery of Mel's body, was still open, but was now at a standstill, pending the discovery of a handgun.

"They never found it?"

"Ben couldn't search the house. No probable cause. Seth and I don't think it's there anyhow. Ben doesn't either. John's too smart."

"I'd go along with Ben's thinking. He's been a detective for a long time. That's what Charlene told me at the wedding. The man's really good at his job."

"Then you're coming, for sure?" She changed the subject.

"I'll see you in two weeks. Sal and Gwennie will be staying at the house with me. Sal wants to cook dinner. Is that okay with you?"

"Absolutely, we'll have a party."

"Love you, Maggie Pie."

"Ditto, dad." She placed the receiver back into the cradle.

Peggy had no idea her father would place another phone call when their conversation ended. She didn't know he had Charlene Winter's phone number or that he would make such a request.

***

It was well after dinner when Ben arrived at the Peggy's house on Easter. He was greeted first by Seth and Peggy, and then by the Put-in-Bay trio and Charlene Winter. Megan and Brad had not yet arrived from the Croft family affair.

"I'm glad you're here," Charlene began. "I think we should get this over and done with. You're going to be pissed in any event."

"What have you done?" Ben asked, surprised by the woman's comment. "Why am I going to be angry?"

"As you know, Peggy told Cal the whole story of her kidnapping…right to the discovery of Mel's body. Apparently, this weighed heavily on his mind, since the case seemed to be going nowhere. When Cal called and told me about it, he wanted to know if I would be willing to search my neighbor's house for the gun."

"Oh. God," Ben groaned loudly. "Don't say anything more to incriminate yourself. I don't want to know."

"It's okay. Really." She tried reassuring the man whose bulging eyes were popping out of their sockets. "I wasn't alone. Sal was with me." Charlene thought knowing she had company would make Ben feel better.

"No. No. No!" Ben shouted at the woman. "Breaking and Entering; I don't want to hear about it."

"Oh, for Christ sake, untangle your shorts. I had a key! John went out of town and asked me to look after his house. So I did." She paused for a nano-second.

"Actually, I was more interested in seeing if that little bitch stole more than my husband's cufflinks." Almost instantly, she turned to face Cal, "Don't ask."

"I made a thorough search," Sal addressed the detective. "If the man owns a gun, then it's stashed somewhere else. There are no firearms in the house."

"But I did find something," Charlene reported. "He had a record of Victoria Reynolds' real estate holdings on his computer. Why would he have that? Why would a stockbroker want a record of her wealth?" She looked at Ben.

"Is she aware of it? That would be a better question," he replied. Now Ben was curious. He should have returned her phone calls. Maybe a relationship with him wasn't her objective after all.

"Hey! What have we missed?" An enthusiastic Megan shouted as she entered the room.

"I was wondering who was taking us to Niagara Falls," her father answered. "Isn't that's where you take visitors to the area? I want to see the Canadian side too. I hear it's really beautiful."

While Cal was rattling on about Niagara Falls, Seth and Peggy began to laugh hysterically.

"What's so funny?" Cal demanded.

Seth and Peggy grew serious for a moment and then started laughing all over again.

"That's where you went after the wedding!" Megan guessed. "Two Buffalonians going to Niagara Falls for their honeymoon! That's priceless!" She clapped her hands and started laughing with them, causing the rest of the family to join in.

"It beats staying in town. At least they had beautiful views and great places to eat." Gwennie agreed with the couple's choice. She had visited the tourist attraction many years earlier and loved it.

"You don't find that strange?" Peggy asked of the honeymoon site so close to their home.

"I wouldn't mind going back there myself," Gwennie replied. "It's beautiful."

"That's what we thought." Peggy caught Seth's nod. "Let's visit tomorrow and have lunch on the Canadian side." She waited silently for their agreement.

"Am I invited too?" Charlene asked.

"Are you kidding? You're going to be our tour guide," Sal quipped.

"Then we're all set." Brad started counting the number of cars needed to accommodate the group.

"Not quite," Ben explained. "I have to work tomorrow." He caught Megan's frown of disapproval. "I need to talk with you, privately," he said and led her to another room in the house, a distance far enough away, so their conversation would not be heard by the group in the family room.

***

"Now young lady, tell me about the 'adopted daughter's story' and everything you know about Victoria Reynolds."

"What do you want me to say? I told you before: you're more my father than he is." She reiterated her feelings for him. "You can't make a person love you, and he can't make me love him. That's how it is. You've always known how I felt about you. I happen to love and respect you, so I told the people at the station I'm your 'adopted daughter.' You're too old to be my lover, so the father bit was more believable."

"Ah, Megan." His eyes fixed on her and he felt utterly confused. Ben felt sorry for the young woman. She found it hard to accept her own biological father; and yet, the fact, that she cared more for the detective, awakened feelings deep within him, emotions, he thought had died a long time ago. In her own way, she really was like a daughter to him. Megan came to him for help; she came when she was in need; and she came for answers to embarrassing questions; but most of all, Megan came because she knew he would always be there for her. Yes, he and his dead wife, Julie, would have loved having a daughter like Megan. So how could he object, if she wanted to be his 'adopted daughter?'

"So, on the other issue, are you and Victoria…?" She ogled him.

"Megan, get off the romantic kick," he growled, his eyes the size of two Frisbees. Megan knew she had touched a raw nerve and now wished she could retract her statement. "What do you know about her social life and business dealings?"

"She owns a lot of property in town. Some of her rentals are on Delaware Avenue and I think she's invested in stocks and bonds. Well, her family was. I know she inherited a lot of money, but she's made a bundle on her own."

"Who handles her investments? Do you know?"

"No, but I can call and ask for a reference. I know she'd tell me."

"I don't want you to do that," Ben said firmly. "Who is she seeing socially?"

"Other than you? No one that I know of." She smirked

Ben gave Megan, his 'if looks could kill' face. "I wish we could have a sensible conversation about women, without your thinking, 'I need a relationship or am in one.'" He chose his words carefully. "I think the woman may be worried or is in some kind of trouble."

"And you wanted me to call her and find out what it is."

"No. I want my 'adopted daughter' to stay out of it and keep her mouth shut about this conversation, and what I am about to tell you."

The information Ben imparted had a profound quieting effect on Megan. Now she was privy to everything that went on, beginning with her sister's kidnapping to the search of John Beck's house and the information stored on the man's computer.

"Oh. My God! I'm shocked. Poor, Peggy… Poor, Seth. What can I do, Ben? Tell me. I have to do something."

"It's imperative, you tell no one about this. I understand you and Victoria Reynolds are friends. She told me at the New Year's party about your knock-down drag-out with Winifred Pitts, and how you became friends afterward. I want you to call her for coffee and, during that conversation, casually learn about her business dealings." He neglected to mention Charlene Winter's comment over lunch about John Beck being Victoria Reynolds' stockbroker.

"So you want me to pump her for information." After making the comment, Megan began to giggle. "I'm going to be your informant."

"Yes," Ben said dryly, "a real father and daughter team."

"That is so frigginly cool!" she shrieked. "Can I tell Brad? I promise…no one else."

"Tell Brad what?" Her tall handsome husband entered the room. "You two have been gone forever."

Megan ignored his comment, listening instead for Ben's answer.

"Only him," Ben emphasized. "I mean it."

"I understand." Megan approached the short pudgy man and threw her arms around him, hugging and swinging him sideways to face her husband.

"Do I have a story for you!"

"Actually…" Ben corrected her quickly and, in a soberly fashion, said, "My 'adopted daughter' has several."

"Adopted daughter? Several?" Ben heard Brad ask, as he left the room.

***

"Well, look who's back." Charlene met Ben's stare. "Mission accomplished?" Her demeanor told him she knew of the disclosure.

"I think so," he hesitated. "Given time, I hope it was the right path."

"Given the relationship, it was a smart move." She agreed with his assessment.

"What are you two talking about?" The conversation made no sense to Cal who was listening to their cryptic questions and answers.

"It's all part of a neighborhood canvass, Ben and I talked about months ago over lunch," she said indifferently. "No matter...who wants another drink?" She sauntered over to the bar. "C'mon Sal, you're a bartender."

Although Peggy and Seth watched Sal whip-up the drink orders, they were wondering how Charlene Winter fit into the pieces of Ben's puzzle.

Megan also watched the group but remained silent. She couldn't wait to tell Brad about the conversation she had with her 'adopted father.'

***

After the party wrapped up and Gwennie went to bed, the two men were still sitting in the family room, when Sal dropped a bomb. "Victoria Reynolds' inventory list wasn't the only thing in John Beck's house today."

"I hate it, when you do this," Cal grumbled. "You're playing me again."

"I'm not this time. He has at least forty grand...in cash. Charlene was in the other room at the computer. But I saw this round table with a drop-in top and a big turnip lamp on it. It seemed out of place to me, so I looked inside. There it was...his stash."

"What did you do, after you found the money?" Cal salivated with interest.

"I put the lamp back," Sal answered, knowing that kind of ending would piss-off his partner, but he just couldn't resist.

Chapter 15
Evidence

It was nearly ten o'clock when Ben pulled into the driveway of his home. He noticed the mounds of snow still lining the driveway and was glad he used the snow blower before he went to Clarisa's for the Easter holiday. The day seemed strange without Seth. There were only three of them at the dinner table this year. He missed the camaraderie and jokes Seth brought to the group. Yet, Ben knew he would feel the same way Cal Burkett did, upon finding his daughters after a twenty-six year absence. The father wanted to spend as much time as possible with them, and Easter seemed like a perfect holiday, since it didn't seem to interfere with the start of their tourist season at Put-in-Bay.

Entering the house, Ben threw a set of car keys on the kitchen table and, stretching his jacket around the arms of a kitchen chair, pulled a bottle of single malt scotch from the cupboard and poured himself a drink. He looked at his watch, dialed a phone number and identified himself. "Sorry for the hour. You called three times so I assumed it must be important."

"It is. I'd like to see you." Victoria Reynolds expressed urgency.

"Do you want to come by my office tomorrow?"

"No. I'd rather have lunch at some private place."

"Are you familiar with Jameson's?" He heard her pause. "Take 324 to Young's Road in Amherst and drive through the tunnel. You should see it on the right." Ben gave an approximate location of the restaurant. "It's a quaint place near the airport and it's very private. The food's very good. Say eleven-thirty?"

"I will meet you there." She ended their conversation.

***

Ben sat on the sofa and sipped his scotch slowly. The phone conversation with Victoria Reynolds puzzled him. She seemed very calm during their conversation and he couldn't understand her urgency to see him. Granted, she did try to monopolize his attention several times at the New Year's party, but since so many other women came forward, he was seldom alone. Had he rushed to return her call sooner than necessary? When he learned John Beck had an inventory of her properties on his computer, Ben thought there might be a connection between her knowledge of it and the number of phone calls to him. Now, he wasn't sure. If Victoria Reynolds was ignorant of John Beck's computer list, why would she want to see him? More important, why did she need to meet at some restaurant hideaway?

His thoughts ran from his scheduled meeting with Victoria Reynolds to the evening party at Peggy's house. It seemed like a cohesive gathering outwardly. But Ben knew that was not the case. He noticed the underlying current of distrust that ran through the night's superficial conversation. Whatever her father said, Megan ignored. What was it about the man that caused Megan to distance herself from him? Perhaps distancing was too strong a word. Megan was very cordial outwardly. But she was not the loving daughter he wanted or hoped he'd find. Given time, Cal Burkett thought Megan would come around and accept him as her father. Unfortunately, he did not know the temperament of his daughter. Megan was the antithesis of Peggy. Where Peggy would be calm and accepting, Megan would offer volatility and rejection. Those few, who really knew and understood Megan, realized her explosive nature and unpredictability; she would reject anyone trying hard to get close to her. In her suspicious mind, everyone had an agenda. And Cal Burkett was no exception. He was trying to close in, much too fast. His other mistake was hoping she would love him like a father. She didn't dislike him, but he was not on her list of favorite people either. If he continued forcing his affections in her direction, Cal Burkett would run the risk of losing Megan completely. Was he that stupid about relationships or just anxious? What could he not understand about the concept of trust? His daughter did not trust him. Until she did, their relationship could not go forward.

His thoughts went back to Victoria Reynolds and Ben wondered if he should have Danny Boyle do an MYA again. He was uncertain about doing that, particularly, if the woman wanted to discuss something secretly and felt reluctant to talk about it. Ben had witnessed that situation before. Drawing-out someone with pertinent information took time, and Ben realized he could be with the woman for several hours. The idea of spending hours with her did not sit well with him. She had eyed him like a piece of meat ready for slicing at Croft's New Year's Day party. At least, that's what he thought at the time.

"I'm reading too much into a simple date for lunch," Ben said to himself, but he didn't believe it. "I'm going to bed," he said aloud, then placed the empty scotch glass on the counter.

***

The next morning, Ben left the station twenty minutes early for his appointment with Victoria Reynolds. He wanted to select a corner table that offered more privacy; one that had less chance of their conversation being overheard and farther away from the normal restaurant cluster. He had not been waiting long before Victoria Reynolds approached him.

"Hello." She greeted him wrapped in a mink coat and a matching hat whose wide brim looked like an open umbrella.

"Glad you could make it," he said, standing-up immediately to remove her coat and seat her. Ben wondered if he should have dressed more carefully, when he noticed her black dress dripping with gold jewelry. "I got the impression that our meeting was important. Did you have something to discuss with me?"

"I would like a drink; then we'll talk."

Ben waved to the waitress who took their drink orders and gave them menus. After she left, Ben studied the woman sitting across from him. She had clear brown eyes and a smooth unlined face, making him wonder about cosmetic surgery. Although he couldn't quite see her hair under the wide hat, Ben knew it was dyed a dark brown color. The shape of her body had stuck in his mind at the New Year's party;

it reminded him of a stick figure, cinched at the waist with a belt. All in all, she was pretty well-preserved. And why not? She had the money for all kinds of cosmetic work. But no matter how youthful she tried to look, Ben knew they were approximately the same age.

"Whatever you want to discuss must be difficult for you. At least that's my assumption." No sooner had Ben made the statement, when the waitress appeared with two cocktails. "We have not looked at the menu yet." He addressed the waitress who slipped away quietly.

"Here's to you, Ben. You may hate me after this." The woman dinged his glass and took a gulp, causing him to wonder where the conversation was headed. She placed her drink on the table, looked him straight in the eye and asked him directly, "Would you want to go to bed with me?"

"I beg your pardon." Ben coughed, his eyes bulging more by the minute.

"I don't mean right now. No. That's not what I mean." She took another gulp of her drink. "Look at me. Do I look like someone you would hit on? This is going so badly. I should leave."

"No. Victoria. Please stay." His hand crossed hers, reassuring the woman before taking it away. "Let's just have lunch and make small talk," he said calmly and, in a quiet manner, called the waitress to place their order.

Victoria found his soothing plea comforting. Perhaps Ben would understand her dilemma if she could explain it coherently. She knew he had a history as a great detective. But more than that, she had a sense about the man, since meeting him at the New Year's party. The detective must have witnessed the foibles and frailties of many people over the years, and she felt certain he would understand her problem.

"Tell me," Ben said in a quiet methodical way, knowing he had her full attention. "Do you think someone is trying to take advantage of you?" His eyes never left hers when he asked the question. Depending on her answer he could determine its relevance.

"Yes, but emotionally," she insisted. "And that's the problem. Seriously, if you had a choice of sleeping with someone, would you select me? Of course not," she answered, before stabbing her salad.

"So you think someone is after your money," he said simply, finishing half of his Reuben.

"How did you know?" She gave an expression of relief.

"Greed comes in different faces. But it's all the same really. It all hinges on two things: who has the money and how can the other person get it."

"What can I do? It's getting sticky and Winifred is becoming very angry."

"Winifred Pitts? The one Megan Croft socked?" Ben snickered. Now, the conversation was getting interesting. It was Victoria Reynolds who told Ben the story of Megan's pugnacious performance the previous year.

"That, very one. We have been going to social gatherings for years, sometimes together, but more often, alone. He's obnoxious, I know. But he's stopped picking on me for some reason. Now, however, Winifred's angry. He learned I was seeing someone and said the man was only interested in my money. Winifred looks after some of my investments."

"How did he know you were seeing someone?" Although Ben asked the question, he was curious how the middle-aged woman had two men on the hook.

"I have no idea. Maybe he had me followed. If I am, I'll hear about seeing you and then I'll know. He can't say you're after my money. I initiated this meeting."

"Slow down, Victoria. How long have you been involved with Winifred Pitts?" For some reason his question hit a nerve.

"Why don't you just ask if we've been sleeping together? That's what you want to know, isn't it?"

"You are one strange lady." He took offense at her reply. "If I wanted to know about your sleeping arrangements, I would have asked. I don't care if you're sleeping with a goat: I'm trying to help you." Ben could see his reprimand hit home with her.

"Maybe ten years. As I told you before, sometimes I'd go alone; other times, we'd go as a couple, but we never...coupled, so to speak."

"What was it like when you were together?"

"I don't understand, Ben. What do you mean?"

"Was he kind, gentlemanly or obnoxious? Did he embarrass you when you were together?" Ben threw a barrage of questions at the woman.

"I never thought about it. But you're right. He was different when we went as a couple. He was very considerate. Come to think of it, he didn't like it when I refused to go with him to another function."

"Then you haven't thought through the real issue. 'He's considerate,' your words, when you are together. You two have been together, maybe ten years. Now someone else is moving in, and Winifred is angry. Why do you suppose that is?" Ben did not wait for a response. "Obviously, Winifred's jealous because he cares about you. But there's a second issue to consider. Is Winifred Pitts independently wealthy?"

"He has a large law firm that's rather prestigious, in addition to old family money. He also owns a big house in the city. Why?"

"He may feel this person you are seeing is unworthy or doesn't have the scope of your living or the money. It's his way of protecting you."

"What should I do, Ben? I'm really not sure I would be happy with Winifred, but I don't think John's been honest with me either. The age difference is just one factor."

"John…?"

"John Beck, my stockbroker. He's a widower. His wife died four or five months ago in a fall. It was ruled an accidental death. He just listed his house for sale and asked me to hold some valuables until he moves to the city. He visits me more often now and Winifred is really annoyed."

"What kinds of valuables?" A bell went off in Ben's head. Could it be possible? He did not want to get too excited. It could prove to be nothing.

"Two big envelopes, one is smudged. I don't know what's in them. Is it important?" She could sense Ben's mounting curiosity.

"Where are they right now?"

"He asked me to put them in my safety deposit box," she explained.

"Where's the key?"

"On the ring in my purse. Why?"

Ben grabbed her fur coat off the chair and, holding it open while she slid into it, expressed his thoughts. "Victoria," he said, dismissing the whole idea of a continued lunch, "it's imperative that we go to your bank. We'll drop off my car and use yours." He rushed the confused woman out of the restaurant.

"I don't understand what we're doing." She stood by her vehicle.

"Sometimes it's better that way. But, believe me what we're doing is very important."

"You're protecting me from something, aren't you?" Her eyes riveted his, as she asked for clarification.

"I'll know better after we go to the bank. Follow me to the station." After making a quick phone call requesting a favor and checking the side car pocket for a pair of latex gloves…just in case, he started his car.

The waitress who left the restaurant bill on the table could not have been happier. The man left a twenty-five percent tip.

***

Ben Burrows and Victoria Reynolds sat in the small room facing her safety deposit box. Upon opening the hinged box, they stared at the two large bubble-wrap envelopes lying on top of its multi-layered contents.

Pulling-on the latex gloves, Ben took the top envelope and attempted to feel its contents by pressing the outer edges toward the package center. Almost instantly, he knew it had the feel of a gun. But was it…the gun…John Beck's gun? He took the second envelope and repeated the same process. He suspected the contents belonged to Mel Travers. He sat in silence facing Victoria Reynolds. The question running through his mind now was why? Why did John Beck give them to her? Mentally, he coupled the envelopes with Victoria's property list on John Beck's computer. How were these two related?

"I'm going to need those envelopes." He told the woman who closed the hinged box. "And I want you to drive me back to the station."

"They're related to a case, aren't they?" She caught the glimmer in his eyes. "You don't think his wife's death was an accident."

"We need to talk," Ben said. "Right now, I want you to give me the envelopes voluntarily and take me back to the station."

"If the envelopes are related to anything criminal, I don't want them. Not only will I give them to you, I'll put it in writing. I do not want to be incriminated. Winifred will kill me, if he thinks I'm involved in some criminal activity."

"Think of it this way…It may just give him the motivation to disclose his feelings." He ushered her out of the bank and into the car. The two envelopes rested in Ben's gloved hands.

***

When they reached the police station, Victoria went with Ben to an area for preparing evidence.

"What do you have there?" Danny Boyle watched Ben look inside an envelope he held in his gloved hands. "Looks like a nine mil," Ben said, sliding it on the table with a pencil. "No fingerprints, wiped clean. I'll need a bullet match. Take a picture."

After Danny Boyle took pictures of the gun, Ben placed it into an evidence bag.

"Is it connected to the body on 79?"

"I'm hoping." Ben nodded, as Danny took a picture of the second envelope's contents. "Chain of evidence should be complete now."

"Sally's still here. I'll get her." As Danny was leaving, he heard Ben's muffled voice speak to someone on his cell phone.

Within minutes, a tall stout woman from the crime lab addressed Ben. "You have something for me?"

Ben picked up both evidence bags and gave them to her.

"You keep disappointing me, Burrows. One of these days, I'm going to stop asking."

"One of these days, I may surprise you," he cracked back.

"You notice I'm not holding my breath." She walked away.

Once Ben completed his task, Victoria began to regret her actions. "When John finds out I gave you the envelopes, he'll come after me." Tears began welling in her eyes.

"Nothing is going to happen to you. Do you understand? Come with me." Ben led her to another room.

Once inside, Ben began taping a question and answer interview of the time Victoria received the two envelopes and of the person, John Beck, who gave them to her. At that time, the man asked her to hold his valuables until he changed to another permanent residence. Her sworn statement also indicated she had not opened the envelopes, nor was she aware of their contents.

A woman entered the room with the transcribed document which Ben and Victoria reread. Finding it satisfactory, Victoria signed her statement and dated it. The woman took the document away. She would place it in Ben's comprehensive case file.

Ben took Victoria's hand and led her to his office. "Now, let's get to the matter at hand. The gun in the envelope may be related to another murder case. This is not about John's dead wife." He paused, witnessing her shock. "Are you concerned for your life now? Do you think John may want to kill you?"

"Ben, I've just given evidence that could put him in prison for murder. What would you think?"

The detective knew the look of fear. It was written all over her face. However, he couldn't tell her his true feelings…what he thought might have been the real purpose of her holding John's envelopes.

Although Victoria's statements were true, John's inventory list of her properties indicated something even more sinister. If they married and she had an accident, he would become a very wealthy man. The envelopes could remain safely hidden until he disposed of them at a later date. But how could he get her to marry him? Could he incriminate her with the envelopes, by using aiding and abetting, to force her? That scenario seemed crazy to the detective. No. John was more likely to charm the woman into a hasty marriage and take her somewhere with a planned accident in mind. Ben would keep those thoughts to himself…for now.

"How was it left between you?" It was necessary she talk of their relationship. He already had the story on Winifred Pitts.

"John would call, or sometimes, he would just stop by the apartment and take me to dinner. The doorman is very friendly to him."

"As friendly as Winifred?"

"Oh. No. He's more…formal with Winifred." Her hesitation told Ben volumes. John Beck had easy access to her penthouse apartment…in a building that she owned. Would the doorman allow John inside her apartment when she was not there? That thought worried him.

"Do you have a regular schedule?" His unexpected question surprised her.

"I have a regular routine…exercise in the morning, have lunch with my friends, get my hair done, that kind of thing."

"But you don't have to be at a particular place, at a certain time," he said.

"No. I am free to go anywhere, why?" She couldn't understand where he was going with this.

"I want you to hire someone I know and trust. I want you to go away with him for awhile. Have you some relative you can visit? You could say your cousin's husband happened to be in Buffalo for a meeting and you're leaving with him to visit her. Tell your doorman that story when you leave with your luggage tomorrow. Do not mention a city or a location."

"Tomorrow?" She was shocked with his proposal.

"If Winifred should call you about me, tell him you asked for my help because you thought you were being followed. Remember, he knows we met at the Croft party."

"What if John Beck had me followed?"

"John wouldn't hire someone. He would do it himself, and I don't think he has that kind of time. My money's on Winifred," Ben said, waving a tall middle-aged man his way, unaware he overheard their entire conversation.

"Victoria, I want you to meet Medoc Hast." Ben made a short introduction, hoping the woman wouldn't notice his own shock.

The detective had expected Clayson Black, and not, Medoc Hast. The job of bodyguard seemed beneath this man of many talents, who now stood before him, and their first meeting flashed through Ben's mind. However, he remained silent and watched Medoc slip into guardian mode.

The handsome man took Victoria's hand. His clear brown eyes met hers and he studied her tight cosmetic face. This was a woman who took care of herself and would not allow time to take its toll. He lowered his eyes to study her body. Although the woman was quite thin, she was also without many curves. Nevertheless, her clothing and jewelry imbued a posture of wealth.

"We'll be fine, together." His comment told Ben everything he needed to know. "I'll go with Victoria in her car. Tomorrow, we'll park it and take mine. We'll pace ourselves, no need to go on a run."

"You're staying with her tonight." Ben ciphered the man's conversation.

"I brought my shaving kit and clean underwear, for now."

"No pajamas?" Victoria questioned the man whose brown-eyed stare pierced her clothing.

"Your cousin sleeps nude." He slipped the mink coat around her shoulders, the hat on her head and gave her a purse to hold.

"Any last instructions?" Medoc waited for the laconic detective to speak.

"Don't let anything happen to her," Ben said simply.

"You're no fun!" He ushered the woman out of the building and into her car.

"Okay. Where would you like to take your cousin to dinner?" Medoc Hast and Victoria Reynolds sat in her car and laughed hysterically.

***

As soon as they left, Ben made a phone call. "I want to speak to my informant," he said when Megan answered the phone. "You are not to call Victoria Reynolds. I changed the plan for now. No phone calls. No communication." Megan listened to his instructions then asked a question that touched a nerve. "You will be the third to know, when it happens," he replied, referring to her question about finding a gun. "It's the logical thing to do. Peggy and Seth should be told every-thing first." He pressed the end button.

Chapter 16
Medoc

Medoc Hast was not an ordinary man in the ordinary sense. Aside from being tall, thin and handsome by some standards, his crop of shiny black hair framed a fair-skinned chiseled face, whose facial lines belied his mid-fifty years. However, they did add a little more dash to the attractive man, whose comely smile would cripple any non-believer of love at first sight. His wardrobe smelled of quality and he presented himself as an educated man from old family money.

Anyone looking at him would say he spared no expense on clothing, or anything else in fashion that would add to his meticulous appearance. And today, this male enigma, whom Ben called upon, did present himself as a man of worldly tastes; however, they both knew, well ahead of time, the precise role Ben wanted him to play. His job description was clear. What wasn't clear was the appearance of Medoc himself. The man headed a family of five thespians: the name Ben gave the group many years earlier, because this collection of "actors," in reality, could have been much more lethal than the every-day roles they portrayed.

Actually, when Ben thought about it, Medoc was the designated head because he owned the house the four others shared. To this day Ben was curious about the men who lived there and the reasons they gave for moving in with him. Were they personal, or did they just renounce a society that forgot them a long time ago? Or were they just a bunch of old guys with no place to live for one reason or another?

It occurred to Ben that he and the men were approximately the same age, at least Medoc Hast and Clayson Black were. The other three had to be in that relative age category: old enough to have experienced very skillful training, and yet young enough to still have clarity of thought. That these middle-aged men were military years earlier could have raised more questions, than a rag-tag group living together because they were terminated by a steel mill company. And yet their being together was logical, if they were "pasteurized" from the same unit at different time intervals. All they ever wanted was anonymity. So who was he to deny their request?

Ben thought Clayson Black would be guarding Victoria Reynolds when he phoned initially, from his car, for a bodyguard. The second call merely confirmed his presence at the station. He was shocked when Medoc appeared. He thought the man took on more "challenging" assignments. At least, that's what Ben assumed after their first encounter. Medoc was too qualified. Yet this highly intelligent man, this trained chameleon-like assassin, would fit into any role perfectly by assuming different identities. Although his roommates must have been excellent in their line of work, Medoc had to be the best. However, as he stated in the last part of their cryptic conversation, "on a run," meant Clayson Black was involved in something else, and therefore, not available. Taking this job was his means of repaying Ben for not trying to arrest him. Of course, both men knew it would never have come to that. Medoc would have killed him first. Medoc came to return the favor for his silence, and Ben was smart enough to let that event fade from his mind. It was never mentioned…ever.

Ben's thoughts drifted back several years earlier to the wedding reception of a local politician's daughter. How Medoc came by an invitation was a mystery. Of course, Ben's whole group got one: they had donated a large sum of money to the man's campaign. Ben objected to that kind of thing, but he knew how the game was played and refused to comment on political theater.

Somehow, Ben drifted into a solitary room to find Medoc removing a thumb drive from a computer. He moved swiftly but not fast enough before Medoc held a knife to his throat.

"I'm not interested in bloodying-up the carpet or back yard, but I will." He turned Ben's pudgy body to face the French doors.

"I'm detective, Ben Burrows." He introduced himself.

"Well, Ben Burrows, do you want to be a live detective or a dead one?"

Ben never answered Medoc's question. Noises were heard approaching and both escaped notice. Ben went back to the reception and Medoc disappeared completely.

A week later when Ben was walking toward the station parking lot, a passing car came to an abrupt halt and the driver told Ben to get in.

"How did you find me?"

"It's not hard to find a detective," he said. "My name's Medoc Hast. I always return a favor. That's what I was doing when we met." He gave Ben a small white card with a phone number. "When you call, mention your name and verbalize your request with as few words as possible. Do not discuss our conversation with Clarisa or Poag." His eyes darted to the door, signaling Ben to exit.

Ben understood the subtext. Their conversation never took place.

Approximately a month later, Ben drove across a set of abandoned tracks on Railroad Street in Clarence, then along a gravel driveway, narrowed by a dense overgrowth of shrubs and brambles, to a large New England style house of weathered clapboards. On the driveway sat three black vans.

When Ben slid out of the car, Medoc Hast wasted no time in confronting him.

"What are you doing here?"

"You mean how did I find you?" Ben rephrased his question. "I saw Tony's pizza box on your back seat. There's only one Tony's. It was a question of biding my time and following you."

"What the hell kind of detective are you? I spotted you three times before I allowed you to follow me," Medoc said calmly. "Now answer my question. You have four guns pointed at your heart or head. Nobody's really concerned which area to hit."

"I may need help, sometime." Ben was at a loss to give a further explanation for his presence.

"We're not the Red Cross, Burrows," he said hastily. "We're just a bunch of old guys trying to make a life for ourselves. I know I owe you." He remembered giving Ben a card. "One of us will help you, if we can. One more thing; forget this address if you want our relationship to continue."

Everything about Medoc Hast was strange. When they first met at the reception, he was clean shaven and gray. At the station parking lot he had a mustache and dark hair. Then at his home, his long dark hair circled a bearded tan face, while a short-sleeved polo shirt exposed the dark tan of his arms. Although Medoc Hast wore a faded pair of jeans, Ben assumed the rest of his body had the same deep tan one gets from the beach or a boat. Yet, Medoc took on a different appearance every time Ben saw him. Today, he was the picture of a man who enjoyed the finer things in life, a man of good taste and money.

Ben thought he knew everything about Medoc Hast according to a confidential report he managed to acquire quietly after his house visit. However, somewhere deep within his brain, a gnawing hungered for more detailed information. There was more to the man, something not included in the file, and he wondered what it was and why it would be hidden.

He called his retired friend who sent the report and requested a deeper dig. As usual the request had to be cryptic: Ben had to follow the rules. This was a result of the man's former life…whatever it was. They had met on a fishing trip and, becoming fast friends, the man offered to help the detective, if unfiltered information was needed on someone. Ben accepted his offer after meeting Medoc Hast, but felt something important had not been disclosed.

"Unless we're going fishing, I'm not interested." Reuben Mendell yelled into the phone.

"Where's your hearing aid?" Ben shouted back.

"Can't hear crap," Mendel screamed openly. "I need a new specialist."

"Don't use Hast again. Work's incomplete." Ben directed. "I'll call back in two weeks to check on you."

He pressed the end button, knowing that Reuben understood his request for more information on Medoc Hast. Then Ben's thoughts turned to Clayson Black.

***

Ben wished Clayson Black could have come instead of Medoc. He made the call with a short request: suave bodyguard. A very charming Medoc certainly fit the bill. But for this particular assignment, Ben preferred Clayson Black, the man with laughing dark eyes and an easy gait that matched his conversational skills. He wasn't as tall as Medoc, and not quite as handsome, yet there was a quiet, calm manner about him that caused people to trust him. No one would ever suspect that he, too, was militarily trained to kill. Still, Ben preferred Clayson for this job and he had a good reason. It was immediately obvious that Victoria Reynolds found Medoc very attractive. That alone could create serious problems for Ben. He had grave misgivings about this one-sided couple.

His thoughts returned to Clayson Black. He came upon the man possibly a year earlier on a missing child case. He had made the phone call with four words: missing child, suspect uncle. Since time was a factor, Clayson appeared almost immediately and, assisting Ben on the periphery, found clues the detective could not legally pursue to further his case. Ben found the child unharmed and arrested the uncle for the abduction. Of course, Clayson disappeared as quickly as he came. However, it was during a very brief conversation with him, that Ben learned the men were military at one time: a special-forces unit put to pasture. Death, divorce or something of a personal nature grouped these men together. Since their lives were "messed up," they had nowhere to go. One by one, they moved in with Medoc and shared expenses. They just wanted to be normal again and left alone. They lived together, raised hell together on a jointly-owned boat, and would probably watch each one die of old age. But they would still be together. Ben looked upon this sadly. There was no one of real importance in their shallow lives.

In his own mind, Ben knew they trusted him, although he had never met the other three. Clayson once referred to Thorsen Greer, their somewhat limping yardage star. At first, Ben wondered about the nickname, but after a sudden epiphany he developed a keen understanding of the man's skills. Yet he wondered if Thorsen Greer ever used his long range talents.

The question Ben had been asking himself, after he first met Medoc, was the matter of secrecy. Only through his encounter with Clayson and the missing child case, was the answer so apparent. Normally, retired military men, who live in cities scattered throughout the country, do so without speculation. However, five retired military men living together might have raised questions, particularly with their talents. The fact that personal problems had brought these men together was irrelevant. Although they had committed no crime and could have been living on the streets as homeless men, their specialties could have targeted them, which of course, was their reason for maintaining a very low profile. Ben tucked their presence in the back of his mind, thinking the men might serve a useful purpose sometime down the road, if they were available, and not off boating somewhere, enjoying themselves. Their one definitive rule was to leave them alone. If Ben needed help and the availability was right, Medoc might just provide the service. Of course, the price had to be right.

Ben laughed at the thought. Clayson took no money for the missing child case and Medoc was repaying Ben with bodyguard services. How could anyone think this rag-tag team was a threat?

***

Ben's thoughts suddenly shifted when Danny Boyle stepped into his office.

"So, do you think you nailed it?"

"I'm waiting for Sally to give me the word. If there's a match, we might have a go," Ben said. "Depends on downtown. They won't pursue anything, unless they think it's solid."

"So the accidental ruling will stand?"

Ben shrugged. "I have to concentrate on Mel's body and the evidence bags. That's my last hope."

"Well you won't be alone while you're waiting. Your daughter's coming." He left Ben's office with that announcement.

"Megan, what are you doing here?" Ben's question was mixed with surprise. They had a phone conversation, only moments earlier.

"I think we should go to The Tavern," she answered quickly about the restaurant nearby.

"And why should we do that? Are you in trouble?"

"No, but you are."

"What did you get me into now?"

"We took a vote at lunch in Niagara Falls. We want you to join us at dinner. Everyone's there now, so I ran over to get you. Charlene will be pissed if you don't come. I think she has a thing for you. But then, she has a thing for my father too."

"What she has for me is far from romantic," he said, thinking how quickly the day passed.

"I don't really care what she has. I don't like it. She better get closer to my biological father. My "adopted" one belongs to me."

"What is it with you? First you tell me I should get laid, then you don't approve when someone seems to like me."

"You need to get laid, but not with her."

"Would you feel better, if I told you not to worry? It won't happen."

"Promise?"

"Guaranteed."

"Okay. Let's go." She sighed with relief. "I want you to sit between Brad and me."

"I've never felt so protected in my entire life." Ben choked with laughter as they left the building together.

"Good. Now you can tell me what evidence you found today. I'll pretend ignorance when you tell Seth and Peggy, 'first and second.'"

There were times when Ben found his "daughter" incorrigible.

Chapter 17
Victoria

"Where do you want to go for dinner?" Victoria asked Medoc before starting the car.

"Some place terribly expensive, where we will be seen," he said calmly.

"Don't you think it might be better if we had dinner at some out of the way place?"

"Surely, you're not ashamed to be seen with me." His eyes questioned hers.

"Oh. No. I was thinking about being seen by John."

"You need to forget him right now." He calmed her fears. "I'm here to protect you." Then Medoc began laughing. "But I do a much better job when I'm well fed."

Victoria caught his inference immediately. "We'll go to Catherine's Table. It's terribly expensive, well-known and I always run into someone I know."

"Sounds like a perfect choice," he said, ignoring the fact that he had eaten there many times before, but only when he wasn't paying for it.

As they were leaving the restaurant, a few of Victoria's friends stopped the couple as they passed by their table. While she was making the introductions, the foursome seemed focused on her handsome meticulously-dressed date. The two women scrutinized the attractive man, trying to reconcile in their minds how she snagged him. Their thoughts were obviously felt by Medoc, whose arm thoughtfully encircled Victoria's waist in a most caressing manner, giving the two crows more to speculate on. Medoc loved doing that kind of thing. Women could be so bitchy.

***

As soon as they entered Victoria's apartment building, the door-man, Albert Lansing, reported some news that shook her with fear.

"He's up there now? You let him in my apartment? Why would you do that?" She asked a barrage of questions without listening to his explanation.

"Who is in your apartment?" Medoc interrupted her.

"John Beck. Lansing let him into my apartment." She pointed to the doorman.

"No, I did not," Lansing groused and tried giving her an explana-tion, but knew he did not have her attention.

Instead, an angry Victoria Reynolds left the doorman standing by his desk and ran to the elevator with Medoc trailing behind her.

"I go in first," Medoc instructed, taking the key from her hand. "Follow my lead." As he opened the door slowly, a voice rang out.

"Victoria? Don't be frightened," the male voice said.

"Who are you?" Medoc asked angrily. "What are you doing here?"

"I came to see Victoria." John Beck introduced himself. "We're engaged."

"I find that somewhat impossible, since Victoria is my wife and has been for quite some time." Medoc realized his words had a startling effect on the man who for some reason gave no immedi-ate response to the statement. "It had to be kept secret until I could resolve our family's financial arrangements."

"I didn't know." His eyes focused on Victoria. "You could have given me some sort of notice."

"I never encouraged you," she replied. "As for being engaged, that's totally ridiculous. I'm married."

"I will need my envelopes, the ones I gave you to hold for me." He continued his stare.

"Are those the envelopes in the safety deposit box?" Medoc remembered the conversation between Victoria and Ben at the sta-tion. "The contents of the box are with my attorney who is itemizing our holdings. Victoria told me of your heirlooms and these will be returned to you, I promise. I should warn you though, my attorney is very nosy and will take a quick peek inside, but he is honest and won't remove anything of yours."

John Beck rose from the upholstered chair and, after calmly congratulating both of them, fled the apartment with the excuse of a fixed appointment. Medoc knew from experience the man was badly shaken with the news. John Beck knew it was only a matter of time before his crime was uncovered.

"Well, that was a surprise," she said.

Medoc put a finger to his nose to hush the woman, and then began searching the kitchen drawers for a few things.

"What are you looking for?"

"Something protective. Don't move." Medoc cautioned suddenly, hearing a loud knocking at her door.

"Victoria." A man shouted. "Are you alright?"

"Winifred," Victoria explained.

"This must be parade night." Medoc chuckled. "Continue to follow my lead." Medoc opened the door and smiled.

A man dressed in a tuxedo entered the apartment and immediately began a harangue.

"Why aren't you dressed and ready for tonight's opening gala?" Winifred Pitts asked angrily. "You agreed to go."

"But I didn't agree to go with you," Victoria shot back.

"Just a minute." Medoc refereed the conversation. "If you didn't have a date with Victoria, what are you doing here?"

"She wasn't there. I was worried that something was wrong."

"And why would that bother you?" Medoc persisted.

"It doesn't." Winifred was ready to leave in a huff.

"That's the thing with rare diamonds. They sparkle like the stars and are snapped up by people who know quality." Medoc let his statement drop and watched Victoria walk Winifred to the door.

"You will call me," he said.

"It was just dinner," she said quietly.

He pulled her closer to him and whispered, "Maybe for now, but I'd like you to keep it that way."

"Why?" She waited for his answer, but he remained silent. "Goodnight Winifred."

Victoria Reynolds closed the door, leaned against it and smiled.

"Okay, young lady." Medoc sought her attention. Pouring two glasses of wine for a toast, he said, "I overheard the whole conversation. Now we go into stage two, unless you have someone else coming tonight."

"Stage two?" she asked. "What are we doing?" She followed him into her bedroom.

"You are packing a suitcase. I don't know where we're going yet, but take a bathing suit. Have any ideas? You're paying for it."

"Since we're married, do we have to go away now? You know what I mean," she said, then added, "He knows I don't have the envelopes anymore."

"We were given marching orders for a reason," Medoc replied. "A lot can happen in the meantime and I think you better start packing."

He left the bedroom with a wine glass in hand and continued searching the kitchen drawers.

While Medoc searched for something in particular, Victoria began her bedroom quest for clothing in general. She had no knowledge of destination or time frame. The only item Medoc insisted she take was a bathing suit. She would start from there.

Victoria crossed the large bedroom and caught a glimpse of herself in the full length door mirror. The reflection viewed a small-boned, middle-aged woman of medium height, brown hair and eyes, and a smooth face that had been cosmetically altered. Her figure, although thin, was without the hourglass lines women sought over the ages. Whether it was age or laziness, Victoria felt ashamed she had not concentrated on the rest of her body. She certainly had money enough for spa trips. Actually, she had enough money to buy one. She turned sideways and was glad that neither her abdomen nor her buttocks protruded. Still, how could any man find her physically attractive? Would he, a man that handsome?

She moved away from the mirror to her dresser drawers and began pulling-out a week's worth of underwear, two bathing suits and a cover-up, all of which she placed on her king-sized bed. Somewhere in her dresser or chest of drawers lay a pair of unworn Bermuda shorts. She tore into the furniture and found a pair of white shorts with a small embroidered tree along the bottom side of one leg. A matching top with the same design lay underneath them. She remembered purchasing the set for a picnic which was later cancelled by rain.

She crossed the large room again and walked into an enormous walk-in closet, and became overwhelmed by not knowing what clothing to select for an unknown destination. "It's cold here, so I'll need a coat," she said aloud and, pulling a cloth coat off a hanger, began laughing to herself. She could see the humor of wearing a winter coat over a bathing suit! Victoria studied the rack of dresses, many of them much more formal than needed for the trip. However, she spied three suitable ones; one black, another blue, and the third, a small print. She gathered them, along with the coat and placed them on the bed with the other clothing. She remembered her beige silk pantsuit and added it to the rest of her wardrobe. A short time later a variety of sandals, shoes and accessories lay on the bed with her chosen outfits. Finally, she packed her cosmetic bag and concentrated on the last two things necessary for the trip: a passport and cash.

She walked to a wall safe, which was tucked behind a landscape painting, done by an artist she had just met recently, and retrieved a passport and five thousand dollars. Would that be enough cash for them? She had multiple credit cards in her wallet. Victoria thought of taking a check book and decided against it. Instead, she took an additional thousand dollars. That would be enough for a week. If it wasn't, she could always get more from the bank or from Winifred. He would be so angry with her. She placed the cash and passport into her handbag, and then began to pack the clothing on her bed into a large twenty-six inch suitcase. Medoc could roll it to her car, while she carried the cosmetic case. Her thoughts suddenly concentrated on him.

"Need some help?" she yelled.

"Continue packing," he answered loudly, before entering the small private hall of her penthouse apartment. His hands held those things he found necessary for securing a peaceful night's sleep. After fortifying the elevator door, Medoc took the opportunity to phone Ben with an update on John Beck and an explanation of their "marriage" in relation to the envelopes taken from the safety deposit box. Medoc was happy when the call ended. Ben seemed satisfied with the results…so far. However, the detective made it abundantly clear that their departure was still a necessary precaution. Victoria Reynolds would be in grave danger, when John Beck fully realized the threat she presented.

***

Later that night, Medoc left the spare bedroom to check on Victoria. She lay peacefully asleep on her side, taking only one-half of the king-size bed. Thinking her bed was more comfortable than his, Medoc slipped under the covers and pulled the back of her body to him.

"What are you doing?" Victoria yawned, turning to face him. "You're in my bed."

"Married couples usually do sleep together," Medoc answered slyly, knowing the chemistry between them was growing by the minute.

"You're not wearing anything."

"You won't be either." He threw her piece of nightgown fluff on the floor, pulled her gently to him and kissed her. Medoc could feel her body slowly yielding to his, as he rolled over on her and edged her lips open with his tongue, mirroring his next step. She was surprisingly tight when he entered her, and he had to take long slow strokes, before he felt her hot, wet readiness. He knew this was going to be a good release…for both of them.

"Oh. Medoc," she sighed, moving to the rhythm of his body movements.

"You're so tight… It's so good," he whispered, increasing his pace.

***

"Hi, sleepy head." Medoc brought her a cup of brewed coffee. "Feel rested?" He caught her nod. "I'm giving you a choice, Vegas or Hawaii?"

"You choose," she said, placing the coffee cup on the nightstand. "Was I alright?" She needed reassurance. "I mean…"

"Let's get settled first…after that…we'll talk." He kissed her and left the room.

However, his thoughts were not on getting settled. They were more on how a piece of ass could get him in so much trouble. Granted, he hadn't had anything that tight in years. She was almost virginal. Medoc's thoughts suddenly exploded. It couldn't be, could it? Was he her first? At her age? Or had it been awhile since Victoria was laid? She sure as hell wasn't bed-cozy with Winifred Pitts. Medoc could almost believe the man used his tool for peeing and nothing else.

***

Medoc was sitting on the couch watching television when a fashionably dressed Victoria entered the room with her luggage.

"You look positively gorgeous." Medoc smiled approvingly and felt an arousal growing within him. "Remember, I'm your cousin, if asked by the doorman, and you'll be out of town for a few days, but don't mention our destination. If anything pops up, tell him to call Winifred. That should fire up his innards."

"Medoc, you are terrible! But I love it." As she bent down to kiss him, he pulled her on his lap and pressed her lips with his.

"You are a strikingly beautiful woman," he whispered, slipping his hand slowly up her dress. "I was, wasn't I?" He stroked her hairy treasure.

"Yes," she whispered, embarrassed by the confession and, lowering her face, continued to stare at her hands.

"I want you. You know that, don't you?" He removed his hand from her dress and lifted her face to his.

"Yes."

"I knew it was bound to happen when we met. I felt the attraction immediately."

"I was nervous."

"And now?"

"I'm not."

"We seem to fit," he mused. "But climbing into bed with a strange female is not something I do."

"You're telling me this because…"

"I want you to know the kind of person I am. What happened last night was unusual…but why it happened, escapes me."

"Are you sorry?"

"How can either of us be sorry when there's so much chemistry between us? Admit it. You wanted me." He waited for her response.

"I did, Medoc." She looked directly into his eyes and kissed him. "I didn't know what to expect but I didn't want it to end."

"It won't," he whispered, terminating their conversation.

She slid off his lap slowly, straightened her dress and reached for her coat. As she rolled her luggage toward the door, Victoria took a last minute glance of her apartment when the phone rang on her landline. But Medoc stopped her from answering.

"Victoria, Winifred." His distinguished voice identified himself. "I am worried about you. If I can't get you on your cell, please call me." His phone call ended.

She turned to Medoc. "Why couldn't I answer?"

"That's easy. He needs to understand his reason for concern." He caught her quizzical look. "In laymen's terms, 'it's time to get off the pot.' He's been doing nothing with you but getting older for the past ten years."

"He won't do anything, I guarantee it."

"But I will." He winked.

"Where's your shaving kit?" She began checking the luggage.

"Inside the suitcase with my shorts and your panties," he answered simply.

"You are a terrible man!"

"But you love the things I do to you. C'mon admit it." He brushed the breast portion of her dress, like some helpful person removing crumbs from clothing.

"You are such a horny toad."

They walked down the small private hall outside her penthouse, shaking with laughter. When they reached the elevator, Victoria watched Medoc dismantle some noisy contraption crossing the elevator door. "Is that a bodyguard thing?" she asked but was silenced by the bell.

"Remember what to say, if asked." Medoc stressed the last two words of his statement.

Chapter 18
The Search for John

Ben was already in his office when Medoc and Victoria arrived with their itinerary. He thought they would have left town earlier, but Ben knew Medoc had reasons for a late start and would share those with him.

"Do you have anything new since last night?" Medoc greeted him. Ben offered Victoria a seat and took Medoc into another office for a private conversation.

"I'm waiting for the test results. I know he wiped the gun clean, but I think John's fingerprints are on both envelopes and the wallet that belonged to Mel Travers." Then Ben dropped the subject to raise a safety issue. "Where are you taking her? You know she has to be watched."

"What aren't you telling me?" Medoc groused. "I told you he was waiting inside her apartment when we got there. He knows she doesn't have the envelopes." Medoc stopped speaking suddenly. "Beck knows you have them and plan to use her as a witness after his arrest. That's why you want her protected. That's why he may come after her."

"Without her, a high-priced attorney could have a field day in court. We've both know how that works," Ben added.

"I'm thinking Kauai, maybe a hotel in Hanalei. It would be a quiet vacation and I'd have more control. I've never been a bodyguard, but you already knew that."

"Cut the crap." Ben's eyes bulged. "You could probably do a carving in less than a minute."

"I still have a few tricks."

"That's why I need your help guarding her. You owe me that." He took a firm stand, knowing the man would acquiesce to his wishes.

"I wasn't backing down," Medoc explained. "But I'm not at the top of my game anymore."

"Well, you sure as hell must be sharp at something. I have never seen a more glowing smile on Victoria Reynolds' face…ever."

"Women who feel desirable by men always take on a different look. They feel more beautiful because men find them attractive. Let's face it. Every man wants a piece of ass, but who wants to screw a moose? So I'm taking the job of guarding her body very seriously." He knew Ben would catch the inference.

"Spare the details," Ben interrupted, bringing that portion of the conversation to a close. "I need a departure and arrival time. Is the reservation firm?"

When Medoc remained silent, Ben understood his message. Keeping the reservation fluid was part of his plan. They would stay somewhere safe. That meant he would have scouted the area first. But how could he have done that? A sudden thought hit him. Was Clayson Black in Hawaii for some other purpose and told to check the area on Medoc's behalf? That would have accounted for his unavailability. Ben's attention returned to their conversation, knowing he would never be told if his thoughts were correct.

"I'll call you." Medoc followed Ben back to his office where they left Victoria. To their surprise, they found her busy on the phone.

"How many times must I tell you? It was only dinner." They heard her insist. "No. Don't call me. I'm going out of town. Yes, with him. I may even go to a spa afterward. If I need money, I'll call you." Then she listened to his response. "Winifred. What a nice thing to say. Thank you. I will." Victoria pressed the end button on her cell phone.

"I'm astonished," she addressed no one in particular. "He told me I was beautiful enough without spa treatments." She caught the twinkle in Medoc's eyes. His ploy to move Winifred forward was beginning to gel. Then she turned her attention to Ben, "Are you still having Medoc take me somewhere safe?"

"Medoc's come up with a very good plan. He will take care of you while I try to get this case wrapped-up for an arrest." Ben hoped he sounded convincing since he had no details of their trip.

"You haven't arrested him yet?" Her eyes widened with shock.

"We just got the envelopes yesterday," Ben reminded her.

"It seems like such a long time ago," she said softly, almost to herself.

"It's important that you stay safe and let me do my job."

The three of them strolled out of Ben's office toward the building exit with Victoria's luggage in tow.

"We'll be in touch." Medoc gave the detective a set of Victoria's car keys. "Our ride's here and so is my suitcase."

Ben watched the couple stow the luggage and enter the dark van. Although the detective could not identify the driver, he wondered which of the three men, ones he had not yet met, was today's chauffeur. He checked the set of keys in his hand. In addition to the ones for the car, Ben felt certain he also had keys to Victoria's penthouse apartment. That would make inspection so much easier. But for now he had to put a sticker on her car so it would not be towed away.

***

Sometime mid-morning, Ben received the phone call on a matter that was foremost on his mind.

"They're a match," Sally said, referring to the bullets taken from Mel's body and the gun used to kill him. "The gun was wiped clean but the prints on the envelopes and wallet belong to John Beck. Are we good with that?"

"You're perfect," he said to the lab technician. "We're lucky to have you."

"Yeah, yeah, yeah, you're all accolades and no action."

"I told you one of these days, I may surprise you."

"You've been singing that song for years, and I'm tired of needing my piano tuned," she answered. "I'll fax the report."

"Appreciate it." Ben placed the phone back into its cradle.

A short time later, Ben took Sally's report from the fax machine and walked into his chief's office with a file documenting the evidence against John Beck.

***

"You're going where?" Danny Boyle watched Ben holster his gun and pocket some personal items from his desk.

"We're picking-up John Beck."

"We?" he asked, somewhat surprised.

"Grassley's coming with me." Ben referred to another detective in the unit.

"Good luck with that," Danny said.

"He's going through a rough patch. The divorce left him broke." A frown crossed Ben's forehead. "Don't." Ben stopped the young police officer from spewing a litany of the man's notorious drinking habits.

"We all know why he doesn't have your pay grade." Danny became silent when he saw Moynan Grassley approaching them.

"We'll take my car," Ben said pointedly, when they left the building. Without any further explanation, Ben's driving statement was clear. They would be arresting John Beck as a murder suspect and not stopping at some local bar.

When the two men approached John Beck's home, they immediately noticed the 'For Sale' sign in the front yard. After checking the house and grounds they began to question the neighbors. Moynan took the house on one side of the Beck home, while Ben chose the other, the one belonging to Charlene Winter. Of course, Ben had seen her the previous night at dinner, but he was sandwiched between Megan and Brad, and never had the opportunity to talk with her about John. Megan was only interested in having Charlene pair-up with her biological father. Still, Ben questioned Megan's motives for not wanting him to be with Charlene. Not that he wanted to. She was a very nice woman, but he was not interested in her romantically, nor was she interested in him that way. They were merely friends. Of course,

Megan didn't agree with that opinion. A friendship could always develop into something more meaningful: that was her philosophy. The thought amused him. He did, however, wonder why Ann Quigley was there. He had not seen the university librarian since Megan's Thanksgiving dinner, nor did he have the opportunity to speak with her. Was there something going on between the librarian and Megan, something concerning him?

"You just can't seem to get enough of me." Charlene laughed when she answered the door, wearing a long caftan and holding a very long cigarette holder encasing an unlighted cigarette. "I was rehearsing."

"I'm looking for John. Have you seen him?" Ben ignored her saucy comments, but was, nevertheless, amused by the banter.

However, his question meant only one thing to her. The detective had found some new evidence against her neighbor. "When I came home last night, I noticed his car in the driveway. I think the light was on in his bedroom, but I couldn't swear to it on a witness stand."

"Did you see him today? His car's gone."

"I've been busy with my lines. Now, I'm getting ready to meet the group for chicken wings. You know they're leaving in two days. Would you like to join us? Don't look at me like that," she groaned. "I'm not asking you to join us for a pot party." She made a face and became serious. "I know. You're working."

"If he should come back to the house tonight, call me. That is, if I don't find him first." He gave her a card with his cell number on it.

"Okay, Sherlock, you'll hear from me, if Johnny comes marching home." She started laughing again.

"Funny," Ben said dryly and left the laughing woman, as she slowly closed the door. He really enjoyed her humor. Why couldn't Megan just accept that?

Moynan's voice interrupted his thoughts as he walked down Charlene Winter's driveway. "Nobody seems to know anything," he reported. "What do you think?"

"We should go to his office," Ben advised. "Someone there should be able to give us his schedule, if he has one."

They left the Wellington Woods address for the city and within forty minutes, they were with the manager of Pace Securities, who knew absolutely nothing about John Beck's current schedule.

"He left here yesterday afternoon to meet a client." Earl Rogers told the two detectives. "He mentioned going to Chile next week. That's near Rochester," he explained carefully. "But I can't help you with his schedule for today. I'm sure it's business, wherever he is."

The two detectives thanked the manager and, after questioning several other stockbrokers in their respective offices, left with no clues to the man's whereabouts. Intuitively, Ben knew someone was lying; someone who did not want to get involved with the police.

Ben retraced his steps to see the manager once more. "Who is the newest stockbroker in your office?"

"Mandy Pitkin. She started less than a year ago. Why?" he asked.

"You assigned someone to train her in the mechanics of the office. Who was it?"

"John Beck worked closely with her," he answered cautiously.

"Why didn't you tell us before?" Moynan joined in.

"I didn't want to get her in trouble."

"Was anyone else assigned to him?" Ben studied the man's response.

"There was no need. The others have been here for a long time. Mandy needed help, but she's not in the office today. She had an appointment in the city and should be back tomorrow."

"I will need her address and phone number." Ben watched the man take a small card from his desk drawer and scrawl the requested information from a ledger on his desk.

"You will keep me informed." He gave Ben the card.

"We always try to be cooperative," Ben offered and left his office with Moynan trailing him.

"Should we go to her home and wait?" Moynan asked.

"Mandy Pitkin won't be home, and she won't be in the office tomorrow either. Earl Rogers' is on the phone with her right now, pumping for information about John Beck. He's telling her to say nothing until an attorney is present when we question her. Remember, we're dealing with a brokerage that specializes in the "Carriage Trade." They dislike scandal...of any kind."

"What are you suggesting?"

"We get the addresses of her parents and relatives. If we shake the family tree hard enough, someone will talk with us."

***

It wasn't often that things "fell into place" for Ben, particularly in a murder case. But after an exhaustive round of visits to the parents and brother of Mandy Pitkin, a series of events took place. First, no one knew anything about John Beck, other than he was the young woman's mentor. That was the story from her parents. However, a different narrative came from her brother. Yes, the man was her mentor who helped her a great deal. But he came to rely on her more and more after the death of his wife. The brother was afraid a relationship would develop. John Beck was too old for his sister and he was not Jewish. On the horizon was someone who had all the credentials; someone much more suitable for her. Then, when the brother learned John Beck was a murder suspect and the detectives were only interested in the places the man frequented, he became very cooperative. Ben suggested his sister bring a lawyer, if that made her more comfortable during her interview at the station. They needed to find and arrest this man.

So, Ben Burrows was a very surprised detective when Mandy Pitkin phoned and made an appointment to see him. At the appointed hour, Mandy Pitkin and her brother, David, walked into the police station, without an attorney, and met Ben and Moynan in the room they used to question suspects. Where Ben was cordial upon meeting them, Moynan remained distant and allowed Ben to question the woman.

"We appreciate your coming here," Ben said to both of them. "It's imperative we find John Beck and hope you can help us locate him."

"There isn't much I can offer," Mandy began. "He called my cell this morning and told me he wouldn't be in the office because something came up unexpectedly."

"Did he explain what it was?" Ben asked.

"Not really. John thought he was going to come into some money, but I guess that fell through. I got the impression he was really depressed."

"Did he say anything about going away?" Ben continued. "Did he mention taking a trip?"

"Come to think of it, he did make a funny remark. He said, 'Win or lose, I still have a way out.' What did that mean?"

"Did he mention going home at all?"

"Yes, but only to get some things. That's what he said. He was going home to get some things and then, he made that funny remark about having a way out."

"Did he say when he was going home for his things?"

"I thought maybe tonight. John told me he was tied-up with clients all day, but there was nothing written on his desk calendar. In fact, there was nothing posted this entire week. That surprised me because he always had something written."

"I know this will sound strange, but do you know what places he frequents, taverns, bars, or restaurants?"

"They all talk about Ballentines, a bar near our office. I never go with them, but I think they eat dinner there too. I don't remember hearing any other place, but then, I'm never asked. I'm not part of their click." Her eyes took a downward turn. It was obvious that she felt hurt by their rejection.

"Maybe you should stay with your brother tonight, just in case John tries to contact you again."

"We have room." The married brother agreed.

"That would be good." Ben concurred. "We want your sister to be safe." He rose from his chair. "I want to thank both of you for coming." Ben shook David's hand and thanked Mandy again.

"Yes." Moynan agreed. "You have been very helpful."

The two detectives walked the brother and sister to the front door of the building and watched them drive away.

"What do you think?" Moynan raised the question.

"The woman knows more than she gave us."

"I agree with that." Moynan nodded. "Think he'll go back to his house tonight?"

"He's already been there. Then he covered himself with the sob story she bought into, but I don't know if she's dumb enough to help him. The brother won't."

"What about her apartment?"

"No. John knows we wanted to interview her. I'm sure she told him. He might think we're watching her place. We should go to Victoria Reynolds' apartment right now. She gave me her keys."

"I suppose you have a good reason," Moynan said.

"The best. I want to see if John Beck's been there already."

Chapter 19
Rampage

"Hey!" Charlene breezed in, greeting the seated group at Duffeys. "Am I late?"

"We just got here," Sal said, looking over the menu.

"He's been chewing at the bit for chicken wings, but they are good here," Gwennie admitted.

"You look nice." Cal complimented her. "What have you been up to?" The question caused him to laugh "Can't be much, seeing that we've been together almost daily since we got here."

"You need to emphasize the daily," Sal said. "Not nightly, but daily. What's wrong with you?" He quizzed his partner. "Maybe you're taking sleeping pills like Gwennie."

Gwennie shot Sal a dirty look and immediately clarified the remark. "I haven't felt rested this trip, but damned if I know why."

"I do have some news." Charlene ignored Sal's inference. "I saw Ben this morning. He was looking for John Beck. I think our famous detective friend has the goods on my next door neighbor. He wouldn't be searching for him, otherwise. Do you think he found the gun?" she whispered. "That's the only thing I could think of."

"If the gun turned up and the bullets match, Ben has probable cause to arrest him," Sal offered his opinion. "I only hope he has a good picture of John Beck."

"Just listen to the lawyer here," Cal quipped, mocking his partner.

"That wouldn't be a problem. I saw John's picture's on the computer with Pace Securities, but that's not what you meant, is it?" Charlene asked. "What's the issue here?"

Her question surprised Cal. "Sal's just saying Ben has a strong case against your neighbor, if the gun and bullets match."

"I know all that," Charlene challenged. "But there's more to the story…like finding him. John wasn't home when Ben came by. So, I'm sure he went to his office next. But…," she paused. "Here's the kicker. Ben wanted to know if John was home last night. Why do you suppose he asked that question?"

"Ben thinks he's skipping town!" Gwennie chimed in, expecting agreement from everyone. Cal and Sal eyed each other, their thoughts on the hidden money.

"What's going on? Am I missing something?" Charlene's question rang hollow when the men remained silent. "There's no reason for him to go after Peggy or Seth, if that's what you're thinking," she said, totally unaware of the difference in their thought paths. "If John is leaving town, he must have made some kind of plan, even a hasty one. Wherever he's going, John's not coming back."

"Maybe you're right," Cal agreed, avoiding the issue that was clearly on his mind. "But I think I should call Peggy with the information." Cal walked away from the table and dialed a number on his cell.

"Okay, lets order." Sal waved the waitress over. "Beer first," he said.

"What about Cal?" Gwennie asked.

"I already know what he wants," Sal replied, winking at the waitress and placing his order.

Cal returned just in time to add his food request and waited until the waitress left them alone. "Peggy's not worried. She's confident Ben will find John. She's not worried about Seth either. He has Gabriel."

"The German shepherd," Gwennie said. "He's been trained to attack. At least that's what I've heard."

"Are we meeting them for dinner?" Sal changed the subject.

"They're coming." Cal nodded. "They want to go to The Tavern again. Is that ok?"

"I liked The Tavern last night. The food was good," Gwennie offered her opinion. "Are you coming with us?" She turned to Charlene.

"I'm out for tonight. I have an appointment."

"Ah ha…cheating on us already!" Sal challenged.

She nodded and laughed. "I do a reading at Riversal on Tuesday nights when I'm available. It was set up weeks ago."

"Riversal?" Cal questioned.

"It's a retirement home in Clarence. It's beautiful, clean and the people and staff are great. And they are very appreciative."

Cal looked at the woman in amazement. She was accomplished, independent and beautiful. He knew Charlene had been married and was now a widow. But she did not seem lonely. The woman was enjoying her slice of life: she wasn't looking for someone else to share it with her. Truth be told, Cal was very impressed with the woman. However, his thoughts were brought-up-short by his partner's loud cheers.

"Hey! Hey! Here we go," Sal shouted when two waitresses heaped buckets of chicken wings with celery and blue cheese on the table, along with French fries and coleslaw.

"Another round?" The waitress referred to their beer order and caught Sal's nod.

"I am so loving this! "Sal bit into a chicken wing.

"So is your cholesterol." Gwennie winced.

***

Ben and Moynan had no problem getting into Victoria Reynolds' penthouse apartment. The doorman checked their badges while Ben flashed the woman's keys. However, Ben did not express shock when he found the apartment in shambles. Furniture was overturned; drawers, searched; and items pulled off closet shelves. John Beck had been there. Of that, Ben was certain.

"You can either sit here or come with me," Ben told the gray-haired detective. "If you stay here, don't touch anything. I want the lab to dust for prints." While waiting for Moynan's reply, Ben dialed a number.

"You're going to question the doorman." Moynan understood his logic and remained silent while Ben spoke to a lab technician for help.

"Right," Ben answered, just before his cell phone rang again. "Oh, shit," he said.

"Hello Ann," Ben addressed the woman he had seen, but not spoken to at last night's dinner. His face grew pale as he listened to her side of the conversation. "I have to call you back later on that. This is not a good time to talk. Yes. I know you understand."

"Let's go," he addressed Moynan. They took the elevator to the first floor and approached the doorman.

"What time did you come on duty today?" Ben asked the elderly doorman.

"I've been here since this morning, around six."

"Who was in Victoria Reynolds apartment today?"

"No one that I know of," he said.

"I wouldn't lie about this, if I were you. You are in a lot of trouble. Her apartment has been ransacked. Miss Reynolds will not be happy with you for one thing, and you broke the law by letting someone into her apartment."

"I didn't let anyone in." Albert Lansing pleaded his case. "When I told him she was away, he showed me a key and said that he would be checking her apartment. Miss Reynolds had a suitcase with her, but never said where she was going."

"Who was the man? Can you identify him?" Moynan asked.

"Mr. Beck. He's been here before."

"I want your name, address and phone number. We may need to question you further." Ben watched the man as he wrote the requested information.

"Should I get a lawyer?" The aged man was shaken.

"It might be a good idea," Ben said, before retracing his steps to the elevator with Moynan trailing him.

"I have to make a private phone call." Ben told the detective when the elevator stopped. Moynan swept past Ben quickly and left him standing in the hall.

"What the hell did you get me into?" Ben roared angrily. "She needs an escort for some event and you suggested me? Stop laughing Megan. It's not funny." Her response did nothing to ease his anger. "I'm really busy trying to close this case," he paused when she interrupted him. "I wouldn't be looking for him if I didn't," he said. Ben listened again, as she pleaded with him. "So that's why you had her come to dinner last night. What? She asked you?" The color began to drain from his face. "Megan, I am not the solution to every woman's problem." He pressed the end button immediately. His 'adopted daughter' knew he was extremely angry.

Ben continued standing in the hall and made another phone call. However, this was much briefer than his conversation with Megan.

"I didn't call for a Hawaiian time check." Ben spat into the phone when Medoc answered and questioned the time difference. "I'm at Victoria's apartment right now. It's been ransacked. I think John was looking for the envelopes…to make sure, I guess. I'm having the crime lab dust for prints and adding more charges. How the hell he got a key, I'll never know. Tell her, so Victoria knows what to expect when she gets back. I think John's planning to skip town, so he won't be looking for her now. But don't take any chances, he's desperate." Ben pressed the end button, confident that Medoc would handle the home invasion properly. He'd probably hold Victoria in his arms, soothe her calmly…and then take her to bed.

***

He entered Victoria's apartment to find Moynan out on her balcony overlooking Delaware Avenue. "You must be freezing out here." Ben joined the detective whose pale drawn face seemed more wrinkled than ever. They were approximately the same age, both a little pudgy and somewhat gray, but Moynan looked much older. His eyes had lost the luster of living and his body pores reeked of alcohol.

"Must take a lot of money for a pad like this," Moynan mused, ignoring Ben's statement. "You'd think the security would be better."

"We both know the doorman's lying. John probably gave him twenty bucks and away he went. At some point he made keys for the apartment and elevator. But the question is how and when? We know he was looking for the envelopes. He may have thought Victoria brought them back to the apartment. When he didn't find them, he probably searched for cash. His frustration must have turned to rage by the looks of this place. Ah," Ben said. "They're here." He welcomed the two technicians from the crime lab.

***

After the technicians left the Reynolds' apartment, Ben and Moynan drove the few blocks to Ballentines.

"We are going for information," Ben said evenly. "Mandy told us John frequents the place." Ben leered at Moynan sideways with a reminder. "We're still on duty." Ben's directive made it clear to the man who sat in the passenger seat. There would be no drinking on this trip, not with Ben. The man was all business.

There were only a few customers in the tavern when they approached the bartender, pouring drinks. Two men at the far end of the bar seemed more interested in watching television on a set perched high above them, than listening to the two middle-aged men talking to the bartender.

"Oh, I know him. He comes here Thursday nights usually," the bartender said, looking at the picture of John Beck. "He's one of the Pace group. Five or six of them come in together for drinks and dinner."

"Has he been in today or was he by yesterday?" Ben asked, displaying his badge.

"Haven't seen him in a week, but some man was looking for him an hour ago."

"Did he say why he needed to see John?" Ben continued his questions.

"No. But he does paperwork here sometimes, over at the corner table where it's quiet. I think he's a real estate agent. I heard John's selling his house. Maybe that's the connection."

"Can you describe the man who was looking for him?" Moynan joined the conversation.

"Kinda tall, average looking. I don't remember when he left. I was busy. For some reason, everybody came at the same time and, as you can see, I'm alone. The other bartender called off sick."

Ben was getting ready to leave, when a sudden thought occurred to him. "Did the man say anything about coming back here?"

"He didn't say," the bartender replied.

"Thank you. We appreciate your help."

The two detectives left the bar with little information and no alcohol, so neither man was happy with the outcome of the visit.

"You believe him?" Moynan voiced skepticism.

"I think he knows the man's identity, the one who wanted to see John Beck," Ben replied. "The bartender doesn't want to get involved, particularly if he doesn't know the man on a personal level."

"Yeah, but maybe he does know the guy." Moynan raised the possibility.

"If they are friends, he's on the phone right now telling him about our visit. If that's the case, the man will meet John somewhere else. Doesn't matter really, I'm sure Mandy has already told John she mentioned Ballentines to us. So, he knows we'd question the bartender at some point."

"When all is said and done, we're back where we started. John Beck could be anywhere." Moynan shook his head in disgust.

"I wouldn't say that," Ben disagreed. "We know a lot more now. He won't go home. And he won't go back to the office. I alerted the airlines and bus stations, after Sally called with the evidence this morning." However, Ben never alluded to the bitter exchange between Medoc Hast and John Beck in Victoria Reynolds' apartment.

"I think we should check Mandy Pitkin again." Moynan voiced his opinion.

"If she hasn't heard anything by now, he's either leaving town tonight or has already left."

"I think we're on the same page," Moynan agreed. "But I still don't trust her. I think we should swing by her place on the way back. If she's there we won't have to call her."

There was no one at Mandy Pitkin's address when they parked in front of her apartment and looked around. The neighbors had nothing to report.

Later when Ben and Moynan arrived at the station, there was a note on Ben's desk from Mandy Pitkin asking him to call her. However, the only thing she reported was a phone call from John Beck, saying he would be in the office the following day. Ben could hear her brother's voice in the background, insisting she tell him her entire conversation with John Beck, including the mention of his patronage at Ballentines.

"What do you think he's up to now?" Moynan asked.

"He's finalized his plans for leaving town. And we have no idea where he is or where he plans to go."

"If we had a clue, we could do a stakeout," Moynan offered.

"Where, Ballentines? He'll know we talked to the bartender, so he won't be there. He'd be somewhere near, maybe, but we can't keep patrolling the city blocks."

"I'm going home," Moynan said, "unless you need me."

"I'll walk out with you." Ben agreed with the man's thinking. Nothing more could be done until they got a break on John Beck's location.

***

On his way home, Ben thought about the case. When Ben could arrest John Beck physically, he had no real evidence to make a case. Now that he had evidence for an arrest, Ben could not locate the man. No question, the man was smart. He had connections and was probably using them to escape prosecution.

After his meeting with Victoria and Medoc, John realized the envelopes were gone and the police were closing in on him. From his point of view, whether it was Victoria or Medoc's attorney who gave the envelopes to the police, John Beck was certain of one thing. It was only a matter of time before he was arrested. So, why did he go back to Victoria's apartment? Only two things came to mind. Either John went there to check again, hoping her story was false, or he went searching for money while she was away. Victoria had previously mentioned the cozy relationship between the doorman and John Beck.

After Ben pulled into his driveway, he checked the mailbox and found a letter from Reuben Mendell. Upon entering the house he opened the letter which contained two newspaper clippings and a detailed note that ended with two words, "Hast enough?" Mendell's clever question made him smile. No translation was needed. Ben scanned the note and two articles briefly. Now he had a clearer understanding of one Medoc Hast, whose real name was Madoc Devon Hast. He had merely changed the letter, a, to an e in his first name. Ben grasped the Napa Valley switch immediately. The one article covered the wedding of a wine owner's son, Cory Langsford Hast, to wealthy banker's daughter, Melissa J. Graham. Along the side margin Mendell scribbled a note. She had been engaged to Madoc, the wealthy younger son, who was rumored to have enlisted in the armed services after the wedding. The second article, dated a year later, indicated the woman's drowning death in a boating accident. The separate note gave him even more insight to the troubled life of Medoc Hast.

Medoc's way of living seemed clearer now. He had lived a life of wealth and had been burned by the family and rejected by someone he loved. The truth of that statement would lie somewhere in between. Ben thought this was probably true of the other men who lived with Medoc. They had nowhere to go, for one reason or another, and having bonded as friends in the service, found it much easier to continue living their lives together. Ben's thoughts now turned in a different direction.

He remembered his promise to return Ann Quigley's phone call. But as usual, before doing anything, Ben needed his nightly fortification of single malt scotch. He scanned the evening paper a little more thoroughly than usual and turned on the television and surfed all the news channels. Finally, when he could think of no other diversion to delay the phone call, he dialed her number.

"Yes, you caught me at a bad time today," Ben admitted and listened to her side of the conversation once again. "Ann, please don't be embarrassed. Megan already explained. What exactly does that involve? And it's where? No. I would not dream of meeting you at the restaurant. I will come by at six-thirty. My understanding is cocktails at seven and dinner at eight. Is that correct? No. I'm not upset," he said. "It will be a lovely evening." After saying goodbye, Ben pressed the end button on his cell.

Of course, he wasn't upset. Pissed couldn't begin to cover it. Ben just hoped he wouldn't be drawn visually to the woman's saggy breasts. He remembered Megan's conversation about them during their first interview…when Peggy had been kidnapped. She wanted to tell her librarian friend, who helped her so much with her research papers, to buy a sturdy new brassiere for her saggy breasts. Megan railed about them, just lying there, resting on her abdomen. So every time Ben saw Ann Quigley, his eyes were drawn to her breasts. That was the case when Megan and Brad hosted dinner the past Thanksgiving holiday, their first shot at family entertaining.

When Rosalie and Franklin junior were called away that Thanksgiving week by her father's health problems, Megan and Brad replaced them as hosts. Megan invited Peggy, Ben and Ann to help her sail through the dinner, since she felt uncomfortable entertaining the Croft family on her own for the first time. That Thanksgiving was Ben's first inspection of Ann Quigley's breasts. Things of that nature looked normal to him and he forgot about them until now.

Ben didn't recall a breast inspection at The Tavern restaurant the previous night either. But then, there were a lot of people around, distracting him with conversation. The idea of eyeballing her breasts seemed farfetched. But now, this would be their first experience as a couple. A couple! The idea of pairing with her scared the hell out of him. He had absolutely no interest in the woman. In fact, he couldn't remember having one real conversation with her. Being her escort was going to be problematic.

He didn't want to be with the woman, let alone have a conversation with her. Yet, that thought made him somewhat ashamed. If truth be told, he wasn't the most handsome man, nor was his five-foot-seven inch height considered tall, even for a pudgy middle-aged man like himself. And the only things increasing about his stature were wrinkles and gray hair. He was doing her a favor and they both knew it. The woman seemed nice enough, but that was not the important issue. Her honesty was.

When she spoke with Megan the previous night, Ann mentioned being honored at a dinner the forthcoming Saturday evening. Her plight was no escort. And of course, Megan suggested Ben. But Ann Quigley was a very smart woman. The librarian knew from her Thanksgiving experience with him, that there was no chemistry between them, nor would there ever be. So what remained was the question of his being her escort for that function. Megan made the arrangements, but it was without Ben's knowledge. When Ann discovered Ben's ignorance in the matter, she phoned him at work to let him off-the-hook, so to speak.

What was Ben to do? He could refuse and let Megan call him a "shit" for being so mean spirited, when he had nothing on that evening. Ann Quigley would be hurt even more, by his rejecting her. He was between a rock and a hard place. He didn't want to be the woman's evening escort, and he didn't want to alienate Megan, although she was the source of his aggravation. His only option was to acquiesce, smile and prevent Megan from providing future escort service for her unaccompanied female friends.

Ben thought about Megan and smiled. Not only was his 'adopted daughter,' his informant, she was also his pimp.

***

"How did you manage to get a round table?" Megan asked, as she and Brad strolled into the restaurant and joined Peggy, Seth and the Put-in-Bay threesome. "So where's Charlene? Is she coming?"

"She has a reading or something of that nature at Riversal, the retirement home," Cal said. "Charlene told us at lunch."

"I didn't know she did that kind of thing." A surprised Peggy remarked.

"She's always busy," Megan added. "Charlene takes all the acting roles that come her way. That's how she makes a living. But she does the retirement and nursing homes, and also the sick children's wards on her own dime, when she's available. She just doesn't talk about it. I think she lost someone a long time ago and feels closer to that person when she's doing a charity performance."

"But that's not the only thing she told us," Gwennie said. "Apparently Ben was by her house today looking for John Beck."

"Tell them about your conversation with him." Brad urged his wife.

"When we talked later today and I learned he was looking for John Beck, I asked if he had some new evidence. Ben said, 'I wouldn't be looking for him if I didn't.' So I took it to mean, Ben found what he was looking for."

"The gun," Seth said. "Ben found the gun that killed Mel. That's no longer supposition." He thought of Cal's call to Peggy earlier that day. "And if the bullets match, he's got a case. Otherwise, he would have nothing. His search for John Beck can only mean one thing: the bullets match."

With that thought, a flood of relief swept over Seth. In the scheme of things, Judd's murder would be avenged. John Beck would be sent to prison for murdering the man who killed Judd.

"So, we know John Beck's not at home and he's not stupid enough to be holed up in his office. Where would he go, if he hasn't already left town?" Sal asked.

"Didn't Charlene say that he went to some bar near his office? Ballentines or some name like that?" Gwennie asked. "He'd have friends there, wouldn't he?"

"That's possible," Cal agreed.

"Okay, enough with the detective work, let's order." Sal interrupted the conversation.

"Amen to that. Ben will tell us in due time." Seth stopped talking and began reading the menu.

"Do you know what you're ordering?" Peggy asked.

"Do you mean now, or later?" His smile widened as Peggy caught his inference.

Chapter 20
Street Justice

It was late when the Put-in-Bay trio got back to Peggy's house from The Tavern Restaurant.

"Anyone want something to drink?" Sal asked.

"I am eating and drinking too much," Gwennie complained. "I must've put on five pounds since we got here."

"On you, it looks good." Sal embraced her, sliding his hands down her hips. "You always feel good to me." He shifted his position and studied her. "Gwennie, you look tired."

"I'm going to take another sleeping pill. Was I snoring a lot last night?"

"No," Sal answered. "Why?'

"I just zonked. Never woke up until this morning," she said. "I don't know what's in those pills, but they sure as hell work." She kissed Sal and started up the stairs. "Do you mind if I go to bed? I'm tired. No Blue Whale tonight."

"Then I'll be on your breakfast menu," Sal shouted, watching her disappear up the stairs.

"That went well," Cal said, getting up from his seated position on the couch. He checked his open laptop that sat on the dining room table and clicked on a link.

"Did you get it?"

"Right after lunch with Charlene." Cal flashed John Beck's picture on his computer screen. "I also have it on my cell phone."

Sal watched Cal walk to the refrigerator and remove a quart of milk.

"Leave a note, just in case," Cal instructed, emptying the milk container into the sink. "This is sour." He winked. "We should go to the store for another quart. We'll need it for breakfast. On the way back, maybe we can stop for a drink."

"Sounds like a plan." Sal wrote a note hurriedly. "You drive." He tossed a set of car keys to his partner and took a Kit Kat snack from his pocket.

"I don't know why I have all the cavities. You're the one who eats the candy," Cal complained, watching Sal stuff the empty candy wrapper back into his pocket.

"Bitch, bitch, bitch. Do you know where we're going?" Sal demanded.

"The city. And then, you are going to tell me where to go. You have the GPS gismo on your phone."

"Take the Thruway and get off at Delaware," Sal instructed.

"Then where?"

"We'll go Genesee to Franklin. I don't think Ballentines is far from the there. It's closer to the Stayler Hotel." Sal studied the GPS map.

"I thought the Stayler was on Delaware."

"His office isn't far from there. That's the key. We should patrol the streets inside that little area. We concentrate on Franklin, where his office is, and West Huron back to Delaware. Get us there and we'll do the Mohawk-Delaware area. There are all kinds of bars and side streets in that section. That's where I'd go to meet someone with clout."

"How do you know all this?" Cal was curious.

"Gwennie and I came here for a few days to look around. Never went to Niagara Falls though. I just remember the one way streets being a bitch to drive."

"So that's why I'm elected," Cal groused.

"I've been there, done that. I thought I'd pass it on."

"That's my point. You know your way around," Cal pressed. "You should be driving."

"In you wet dreams, Cal-lio. This is our exit."

The two men took careful notice of all the activity as they slowly patrolled Franklin Street. Then, according to plan, Cal drove the several blocks of Huron back to the Delaware-Mohawk area that Sal suggested. Nothing seemed out of the ordinary until they drove along the third block of a darkened alley. They saw the swinging arms and legs of three men assaulting a man who had just fallen to the ground.

When Cal flashed on his high beams and raced toward them, the three men jumped into a waiting van and sped away.

"What are you doing?" Sal screamed hysterically. "We've been through this shit before. I don't need a reminder."

"Get out and look. See if he's alive. But don't touch anything."

"Let's just get outta here." Sal wanted no part of the mugging.

"No." Cal insisted. "I think that's John Beck lying there. Check it out."

"Shit," Sal blustered, getting out of the car. "I get all the dirty work."

Sal went to the man lying on the ground. From the extremely dim streetlight nearby, his body had a crumpled almost accordion-like look that matched his bloody-blotched face. When Sal checked the broken body to see if the man was still alive, he noticed two things immediately. The man seemed to be breathing and a small attaché case lay nearby. He grabbed the attaché case, jumped back into the car and roared, "Move your ass out of here."

"Is he or isn't he?" Cal sped up the street.

"He is, if someone comes to help him. But I took the attaché case."

Just as they turned the corner, they heard the blaring of sirens approach the first block of the alley.

"Jesus, we just made it." Sal heaved a huge sigh of relief. "I wouldn't want the police questioning us about the mugging. That bloody body looks like John Beck."

"Tell me you didn't touch him or anything else there."

"Give me some credit. The last thing I need would be my fingerprints anywhere near John Beck. The police would try to link me to his attempted murder."

"I'd like to know what they were looking for."

"Who? The muggers?" Sal asked. "That's a no-brainer. Money, they wanted money, but didn't get a chance. They didn't want to be run over by some crazy nut, for maybe twenty bucks, if the man even had that."

"John would have had a lot more than twenty," Cal challenged.

"But who would know? That's the chance muggers take. Some days they make out financially; other days, zilch." He made a hand-slicing throat gesture.

"I wonder why the police came." Cal changed the subject.

"What do you mean?"

"Someone must have called them. Maybe someone was watching us," he said. "But from where? The alley was so dark."

Sal looked at his partner. "What was he doing, screwing around in a dark alley? That's the first question."

"Maybe he planned on meeting someone there," Cal answered. "But how did he get there? Where's his car?"

"He wouldn't have a car, if he's skipping town," Sal explained.

"No. I don't buy that. There's a car somewhere. It might even be a part of his escape plan. I think it's parked in the alley where he was mugged or some spot nearby."

"He wouldn't just stand around waiting for someone. That's asking for trouble." Sal challenged him.

"I think he got out of his car when he saw the van approach, thinking it was his connection to leave town."

Sal gave his partner's story some thought. "Then when he realized his mistake, it was too late."

"I think that's what happened," Cal agreed.

"So we're back to square one. Who called the police?" Sal asked. "We know it wasn't the muggers."

Cal thought about the logistics of it. "I think it was the person John was supposed to meet. Whoever it was, watched the whole thing come down. But I didn't see another car drive away."

"I know what happened if you think vertical and horizontal. No, think about it." He caught Cal's shrug. "We were in the third block. John was on the end of the third horizontal block, and the other person parked on the corner, vertically. He saw the whole thing."

"Who did?" Cal asked.

"Don't be a smart ass. You know what I mean: he…she…whoever. Still, why would he get involved? That would be the last thing I'd do."

"Maybe the person felt he'd be implicated, if John died and he was caught helping him get away. Or maybe, he realized, after watching John get mugged, that he was being watched."

"By?"

"I don't know, Sal. There's just so much we don't know," he said, driving into the parking lot of a 7-Eleven store. "We need milk. That's something I do know."

"You are such a smart ass," Sal hissed, getting out of the car.

It was then a thought crossed Cal's mind. For most of his life, the man who knew him best was buying a quart of milk. This was the excuse to help a friend satisfy a wrong that was done to his daughter.

***

"Okay Cal," Sal said, "Now to the good part."

"I suggest my bedroom."

When the two men entered the house and quietly sailed up the stairs with the attaché case in hand, they could hear Gwennie snoring through the closed door.

"Does she sing that same tune every night?"

"Nah, I turn her over, so her nose's in the pillow. But I know she's alive when I listen to her breathe."

Sal set the attaché case on the bed and opened it. A flood of packaged money filled their eyes. Taking Cal's pen from the nightstand, he moved the top parcel to count the number of banded packs. Each band read one-thousand: twenty bands, twenty thousand dollars. "I don't think we'll find the rest. It's stashed somewhere else or he paid someone to help him run. These are the same money bands I saw in his house. Is it enough?"

"Maybe not, but it will help. Put it on the closet shelf." He pointed to the case. "We'll see what develops."

"Want a drink?"

"I thought you'd never ask," Cal said as they walked softly downstairs.

"Wouldn't it be a bitch, if he planned the whole thing...the meeting and the mugging?" Sal poured each of them a drink.

"And then called the police?" Cal's eyes widened.

"Just a thought." Sal laughed. "I like to muddy the waters, sometimes."

"Too bad we'll never learn the real story."

"Peggy will tell you if she ever learns the truth."

"Yes," he pondered. "I really believe Maggie Pie would. Yet, something about him tells me that possibility is too far-fetched. He's too..."

"Honorable?"

"Exactly the right word."

***

"Burrows," Ben answered the phone, still half-asleep. Suddenly the news of John Beck's capture sparked his interest. "Where is he now?" He listened to city policeman Cleary's story. "Is he awake?" He listened further. "I'm coming in, probably thirty-minutes. You still into Bushmills? You got a bottle coming. Oh, yes. Danny's doing a good job. I've been keeping an eye out."

Thank-God he knew them all: city detectives and policeman alike, both new and experienced. They knew Ben had been trying to close the case for almost a year. They also knew the detective suspected John Beck, but couldn't prove it. Now that Ben had some concrete evidence for a conviction, his suspect turned up beaten and bloody. Was it planned or was the mugging a coincidence? What about the phone call to the police with the mugging location? Was that not unusual? Ben smelled a setup.

It was a quick drive to the city's General Hospital. Parking presented no problem and the guard recognized Ben from previous visits there with wanted felons. After taking the elevator to the fifth floor, he ran into the doctor who had treated John Beck and was on his way to see another patient.

"What's the prognosis?" Ben stopped him momentarily.

"He'll survive, but healing will take awhile. He was semi-conscious when he came in and I had to give him something to ease the pain and make him sleep. You should go home. He won't be awake for hours."

Ben looked in on the bandaged man. Were any of his bones broken? The doctor hadn't covered that aspect. Nor had the doctor mentioned the patient's swollen and bruised face, or his bandaged head. Medical people always had a calm uplifting jargon of their own. The doctor said, "Healing would take awhile." What would he tell someone about a patient near death? "He still has his fifteen minutes of life?"

Ben walked over to the nurses' station to question the one assigned to John Beck. During that discussion the nurse confirmed Cleary's story. The patient came in by ambulance and the injuries were the result of a mugging. Ben left his cell number with her to notify him when the patient became conscious.

After Ben left the hospital, he stopped by the city precinct and read a short CAD report on John Beck's mugging. According to the entry, the alley was deserted and there were no witnesses. The police were notified of the mugging by a caller using a pay phone at the Stayler Hotel. The police went to the alley where they found the unresponsive victim, identified as John Beck from his driver's license, and took the man by ambulance to General Hospital where he was admitted. In addition to his driver's license, his wallet contained a triple A membership, several credit cards and 360 dollars. Other contents found in the pocket of his trousers included a comb, house keys, lip gel and twenty-cents in change. A check of the Stayler Hotel pay phones proved futile. A further investigation indicated apprehension by the police. Detective Ben Burrows, from the Town of Amherst, was working the case.

Ben's level of frustration was high on his way home. In all his years of detective work, he could not believe what had transpired that evening. What mugger would call the police after assaulting someone? Did the mugger know the victim's identity? Was it a planned attack or did the mugger just happen to be in that alley when the victim approached? No. Ben thought further about it. The attack had been planned; otherwise, the mugger would have taken his wallet with the money. Of that, Ben was certain. He had experienced quite a few muggings in his long years as a detective. Still, how did the mugger know John Beck would be in that particular alley at that exact time? There was only one way something that specific could happen. It had to be planned. Now he had to make sense of it.

Ben pulled into his driveway, walked into the house and poured himself two fingers of scotch before sitting down to reason things out.

If someone planned the mugging, then it was only logical that the man's schedule and habits were known. Obviously, whoever did the planning knew John Beck's address. A home address was not privileged information. That information could have been found in a phone book or on a computer. The mugger must have also known John worked for Pace Securities. So if the home address and place of employment were known, the mugger must have also been familiar with the man's routine. The only place John Beck went to frequently was Ballentines.

There was only one logical conclusion: John Beck was being followed. The mugger could have followed him from any of those three places or perhaps, a fourth, Ben knew nothing about. However, nothing could change Ben's thinking. Whoever mugged John Beck followed him into that alley. Then an anonymous person called the police afterward. Someone did not want John Beck to die. But why? That puzzled him.

Ben took a long drink of Scotch. There was the other side of the coin to consider.

Why was John Beck in that particular alley and at that specific time? Who was he meeting? Did the person John was to meet do the mugging? Or did that person watch the beating and call the police from a pay phone at the Stayler Hotel? If John were to meet someone, was it for the purpose of fleeing Buffalo for somewhere safe? Had the money already been exchanged? If his thoughts were correct, the police found only 360 dollars in his wallet. There had to be money somewhere else. Could it have been at his office? Or would he have entrusted it to someone whose friendship proved loyal? Would she tell Ben, if he did? He would question Mindy Pitkin again. Still, Ben had to find the person John Beck was meeting. She would not have that information.

Ben finished his drink and went to bed. He needed a few hours sleep to refresh his thoughts. The days from here on in would be long. He would go to the hospital first, question John Beck and place him under arrest. Then he would request a guard watch him. The man was a flight risk. Maybe that's what the mugger intended the entire time. Beat up John Beck so he couldn't leave town.

Ben placed his head on the bed pillow. He had been watching too many crime movies lately.

***

Early next morning, Ben called Moynan with an update on the mugging and met the detective at General Hospital. They arrived at the fifth floor to learn John Beck was conscious enough to answer a few questions. Ben had mixed emotions with that information. He had asked to be called when the patient became conscious and that request was ignored. Yet he was glad to have the opportunity to question his suspect. When he asked about the patient's condition, the nurse told him that according to the chart, there were no broken bones, and no severe injuries; however, the patient had been badly beaten. Healing would take some time. Ben thanked the woman and wondered if everyone in the hospital sang the same song. He heard that same refrain from the doctor, hours earlier.

The two detectives walked into John Beck's room to find the patient awake. Ben knew he had to start his questions with the mugging first.

"Mr. Beck, we keep meeting under the direst of circumstances. You were mugged last night. Can you tell us anything about your attacker?" Ben took out his pad and pencil and wrote the date and time of his interview with John Beck.

"Three or four," the man breathed heavily. "Not one."

"Did you recognize any of them?" He asked to the man's negative response.

"Why were you in that alley? Were you meeting someone?"

The man stared at Ben, realizing the extent of the question and where it would lead. "No," he whispered. "Short-cut."

"To where?" Moynan chimed in.

John Beck turned his face away from the men, intending to end the interview.

Ben Burrows was having none of the man's theatrics, pain or no pain. He had come too far.

"John, I think you should know we have evidence linking you to the murder of Mel Travers." Ben's statement had a startling effect on the man. He turned his face toward Ben and listened to him speak.

"The bullets found in Mel Travers' body match the gun you kept hidden in an envelope. Inside another envelope, which you also wanted stored, we found the man's wallet and other personal things. Unfortunately for you, inside the trouser pocket of Mel Travers' body was a picture of your wife. And from a mistakenly kidnapped woman and the man who ultimately freed her, we have testimony that you intended to have your wife abducted and killed. Now, have you anything to say?"

The man simply stared at Ben, ignoring Moynan completely, and said nothing.

"You leave me no choice. John Beck," Ben addressed him. "I am placing you under arrest for the murder of Mel Travers." He read the man his rights and then called his boss to release the file to the district attorney and take over from there.

John Beck may have been under arrest for the murder of Mel Travers, but this did not satisfy Ben Burrows. He remained silent as he walked with Moynan down the hospital corridor, knowing his search for John Beck was over. The pursuit may have ended, but too many questions still remained unanswered..

"You gotta be glad this baby's in the can," Moynan said as they rode the elevator down to the ground floor.

"He's not been convicted yet," Ben replied.

"That's not your worry. We're out of the loop, so to speak: the powers that be are in charge now. You going back to the station or taking some time off? You look tired."

"I didn't get much sleep. I think I'll go back to see if I need to do anything, then I'll go home. I am tired." Ben agreed. The two men separated in the hospital parking lot, each going to his respective car.

Chapter 21
Candy

Ben didn't feel he lied to Moynan about going back to the station. In fact, he planned on doing just that…after he satisfied his own curiosity.

He drove around the town's one way streets to the alley where John Beck was mugged. By daylight, the alley looked like a warehouse district with buildings that had been abandoned years earlier. There was little in terms of businesses thriving in the area. Ben parked on the corner, perpendicular to the third horizontal block of the alley, and walked to the area where the mugging was to have taken place. A clutter of street trash was strewn everywhere…empty soda cans, fast-food wrappings, French fry cartons and used condoms. However, Ben ignored the litter, looking instead for some kind of blood trail. He saw an area that looked somewhat clear of debris, where a scuffle could have moved the trash to an outer periphery, and his interest centered on what seemed like droplets of blood. He bent down to take a closer look, when something else caught his eye. Could it be? Would that even be possible? He reached into his pocket for a handkerchief and clasped an empty Kit Kat snack wrapper. He wondered what explanation Sal would give to Ben's "find."

There were days when he hated his job: the days when someone close to you committed a crime and was soon to be arrested. Not that Sal was close to him. No. Ben was thinking of Megan. How was she going to react? He couldn't keep the beating hidden if Sal and her father mugged John Beck. Ben couldn't dispute their reasoning, not after having Peggy kidnapped. If Ben had been her father he would have felt the same way. One of them must have made the phone call to the police.

They didn't want the man to die. They wanted him prosecuted for his crimes. Nevertheless, the beating must have felt good. It was their idea of revenge. Still, John Beck said there were three or four men that mugged him. That made no sense. Why would John Beck lie about something like that? These questions ran through Ben's mind as he slid into his car. Just as he was about to turn on the ignition and drive forward, his eyes took a sweeping view of the scene. What if someone sat in that very spot and watched the mugging take place but remained hidden? The alley was dark. Whoever was there would not have been seen. Was the person meeting John Beck sitting there the entire time? He could have gotten away before the police came. It would have been easy to put the car in reverse, make a turn and drive away.

With these thoughts on his mind, Ben drove back to Amherst, but instead of going to the station, he went to Peggy's house to interview one of her guests.

Gwennie pulled Ben into the house after he rang the doorbell and began talking immediately as she led him to the family room.

"We left a message at the station for you to call us. This is our last night here and we wanted you to have dinner with us. We're leaving early tomorrow morning."

"Hey." Cal greeted the detective. "You are coming to dinner with us tonight. The whole gang will be there, including Charlene."

"Of course he's coming," Sal said. "You want a beer or are you on duty?"

"I need to speak to you privately," he addressed Cal. "Could we possibly go somewhere? It's very important."

Cal slipped into his jacket and followed Ben to his car. Within minutes they were seated in Sessions Restaurant staring at each other over a cup of coffee.

"I needed to see both of you," Ben began. "But I didn't want Gwennie upset by feeling left out, if I asked Sal to join us. Our being alone makes her think the conversation has something to do with Peggy. However, Sal is a very big part of this." Ben removed the handkerchief with the fresh Kit Kat wrapper from his pocket. "I just finished scouting the alley where John Beck was mugged. I want the truth, Cal. I think I've earned your trust. Were you and Sal involved with the mugging?"

"No. Ben. We were not. That is the truth, believe me or not." His eyes met the detective's. "After dinner, Gwennie went to bed and Sal and I drove to the city. We were looking for John Beck, but only to locate him. If we found him, we were going to call you. Mugging was never our intention. Anyhow, we didn't know where the hell we were going, driving all over Delaware and I think, Mohawk. That's the truth. We found ourselves in an alley and drove the distance of maybe three blocks when we saw these men beating the hell out of a man. I turned on my high beams and drove right toward them. Sal was screaming because he thought I was going to run over them. When they saw the high beams they jumped into a van and drove away."

"What did you do, after the men left?" Ben continued his questions.

"I asked Sal to check on him. Sal didn't want to, at first. But I told him I thought the guy looked like John Beck. We got his picture off the computer. So Sal looked to see if he was still breathing. That's when the empty candy wrapper must have fallen out of his pocket."

"What did you do then?"

"We stopped at 7-Eleven for milk. We threw out a carton earlier as an excuse to go out. We didn't want Gwennie to get suspicious if she woke up. That didn't happen. She took a sleeping pill."

"You just left John Beck lying there. You didn't call for help?" Ben demanded.

"Hell. No. Just as I turned off the alley, we heard sirens coming up the block. We had to get out of there. Why?"

"I just wondered who called for help. What color was the van?"

"Black, I think…definitely a dark color. Maybe, I'm crazy."

"What do you mean?" Now Ben was curious.

"When I turned on my high beams and drove toward these muggers, what did they do? They jumped into a van. How can that be?"

"I'm not sure I understand your meaning."

"It was too fast. If you mug a guy, you have to run to your car and start the engine and you know…"

"So, what are you saying?"

"I'm saying some driver came by to pick them up when I was driving toward them with my high beams. Including the driver, there had to be four men involved. That's what I'm saying, and I'm nuts because it happened so fast."

"Where do you think the van came from?"

"It had to be on the same street." Cal became quiet for a moment. "Right, I almost hit the van when it turned. We must have been facing each other."

Cal became quiet again. "It just happened so fast. It was too…"

"Scheduled?" Ben added.

"No. That's not it. Precise would be more like it. It was almost like a planned hit and run. But then, I'm losing my mind, thinking about the precision of a military operation."

"And you saw no other cars?" Ben asked again.

"There were no other cars on the street when we passed by. I don't know about the side streets. We had to get out of there."

"If I questioned Sal, would I get the same story?"

"Come back to the house. No. Gwennie doesn't know. Question him tonight at dinner. You two can go off alone and talk. Maybe he'll remember something I didn't." Cal stopped talking and focused on Ben. "I think you know who mugged John Beck. You just want confirmation," he added. "Peggy kept telling us you were smart. We may not have mugged the guy but I'm not sorry that someone did, after what he put my daughter through. How is the SOB?"

"Alive, hurting and arrested," Ben said. "The case has been turned over for prosecution. So for all intents and purposes, I'm out of the loop."

"No, you're not," Cal challenged. "If you were, Ben Burrows would not be pursuing who mugged John Beck. And if I understood Charlene correctly, John was trying to leave the city. So you want to know who was helping him. Good luck with that. I'm glad he was mugged and I want to see him go to prison. Should we go?" Cal put a tip on the table and took the check. "That's the least I can do for all the help you've given my girls."

As they walked out of the restaurant together, Ben had second thoughts about Cal. Too bad life turned out so badly for him. He would have been a wonderful father. Yet, Ben wondered what he was hiding. His story had one big hole. When Sal checked John Beck to see if the man was still alive, did he really leave the man alone, or was something there for the taking? Ben would never know. But then, he wasn't sure he really wanted to.

Ben headed for the station after depositing a worried Cal at Peggy's house. Cal knew as soon as he opened the front door, Gwennie would be facing him with a barrage of questions. Sal, of course, would remain silent. He would talk to his partner later.

"So what was that all about?" Her mountain of questions began. "Did he tell you something about Peggy?" She couldn't contain her curiosity. "Is there something new on the case? They found John Beck and Ben wanted to relieve your mind. Is that what he wanted to talk about?"

"Close." Cal interrupted before she could ask another question. "John Beck's in the hospital. Someone mugged him last night." His eyes focused on Gwennie as he spoke, but Sal grasped the intended message.

"He couldn't think Seth mugged John Beck!" Gwennie cried in disbelief.

"No. I think, basically, he wanted me to know, so I could tell Peggy."

"Well, for God's sake, he could have told you that right here," Gwennie hissed.

"No. He couldn't," Cal said, trying to stay composed.

"Cal's right. I think Ben felt it was personal." Sal joined in.

"That may be, but I still don't get it," Gwennie said as she walked toward the kitchen refrigerator. "Anyone want water? Where did the milk come from?"

"Cal went out this morning when we were asleep. He thought it was sour." Sal popped a Kit Kat snack into his mouth.

"Watch where you put that," Cal said. "I don't want Peggy finding your candy wrappers all over her floor."

Sal looked at Cal quizzically. "Really?"

"She'll come after you. She knows you eat that brand."

"Oh, for Christ sake, give it to me," Gwennie groused. "What's the big fuss over a candy wrapper anyhow."

"Don't worry, honey." Sal embraced her. "Cal's going through menopause, so we have to be extra kind to him."

"You're right, and I'm sorry." Cal apologized. "I shouldn't be raising a fuss over some stupid wrapper."

Sal more than understood Cal's ciphered message and knew the "show of remorse" was all for Gwennie's benefit.

"I'm going upstairs for awhile. Are we eating out tonight?" Cal walked toward the stairs.

"Do we want to eat Italian, Chinese or steak?" Gwennie asked.

"Call Peggy," Cal said. "See what she wants to do." He continued walking up the steps to the second floor and entered his bedroom.

"I want to take a quick shower." Sal told Gwennie. "I feel sweaty."

Upstairs in Cal's room, the two men had a brief discussion concerning Cal's conversation with Ben. Now, Sal knew what answers to give the detective when questioned at dinner, if of course, Ben decided to join them.

"I told him what I saw."

"Anything asked about our finding?"

"No. And I didn't volunteer."

"We're good." Sal left the room.

***

Danny Boyle greeted Ben as soon as he hit the station door.

"Moynan told us Beck got mugged. Couldn't happen to a nicer murderer," he said, causing Ben to smile.

"Unfortunately, he's only down for one," Ben replied and noticed the chief beckoning him to his office. Ben knew their conversation would concern his evidentiary files and the prosecution of John Beck by the district attorney.

"Everything seems to be in place. At least they were satisfied at this point, but you know how that goes."

"I'll be available if needed," Ben replied.

"With all the evidence they have, it should be a slam dunk."

"I hope you're right," Ben said, knowing their interview had come to an end when the phone rang. Although the detective slipped quietly out of the office, he noticed the man's glowing expression and knew something exciting had just happened at his home.

"What does he want you to do now?" Moynan grabbed him.

"The usual, a holding pattern. It's up to them now. But I have things to clean up. I want to call Mandy Pitkin and tell her John Beck's been arrested. She can tell her boss about it. Then I'm going home." Ben never mentioned the possibility of her being entrusted with John Beck's money. A possibility he raised earlier, before John was mugged.

"Then I'll see you tomorrow." Moynan sailed out of the building.

"Where's he going?" Danny Boyle walked Ben to his office.

"I have no idea," Ben replied.

"When he comes back smelling of whiskey, we'll know soon enough."

Without saying a word, Ben smiled at young Danny Boyle and walked into his office to call Mandy Pitkin.

"You don't say much, Ben Burrows, but your mind's always working." Danny uttered from the Ben's doorway, and then walked away.

***

Ben felt weary. He needed to go to bed. Getting up in the middle of the night, and then trying to get back to sleep, after the hospital visit, didn't do it for him. He did not feel rested. He looked at the clutter of files on his desk. Now that things were grinding down, he just might be able to straighten them out, but not now.

He dialed a number and spoke to a young woman who sounded very relieved with the news about John Beck's arrest. The detective felt certain she would be in her boss' office reporting the arrest as soon as their phone conversation ended.

Ben continued to feel weary. If he had his way, he would go home right now.

"Hey!" A voice greeted him. "I want you to stand up."

Before Ben could say anything, Megan wrapped her arms around him and planted a kiss on his cheek. "You are the best Frog Prince ever! ever! ever!" she chortled and kissed him again.

"Stop." Ben pushed her gently away and stared at her directly. "What did you get me into now?"

"No. That's not why I'm here. It's what you did," she explained. "Ann called and told me what a wonderful person you are for doing this favor Saturday night. She knows your heart's not in it. What I mean is, she knows there's no connection between the two of you, no chemistry."

"I've been preaching that sermon for months, but you absolutely refuse to believe it. I'm not after Ann or Charlene, although they are very nice ladies. You just haven't thought it through, Megan."

"Meaning what?"

"If Brad passed away, would you be searching for a replacement?"

"Of course not. Is that what you think I'm trying to do, replace your wife, Julie? Oh, No. That was never my intention. I just hated to see you alone all the time."

"Megan, I am too busy to be lonely, believe me."

"So what are you wearing?" She changed the subject.

"When?"

"Don't play games with me," she groused. "I'm serious."

"A very dark gray suit which I just had cleaned, white shirt, red tie," he chuckled. "Megan, this is not the first function I've attended."

"I just want my adopted father to look smashing. I like it." She nodded her approval.

"I'm so glad. God forbid, I should embarrass the family," he said, and watched her sit down. He wondered what else was on her mind.

"And?" he asked.

"Two things. I want to know about John Beck and why I wasn't able to talk with Victoria Reynolds."

"Let's take Victoria Reynolds first," he said. "John asked her to hold two envelopes for him. She was unaware they held the evidence of a murder he committed. So I was in the process of sending her away when I asked you not to call her."

"You thought he would come after her."

"That was a distinct possibility. As for John Beck, he was mugged last night and is in General Hospital."

"Did you arrest him?"

"This morning. Now it's up to the district attorney to prosecute the case. I'm out of it, so to speak."

"Good. We can celebrate tonight. Peggy called me to see about Italian, Chinese or steak. What would you prefer? I'd like Pauline's for a change."

"Megan, I am tired. I didn't get a lot of sleep, so I want to bow out."

"No!" she shrieked. "You can't. This is their last night. I don't want him slobbering all over me. I want to be with you. You can sit with anyone you want. Please, Ben."

Ben got up from his chair, slipped into his jacket and took Megan by the arm. They walked to the front entrance together.

"I'm going home to bed." He told Danny Boyle.

"Alone?" The officer eyed Megan on his arm.

Ben stopped, turned, and stared at him…never uttering a word, and then proceeded on.

"Sorry," Danny Boyle shouted as he watched them leave the building. It reminded him of another time. Ben and his 'adopted daughter' looked good together…like family.

Chapter 22
Confirmation

That night, when Ben met the group in the bar at Pauline's Restaurant, he knew this would be his only opportunity to get Sal's version of the mugging. By now Sal knew every detail of Ben's conversation with Cal. Ben was certain an exchange had taken place. Now, it would be a matter of separating facts from fabrication.

Ben waved to Megan but walked toward Sal, leading him somewhat away from the group.

"I'm sure Cal told you about our conversation this morning. I didn't want to involve Gwennie." Ben started his subtle line of questioning.

Sal nodded. "He did. What do you want to know?" The big man looked down at Ben. "Why don't you ask me some questions you didn't ask him?" His tone was snarky. "Or do you people ask the same questions to see if the stories jive?"

"I am sorry if I offended you," Ben said with practiced calm. "That was never my intent. I'm only interested in the person who was helping John Beck leave town. There might be a case of aiding and abetting. That was my only purpose. Did you happen to see anyone?"

"No. That's why I thought it was so strange." Sal began to relax. "We saw three guys mugging someone, and the next thing we knew, sirens were blaring up the street. Who called the police? Do you know?"

"No. But that's not the only thing that's strange. What was John Beck doing in the alley? Was he planning to meet someone?" Ben paused.

"You think someone else was in the alley beside us and the muggers?" Sal added the question to his thoughts.

"I do. That's the only explanation I can come up with."

"Whoever the person was must not have cared whether John Beck lived or died," Sal said simply.

"I don't understand," Ben replied, unable to grasp the man's logic.

"That crazy bastard, Cal, was ready to run over everybody. He puts on his high beams, revs-up the engine and suddenly becomes a NASCAR driver, while I'm screaming my lungs out. Then a van comes out of nowhere, the muggers jump in, and Mr. NASCAR suddenly turns into Goody-Two-Shoes and wants me to check the corpse. No sooner I take a look and sirens are blaring up the ass. Now you're telling me someone else was there. That was no friend. That was a gift."

"And you made this determination on what basis?" The man had Ben's full attention.

"You asked two questions. What was he doing there and was he meeting someone? Obviously, John Beck was in the alley to meet someone. If that someone was helping him leave town, then there had to be a monetary exchange beforehand. If that was the case and John Beck died, then that "someone" would have gotten a free gift with absolutely no effort. I would think the same thing would apply with his arrest. He's not going to identify his accomplice."

"We are on the same page." Ben agreed.

"What are you two talking about?" Gwennie joined them. "You look like you're solving the world's problems."

Sal was the first to speak. "We are. I'm trying to talk Ben into visiting us. He must have some vacation time."

"It would be great if you came with Peggy and Seth," she said. "I don't know about Megan. She's not very accepting. Anyhow, we could go out on the boat. It would be fun."

"Hey!" Megan interrupted their conversation. "I think we're being called to dinner." She took Ben's arm as they walked into the dining room.

"Thank you for the rescue." He looked at her gratefully.

"Isn't that's what daughters are for?" A wide smile crossed her face.

***

Next morning, while Ben was in his office, he received a phone call from Medoc. "What's the word from your corner?" The man asked and listened to Ben chuckle.

"You can come home now, but you already knew that," Ben said, his meaning clear.

"No. The weather's been nice," he said lazily. "We'll round out the week. We like it here, nothing but sunshine and beach clothes."

Ben realized there was no point in arguing with him. Victoria was paying for their trip. So if they wanted to stay, Ben couldn't do anything about it anyway. Then again, if Victoria enjoyed being with him, why stop the woman? She deserved a respite after the way John Beck had used her. Fortunately for Ben, Victoria came to him for help and in doing so, the dream arrest of John Beck became a reality.

Medoc, however, was another story. He knew damn well what was going on, probably engineered it. In fact, it would not have surprised Ben, if Medoc had John Beck followed, from the time of their initial meeting until the night of the mugging, thereby preventing the man's escape. Ben suspected someone in the group called the police from the Strayer Hotel. Intuitively, Ben knew Medoc could also identify the person helping John leave town. But would he? Ben didn't think so. Doing that would further implicate his men.

"Does Victoria know that John Beck's been arrested?"

"No. I'll tell her after we hang up."

"Cute." Ben was being sarcastic. "Are you going to tell her about the mugging too?"

"Beautiful women need to hear positive things, right honey?" He addressed Victoria, ignoring Ben completely.

"You are so full of shit," Ben chided, then heard Medoc's voice again.

"He wants us to enjoy ourselves." He told Ben and Victoria simultaneously and ended the call.

Ben wondered about the purpose of Medoc's phone call. There was only one explanation and no other. Put simply, Medoc wanted to know if Ben suspected his roommates of mugging John Beck. He couldn't ask Ben outright. Instead, Medoc hoped to glean that information through conversation. And Ben was certain Medoc deciphered his two inferences: that Medoc was aware of the mugging long before placing the phone call; and that although the police had no suspects in their crosshairs, Ben had his own suspicions. Cal confirmed them when he negated the word "scheduled" and offered "precise" instead, like a precise hit and run military operation.

So by following the man, Medoc's team not only had a blueprint of John Beck's scheduled escape, they knew the identity of his accomplice and the location of their final meeting. Medoc's men merely intervened, mugged John Beck and kept him in town for an arrest. The identity of his accomplice remained unknown.

**

After Ben spent the morning clearing out his files, he took a break for a late lunch at Harry's for his usual beef on weck. It was going to be a slow day, but Ben needed a day for catch-up at the station. However, as soon as he entered the building Moynan waved him over. Ben approached the detective and could smell the liquor on his breath as he spoke.

"I met Cleary in town for an early lunch," he said. "They found John Beck's car in the block where he was mugged. The jerk walked into some clip-joint around the corner for a drink and got mugged on his way back to the car. He planned to use the Peace Bridge…like we wouldn't find him in Canada. His story checks out though. One of the "girls" tried to shag him but he refused. Go figure."

Ben remained silent, waiting for the detective to continue his story.

"He hung around town because he left an envelope with his passport and eleven hundred dollars in his office. I think Cleary said they found it in his filing cabinet. He had a way in without being seen." At that point, Moynan knew he had Ben's attention. "Aren't you going to ask where we had lunch?"

"You went to Ballentines," Ben said simply.

"I hate it when you do that."

"Stop." Ben challenged the man who was obviously upset by having his surprise ruined. "Tell me what you found."

"He looked like he'd been in a fight. His face was bruised and so were his knuckles. I don't know about his arms and legs. They were covered by his clothes."

"Who was it?" Ben waited.

"The bartender at Ballentines. I think his name is Brett."

"Was he the one we spoke to the other day?"

"No. He wasn't on duty then. Cleary and I wondered if he could have been involved with John Beck somehow, leaving town or even his mugging, but then that thought went dry. Remember, you and I thought there might be a connection at Ballentines the other day."

"I don't understand," Ben said.

"Some men in the bar witnessed a brawl that got out of hand, but they said the bartender put up one helleva fight…"

"Well, that lets him out," Ben agreed.

"Now, Cleary thinks it might have been a random mugging. He thinks someone unconnected with the case saw it happen and called the police. I guess the gang didn't have time to search him. He had over three hundred dollars on him. And whoever called anonymously didn't want to get involved. Nobody wants to get involved today. It's not like the old days. Why is that?"

"Two things, I think. No one likes to be questioned today. And the other is fear of reprisal. A witnesses B and C comes after A. Our society has changed, and not for the better, I'm afraid."

"You think too much." Moynan walked away in disgust.

"Most of the time, he doesn't think at all," Danny Boyle said from his corner of the room. "He's half in the tank already."

Ben never responded to the young officer's comment, although he was well aware of the man's drinking habits.

Once Ben sat at his desk, he began to chuckle to himself. Was Medoc happy or frustrated when he called? From their phone conversation, it was obvious Ben knew the man's roommates were involved in the mugging. However, since the detective never referenced the bartender's involvement, Medoc logically concluded Ben had no knowledge of the men's other activity.

So the real purpose of Medoc's phone call was to determine every-thing Ben had on the case. If John Beck gave the bartender money to help him leave town, and Medoc's men took it after knocking him around, they were home free and a lot richer. That, of course, was providing Ben hadn't made the connection. And in Medoc's mind, Ben only connected his men to the mugging. But Medoc never realized the depth of Ben's quizzical mind. Ben made the connection in both cases but couldn't prove it. And Sal was right on target the previous night. John Beck would never iden-tify his accomplice or mention the money involved.

So, the clip-joint and filing cabinet were part of a plan to cover John Beck's ass. The paid bartender would have been waiting in the alley for his arrival with a forged passport and designated drop-off point. With that plan in operation, everything would have been cov-ered. Then, when the police found his parked car, particularly in that area, he would have already left for parts unknown. The police, how-ever, would think he was still "holed-up" somewhere in town, particu-larly after finding the passport and money.

Now, he simply used the cheap watering hole as a cover for the mugging. That and the contents of his filing cabinet made a believable story. Only Ben didn't buy it. Eleven hundred dollars to leave town for good was chump-change. There had to be more money somewhere else; somewhere hidden from the police.

Medoc's roommates must have watched the whole plan unfold...right before they mugged him. But when did the men, or one of them, take on the bartender? Was it before or after the mug-ging? The detective remembered being told during the interview that the other bartender at Ballentines was off "sick." Somehow, Ben knew intuitively, he should forget the whole thing. Medoc would never reveal their involvement in any of it.

So essentially, John Beck's escape story had two levels: the truth involving Medoc's men, the bartender, and Cal and Sal; and the account John Beck gave the police. There would be no further inves-tigation on any level. Ben would make no more inquiries. He had no evidence. But even more important, he wanted his relationship with Medoc to continue.

As for Medoc's banter, Ben didn't care how long the man played in the sand, his thoughts were elsewhere.

***

The man sat at his desk pondering a page of debits and credits. Even from his seated position, one could tell the man was tall. His head of totally gray hair indicated some measure of middle age, but his clear unwrinkled skin belied any actual year of birth. His blue eyes had a twinkle or two, but for most of the time, particularly when he sat in the position of authority at his office, he was a very staid man, who took his work seriously. And at that particular moment he was on the telephone and engaged in a very serious conversation.

"What do you mean, you want more money," he bellowed. "How could you have gone through so much money in less than a week? I have never known you to gamble, Victoria. Have you taken leave of your senses, or is that animal you're sleeping with, having you pay for sexual favors?"

"No. No." He was emphatic. "I never suggested your being a moose." He hated having his words misconstrued. "I've often said that you are a lovely woman. I just don't want you to be hurt after going on a toot, so to speak."

"No. No." He emphasized again. "I did not imply you needed to pay for companionship." The man realized the conversation was going nowhere and getting him deeper and deeper into trouble. He swung his swivel chair around in exasperation, faced the wall and heaved a sigh, shaking the slight paunch of his rather streamlined body. "Alright, Victoria, if you want to squander your money on a man who is using you for a week's fling, I cannot stop you." He listened to her briefly and was taken-back by her strong language. "Well…I…No. Of course I don't like it," he blustered, challenged by her remark of his caring for her. "You are my client and I have your best interests in mind. Yes, of course…I like all my clients." He listened to her respond but was incensed with her answer. "If that's what you want, I will send the money electronically." He turned his chair around again. This time, however, the man was very angry. He just couldn't show it.

In no time at all, Winifred Pitts was on the phone authorizing a transfer of funds to a bank in Kauai.

Winifred Pitts sat at his desk dejected and depressed. Why would Victoria Reynolds need so much money? Was this man, she was so engaged with, taking all the funds he could get from her? Or was she just too stupid to realize he was just using her? The woman always had a keen business sense. But this was different. Was she so emotionally involved that even the smallest shred of common sense took a back seat to her feelings for this man? How could this have happened so quickly? It couldn't be love at first sight. No matter how attractive she appeared, particularly a woman her age, someone searching for a relationship wouldn't choose her based on looks alone.

Suddenly, Winifred felt ashamed of his inner thoughts. For her age, Victoria was rather attractive. Even without the age consideration, men would find her comely. He never suggested she was paying this Medoc person for sexual favors because she was homely, and he never called her a moose. Where she came up with that thought overwhelmed him. And he never intimated the man was her paid companion. However, he did make the claim that Medoc may have been after her money. That's because Winifred knew his client was paying for the entire trip, hotels, food and entertainment. That fact really bothered him. Granted, it was her money to spend. But why would she spend it on someone who would leave her after their time together was over? There would be no permanency in the relationship. How could there be? They came from two different worlds. Winifred did not know this, factually. It was something he felt after meeting the man. Perhaps it would be in Victoria's best interest if he checked the man's background. Still, why did the behavior of Victoria Reynolds bother him so much? Why?

He never indicated being interested in her. She was just there… always there when he needed a partner for some affair. There was never anything between them, or with any other woman, for that matter. He was known for his notoriously lewd mouth and spewed lusty proclivities to middle-aged spinsters who attended these lofty affairs. But aside from Victoria, no one ever accompanied him to these events. Of course, more often than not, he went alone. To Winifred, this was a chance to see and be seen. It was also a chance to snag some poor unsuspecting female with lascivious banter and perhaps a later encounter.

That last thought made Winifred wonder about Victoria's meeting with Medoc. How exactly did that come about? Was it happenstance or were they formally introduced? Winifred would never know because he would never ask. Why would he? Winifred took a different position on the woman. What was Victoria to him? She was only a client, although a good one, perhaps, and a part-time partner at mutual affairs. But at many society functions, she was just another single woman, along with the rest hanging on the wall, waiting to be pegged by some willing upper-class snob. If someone was pegging her, then why was he so pissed?

The phone rang, snapping him out of his reverie.

"Hello, Barbara." His voice turned friendly as he listened to her invitation. "What date? Let me check my calendar. What time? That will be lovely," he said, ready to end the conversation. "Oh. No. She's on holiday. It's a respite of sorts." He heard the woman go on. "I don't think…." He tried to interrupt. "Yes. She will be back by then." He placed the phone back into its cradle when she ended the call.

"Damn," he said aloud. "Why do women do all the talking and never let us poor devils get a word in? I say she's on a holiday, and Barbara can't wait to see her when she gets back." The woman thinks Victoria had more plastic surgery done and will check at a dinner party two weeks from now! How could he have convinced Barbara Croft otherwise? She did all the talking.

***

"I think you missed your calling," Medoc said, holding a drink in one hand and a cigarette in the other. He leaned back against the bed pillows, a sheet draped carelessly across his naked body, as he watched Victoria change into another pair of shorts. He eyed the front patch of her thong-like panties, the diamond patch that protected her hairy treasure, and felt a swift surge of wanton lust flow through him.

"Take off your bra and panties and come over here." Medoc set down the drink and stubbed his cigarette as he watched the naked woman approach him. He pulled her down and rolled over on her, kissing her face and neck continuously while he slid deep inside her. "I don't know why I have this need to climb your bones," he whispered. He could feel the spasms of her walls tightening around his swollen shaft as their bodies rocked faster and faster. He continued his undulating slide deep within her and covered her mouth with kisses to mask her inevitable scream of joy.

Later that evening, after they watched the Hanalei sunset fade over the water and were walking casually back to their private quarters, Victoria raised a question.

"What did you mean earlier about missing my calling?"

"Isn't it obvious? You have Winifred by the balls. He's upset with your wanting more money. He feels I'm using you, and he's angry because you are enjoying every minute of our very expensive holiday. The man certainly doesn't like the idea of my shagging you."

"But it was your idea to ask for more money. We already have more than enough."

"True, but he doesn't know that." Medoc took her into his arms and kissed her passionately under a cluster of trees. "I want to continue what we started this afternoon." He positioned her against a tree and, unbuttoning the top six buttons of her dress, unhooked her bra and thumbed the nipples of her breasts to a hard nub before suckling them. His hand moved swiftly inside her panty, and as he parted her curls, his fingers inched slowly inward, feeling her readiness. He slid his finger in deeper with an undulating motion and felt her body yielding to it. "I want you," he whispered. "I can't wait."

Startled but pleased by her actions, Medoc watched Victoria remove all of her clothing, piece by piece, and leave a trail of garments as she raced to the front door of their unit; once there, she turned abruptly to face him. To Victoria's surprise, a naked Medoc stood staring right back at her and, lifting her to him, wrapped her legs around his body, and took her immediately to the bedroom.

A short time later, Victoria's thoughts wandered as she lay cuddled in Medoc's arms. Her life had changed so radically since meeting him. He had opened a new world to her, one of loving and being loved.

"I didn't know it could be like this."

"We are so good together. That's a rare gift."

"If someone had to climb my bones, I'm glad it was you."

Medoc responded by pulling her closer to him. "It's not about the sex. I can get that anywhere. It's about you, Victoria," he said clarifying his statement. "I have this need to make love with you…with you tight around me…deep inside. It's like being home…where I belong. I need that. It sustains me."

Grasping the full meaning of his words, she felt a surge of passion stirring deep within her. The unconditional love and wanton lust that flowed between them were emotions she now understood. At that precise moment, Victoria knew exactly where she wanted to be in life…with him…in his arms.

***

"I appreciate your doing this for me." Ann Quigley spoke in her usual quiet manner, when Ben drove her home after the awards dinner. "When Megan told you my friend wasn't available this evening, she didn't know the details. I didn't tell her because I was too embarrassed, Ben. The fact is, he didn't want to come." Her voice cracked in humiliation. "I can't tell you how much that hurts. He refused to be with me when I was being honored by my society as Librarian of the Year."

"Has he ever done that before? I mean not accompany you to some social gathering?"

"We never had the opportunity for this kind of event. But he was always available for the movies or the museum. Places like that. We met at the public library. Can you believe that? He loves to read."

"But you never went to any kind of social function."

"No. He doesn't like parties."

"Did he ever ask for more in your relationship?"

"What do you mean?"

"Come, Ann, surely, you would know if the man is interested in you, particularly when the two of you are constantly paired."

He watched the dark-haired woman's facial expression for some reaction, but as she turned to face him, he noticed only the widening of her large dark eyes. Obviously, someone their age found her quiet way attractive.

"He never said anything, but we do like each other."

As she spoke, Ben rolled his eyes in thought. He had just spent a totally boring evening listening to speeches, and now, he found himself talking to an educated woman with a pubescent emotional level. Could the night get any worse?

"How was it left between the two of you?"

"I'm not sure," she said continuing to reminisce. "We talked every night for almost a year. Short phone conversations about our next meeting," she added. "But we haven't talked since he refused to come with me."

"That was…"

"Five days ago." She finished his sentence. "I haven't heard from Thorsen since." Her voice cracked again and a tear trickled down her face.

The unusual name brought Ben up short. Could it be? Could it even be a remote possibility? How many men living in the area would have had that exact name? Clayson Black mentioned Thorsen Greer's name to him only once. But Ben distinctly remembered his comment about the yardage man. Ben only hoped he wasn't in the man's crosshairs. Getting shot wasn't part of his plan for bestowing a favor. His eyes swept the peripheral traffic moving in all directions. Then his thoughts turned to the woman sitting beside him.

"I think you miscalculated, Ann. I'm telling you this as a friend." Ben gave her his handkerchief. "I would give him the benefit of the doubt. Maybe he's uncomfortable milling around with a lot of people and the introductions that normally follow. Forget his not being with you tonight, if you really like his company. Do the things you both enjoy and skip those you don't."

"You really believe that, don't you?" She asked in earnest.

"Yes. I do. The next time he calls, pick-up where you left off. Forget the awards dinner. A cold statue is no duplicate for a warm friend," Ben said, as he pulled into her driveway.

When Ben got out of the car, he noticed a dark van parked across the street and, remaining totally calm, opened the passenger's side door and accompanied Ann up the steps to the front porch of her house.

"Leave the porch light on for a minute when you get inside. I have to check in. Stupid regulations," he said, pulling out his cell phone to dial a number.

"Thank you so much, Ben." She nodded before closing her front door.

Ben stood on the porch and dialed a number. From his unruffled demeanor, no one would have ever suspected the detective's awareness of the parked van or the person inside it.

"Clayson, or whoever the hell is picking up, it's Burrows!" The detective spat into the phone. "Call Thorsen, right now. I don't want to get shot! Nothing's going on here with Ann. He should call her."

Ben watched the dark van disappear and had one thought in mind. His 'adopted daughter' better stop having him service every problematic female that came her way. Perhaps, service was not the right word, but he knew what he meant, and precisely how he felt at that moment. Although he was competent with firearms, Ben was no match for a trained sniper. Then another thought crossed his mind. The night could have gotten much worse had he actually encountered Thorsen Greer.

Chapter 23
Interim

A week later, Medoc Hast and Victoria Reynolds walked into Ben's office, hand in hand.

"We thought we'd come by to report." Medoc addressed the detective. "The apartment's back to normal finally and nothing's missing. What's going on with John Beck?"

"He's been arrested, but you already knew that. I don't know where it stands since he left the hospital. It's in the DA's hands now."

"Then Victoria might still be in danger." Medoc muttered to himself. "Do you want me to stay with her?" he asked the detective. "Do you think she's safe? He could go after her for revenge."

"I don't think he will, but I can't be certain of that either. Remember, she's on record for giving his envelopes to the police, and the gun proving his guilt was inside one of them."

"Should I stay with her or leave?" Medoc questioned.

"I think you should ask Victoria." Ben turned to face the woman. "Her comfort level is what's most important here."

"I want Medoc to stay with me," she said. "I'd feel safer."

Ben looked at the couple, thinking neither one of them really wanted to separate, and that particular thought bothered him. At some point Medoc had to leave the woman. The longer he stayed with her, the harder it was going to be… for Victoria.

"Keep me posted," Ben said, watching them leave his office.

Danny Boyle came by with his own observation. "They look like two love birds," he chirped. Ben observed the young man silently and said absolutely nothing. "Or not." He walked away.

***

Winifred Pitts was sitting in his office when Victoria phoned, telling him she was back in town and would be doing her own banking.

"Barbara Croft called with an invitation to her dinner party. She tried phoning you," he said, before listening to her side of the conversation. "Then you have already spoken to her." Inwardly, Winifred was disappointed that she already knew about the affair. "Have you accepted?" he asked. "I thought we might go together." He paused, waiting for her decision. "Excellent, I will be by at seven." He listened to her response. "Thank you, Victoria." Winifred heard the click of her receiver.

"Oh, crap!" Victoria shrieked, sitting next to Medoc on the living room couch. "I just agreed to go with him to a dinner party."

"How far do you want to go with this?" Medoc asked.

"What do you mean?" she said, thoroughly confused by his question.

"Do you intend to marry this man? I guess that's the question you have to ask yourself."

"I don't understand," she said. "It's just a dinner party."

"What do you want from Winifred? Do you care for him?"

"He's a good man, but I'm not in love with him."

Medoc drew her to him, locked her eyes with his and grew serious. "We come from different worlds, Victoria. I love you in my own way. But I could never be happy with your friends or the kinds of organizations you're involved in. You need someone who moves in your same circles, someone like him."

"I don't need that." She pulled away from him. "We could be together, if you really wanted to."

"That would work for awhile, but you would become unhappy incrementally. I know that would happen. I've experienced it."

"But you will stay with me this week?" She needed confirmation.

"Of course, we could devise a plan."

"Plan?" she asked confused.

"A plan to snag a groom," he said. "And I have one in mind."

"I'm not interested." She quashed the idea.

"You're no fun," he growled.

"Sure, I am." She stood up, undid her blouse and twirled it on the way to her bedroom.

Medoc watched the woman sashay away from him and leaped to follow her.

***

"Hey!" Megan shook the detective out of his reverie. "I came by to see if you wanted to have a quick lunch."

Ben grabbed his coat and walked his 'adopted daughter' out of the building and into his car. "Where do you want to go?"

"Harry's," Megan answered. "I know you're addicted to beef on weck and I haven't had one in a long time."

"Yes," he said, "I am surprised."

"I didn't say anything."

"Yes, you did, but it was very silent." He chuckled, pulling into Harry's parking lot.

They sat at a small corner table after placing their order and began a conversation.

"What did you want to talk about?" Ben asked.

"How did you know?"

"It's one of those parental things." His eyes twinkled as he spoke.

"You know Cal's gone," she said, referring to her biological father. "But before he left, he gave me ten thousand dollars in cash as a wedding gift from him and Sal. He did the same thing with Peggy."

"And this bothers you, how?"

"I feel like he's trying to buy me off. I can understand giving Peggy and Seth a wedding gift, but why us?"

"I don't see it that way." Ben took a different point of view. "Since he wasn't here for your wedding, he and Sal wanted to give each daughter a gift. Don't forget Megan, they have been gone for approximately twenty-six years. Personally, this is very generous and loving of them. I would take it as coming from the heart."

"I don't believe it. That's just so much bullshit. Where did he get that kind of money and why is he trying to buy my affection?"

"I think they have money. They have a very popular bar in a tourist area. That alone should tell you something."

"Maybe," she said biting into her sandwich. "He also invited us to visit. Makes me wonder if there's a wedding in the making," she added, then changed the subject. "I didn't remember how good this really is." Megan continued eating her sandwich. "What's new on Beck? Is he getting the needle?"

"I doubt it, but I think he will go to prison. There's a great deal of evidence against him." Ben finished his sandwich.

"He should be in jail right now." She crumpled her paper and got up to leave with him.

As Ben was pulling into the parking lot behind the station, Megan remembered something she had forgotten to mention.

"By the way," she said, "I am so proud of you. Ann Quigley called me. She appreciated your being her escort. The woman kept singing your praises to me. She said, 'Ben is such a clear thinking person.' Hell, I could have told her that. But she's a happy camper these days, now that her friend is back with her." She gave Ben a hurried kiss, got out of the car, and waved goodbye. "Next time, Dad, my treat."

As he stood watching Megan's car disappear, a good feeling swept over him. He was glad Ann Quiqley took his advice and was now seeing Thorsen Greer again. He felt certain the woman would limit her activities to the things they both liked. But most of all, Ben was glad he wasn't shot.

When he reached the front door of the building and stepped inside, his boss flagged him over.

"It's done," he said. "John Beck and his attorney took the DA's plea bargain."

"After a week?" Ben expressed surprise.

"I think it was in the shaker at the hospital. No trial. Saves the State money."

"Who knew?"

"Not me. I was just told today. Not important enough, I guess," he said and walked away.

***

Ben went straight to his office, closed the door and made a phone call.

"Put on your pants," he said, "you can go home now. John Beck and his attorney cut a deal with the DA. I wasn't privy to the details. I'll get them later. Tell Victoria." Ben listened to Medoc's side of the inquiry. "That's up to you. I am out of it totally." He ended their conversation.

Although it had been a disappointing case, Ben began to detail the most recent events that unfolded:

John Beck made a deal with the DA; Medoc's men kept the money John Beck gave the bartender to help him leave town; and from the information he interpreted over lunch with Megan, Sal and Cal found a sum of money near John Beck's mugged body and used it to gift Cal's daughters.

Ben focused on the money taken by Cal and Sal.

His thoughts drifted back years earlier when Seth's fiancée, Helen, was killed by a hit and run driver. Ben had gathered a massive amount of evidence against the driver, but the politician's teenage son was given a pass, much to his disgust. He remembered the terrible years of agony Seth suffered after her death. Then Ben thought about the murder of Judd not being resolved, and of Seth, actually witnessing the shooting death of his half-brother. With everything Seth had endured, coupled with Peggy's kidnapping, they more than deserved the money. It was just compensation for crimes that went unpunished.

As for Megan, every "father" wants to see his "child" get ahead in life.

He dialed Seth's number and waited to hear his voice. "I just got word that John Beck made a deal with the DA. I don't know the terms, but I'm sure he'll do jail time. Tell Peggy." He listened to Seth's side of the conversation and said, "We should be able to. I'll ask Poag to check his schedule." A reminiscent expression crossed his face, his thoughts drifting to a happier time.

He remembered their years of fishing together with Poag. It was like a ritual. Poag would give them his schedule; Ben would clear his calendar; and Seth would join them, if he wasn't traveling. He and Seth always shared room three at Poag's motel for an early morning start. After the trip, they returned to the motel and left the following day. Ben's sister, Clarisa, understood her husband's deep passion for fishing. In fact, Poag closed the motel for a week of remodeling three times a year. That was the excuse for those longer fishing trips with Ben. Seth was usually traveling, and Clarisa took that time to visit their children. Now that Seth was married, Ben had doubts about his interest in the sport. Yet, Seth brought it up. Maybe he would go out for a day or two. He did recall Seth joining them when Helen was alive. Perhaps the three of them would still fish together after all. He would check with Poag. It would be like old times.

Within fifteen minutes, a defiant Megan was on the line. "When did you get the news about John Beck?"

"Right after I left you." She heard him chuckle. "I knew you couldn't resist calling."

"Is she still safe? I mean he wouldn't do anything crazy to her or Seth, after confessing, would he?"

"No. Megan. There's no need to worry. They are completely safe."

Ben continued to sit at his desk after their conversation. The case of John Beck was still on his mind. The mastermind behind the whole plan never paid for the kidnapping of Peggy Roberts or the murder of his own wife, Alice. The state could only prosecute him for the murder of Mel Travers. And that was through a plea bargain. Was Ben satisfied with that? Or was he depressed because he couldn't get enough evidence to add the murder of his wife to John Beck's conviction? He had spent months of investigative work, and the evidence of one murder was the only charge that mattered. His mind issued a resounding dissatisfaction with the entire affair.

Still, regardless of Ben's massive disappointment, knowing that a portion of John Beck's hush money went to his victims seemed justifiable for the misery the man had caused. In Ben's mind this was the award given in a civil suit to the injured parties. Of course, Ben was the only person who knew the entire history of John Beck's money management, and he was not sharing that hidden fact with anyone. "You can't prove it, anyway." An inner voice shouted. "That was probably true," Ben acquiesced. Then his thoughts turned to Medoc Hast for some strange reason and he began to feel very uneasy. Just then his cell phone rang.

"It's done," the voice said, ending the call that set Ben's thoughts reeling.

He recognized the voice and understood the message. But the reason completely escaped him. Why did Medoc leave her today? Was it because she no longer needed a bodyguard, now that John Beck pleaded guilty?

No. There had to be a deeper reason. Nevertheless, Ben was glad it had ended. The two were good together, away from Victoria's friends and social calendar, although Medoc would have been accepted anywhere. He would have fit in socially, and not because he came from a background of wealth. That was the beauty of Medoc. He was a real chameleon. But someone, liking change, would become bored easily with the same people, the same organizations and the same scheduled events. Their worlds would collide…with them in dead center. That had to be the reason for the separation. Ben had seen the sparks of chemistry between them and they were real…unfortunately.

***

On the night of Barbara Croft's formal dinner party, approximately two weeks after Medoc left her penthouse apartment, Winifred Pitts was, in every aspect, the perfect escort for the very wealthy Victoria Reynolds. He complimented the gracious hostess, thanked the host and was congenial with every guest the entire evening. Of course, since they all knew one another from various dealings, the easy flow of conversation made the night pass by so quickly, that everyone hated to see it end.

Later, after the dinner party, when Winifred walked Victoria into her building, she paused by the elevator momentarily and extended an invitation. "Would you like a nightcap, Winifred?"

"I think that would be very nice." He stepped into the elevator with her.

"Pour us a drink," Victoria said, upon entering the apartment and flipping a light switch that connected the living room lamps. She placed her evening wrap on an upholstered chair and sat on the couch, while Winifred followed suit by tossing his coat on another chair nearby.

"We need to talk," he said, taking a bottle of scotch and two glasses from the stocked shelf behind the bar.

"About what?" she asked, watching him place the drinks on the coffee table.

"Being coy was never part of your persona." He balked at her facial expression. "Why are you involved with this man, Medoc Hast?" he demanded. "He is making a fool of you and using your money for his pleasure."

"And what makes you think I care?" she challenged. "If I am enjoying myself, for the first time in my life, why should it bother you if I'm paying for it?"

Victoria studied him carefully. Most women would have considered the crass and crude Winifred quite handsome, but she was not interested in the man. Her mind and body had been awakened by the touch of someone else, and she longed for the feel of him again. The thought stirred a deep hunger within her and she ached for Medoc's strong embrace.

"I would be the last person to deny you any pleasure, but not at your own personal expense," he said, nullifying her reverie.

"So you think I'm too old for some romantic adventure, or maybe I'm not attractive enough. I'm old and unattractive."

"No. Victoria," he said quickly, fearing her anger. "I just want an explanation. This whole, what, maybe three weeks, has been so unlike you. Has something happened that I should know about? We've been friends for a long time." He reached for her hand, but she instinctively withdrew it.

"Alright." He folded his arms. "Just tell me what is going on. If you are romantically involved with this man, I will be the last to interfere. However, if you are hiding something from me, something I should know about; then this is the time to discuss it."

"There is nothing to discuss. Medoc is no longer with me," she said quietly. "I hired him to be my bodyguard, so naturally I had to pay him and all of the expenses we incurred. It's a long story, but I'll give you the abridged version."

"So that's why you needed the money," he exclaimed, when Victoria finished explaining her danger with John Beck's incriminating envelopes, Ben Burrows' concern for her safety, and his suggestion of hiring a bodyguard. "And the detective feels you are safe now?" Winifred needed reassurance.

"John Beck's been charged with murder and has taken the plea bargain offered. So, there would be no reason for him to come after me."

"And your bodyguard?" he asked.

"His job is over," she sighed, "and things are back to normal."

"And you're safe. You are sure of that?" He questioned again, and then shook his head in confusion. "That still doesn't explain why a man of means would take a job as a bodyguard."

"What are you saying?" she demanded. Although Victoria tried to remain unruffled, her mind was churning all sorts of depressing thoughts.

"He comes from a family of wealth to put it simply. His family owns the Hast wineries in Napa."

"Don't tell me you had him investigated?" Victoria tried to mask her shock.

That Winifred would investigate Medoc made her angry. She was even more upset with Medoc for not giving her a better explanation of his background instead of the few crumbs he threw here and there.

"Naturally, I was concerned when we first met. After all," he cautioned, "I do handle a portion of your financials, so I had to know what you were dealing with. Spending time in the service could explain his proficiency as a bodyguard." Then he thought about the man's misspelled first name. It must have been a typo he assured himself and promptly dismissed it from his mind. "Ben probably knew his background and trusted him to keep you out of harm's way. But it no longer matters now. His job is over and you are safe."

"Ben Burrows would never have allowed me to be alone if I were in danger. Not only is Ben an honorable man; he is a very good friend."

"You must have great trust in this detective." Winifred caught her nod. "I am relieved. I don't want anything to happen to you. We've been together for a long time."

"Too long," Victoria said impulsively.

"A relationship can't go forward when the chemistry is solely one-sided," he replied. "Sometimes, however, a relationship can develop into something deeper and more meaningful, if one is patient."

Winifred realized his statement came as a surprise to her, and then noticed a tear edging the corner of her eye. He reached for her hand and found she had not instinctively removed it from his grasp.

"Oh, Winifred," she sighed, the tear inching farther down her cheek. "I can't think anymore. It's been such an ordeal." She reached into her pocket for a tissue, ignoring his declaration. "Maybe I shouldn't have gone to the dinner party tonight. I feel drained."

Winifred quickly finished his drink, grabbed his coat and before leaving, kissed her on the forehead. "I'll call you. Maybe we can get a group to fly to New York for a show. Separate rooms, of course," he said, before she could object.

"That would be nice," Victoria agreed. She watched him disappear out of her apartment, locking the door behind him.

When the tall silver-haired man got into his car, he was oblivious of the black van following him to the prestigious Sovereign Club, a limited membership facility for very wealthy gentleman, who appreciated good food, expensive cigars, and beautifully appointed rooms for everything else a member required. An hour later, the same van followed the car to the man's home in the city.

Victoria continued to sit on the couch after Winifred left, her thoughts lingering on their conversation. She did not want to go to New York with Winifred. Nor did she want to be with a group of old hens, cackling about those mundane things that no longer held her interest. Had she changed? Or had Medoc changed her? Maybe she had been away too long from her group of old friends.

Winifred's shocking news of Medoc's background left her utterly confused. Why hadn't he told her? Did he think having money would make a difference? Would it bring them closer, or widen the gulf between them? She wondered. Winifred also mentioned Medoc's military service. Was that Ben's reason for using him as her bodyguard? She would call the detective tomorrow to learn more about Medoc's background. Should she tell him Medoc's real reason for leaving her? Somehow, Ben had already sensed the extent of their relationship. But did he know how Medoc left it with her? She thought not.

He had summed it up so succinctly. She had a life filled with friends, social obligations and community functions. That had been the history of her very wealthy family, and she, as the only child, an heiress, had continued in that vein after their demise. Of course, to those who knew her, Victoria had a reputation for being a very smart business woman. She had accumulated a great amount of wealth in her own right through shrewd real estate investments.

And there it was. Medoc left Victoria to continue her role in the community. He wanted no part of it. He needed the freedom from a structured schedule. "Been there, done that." He told her. "Not doing it again."

Medoc had removed himself from a social and political life to an unrestricted and more open lifestyle. He never liked the social swirl, not that it made him uncomfortable. He enjoyed meeting people but he was not a collector. To Medoc, those social events were collections of people building networks on one another, all to the inclusion of one giant spider, incorporating everyone into its web: the all knowing spider, with dirt on everyone. He was the inevitable host: like a sweet-talking blackmailer.

Pleading with him got her nowhere. It was a useless exercise which made no sense. He loved her: she loved him. Why couldn't they be together? Victoria didn't need a social life: she needed him. Medoc thought she couldn't change her habits of a half-century. She disagreed. They fought. They argued. He finally acquiesced with a directive.

She was to meet him in Tonawanda Park on Sheridan Drive at noon on September first, providing she still felt the same.

The whole arrangement seemed stupid to her. However, knowing Medoc as she did, Victoria felt he had some ulterior motive for the arrangement. But she could not determine what it was. Would Ben know? That was something else she would ask.

***

Two weeks later, Victoria Reynolds made a phone call.

They met in Tonawanda Park facing Sheridan Drive at an appointed time. When they saw one another, they raced into each other's arms and kissed each other passionately without embarrassment.

"I don't want to be without you." She began to sob. "I'm so lonely."

"I'm only thinking of you. You know that." He kissed her again.

"Please take me somewhere Medoc. Please. I feel like my heart is breaking. I hunger for you."

"Follow me. We'll head away from the city."

When they arrived at a motel, Medoc and Victoria spent the entire afternoon making love. This time, Medoc made love to her in a way she had never experienced before. She peaked almost continuously. He had her floating so often she never wanted to leave him. He began by gently exploring and kissing each and every contour of her body, before finally positioning her. Completely shocked by the rapidity of his next move, Victoria found herself clutching the bed sheet and groaning with heightened emotions. Her chick-flick readings had never detailed the wild orgasmic spasms a woman would experience with such an accomplished lover. She had been virginal in that respect also.

They lay in each other's arms, staring at one another.

"How could I possibly want another man touching me after you?" she asked. "I never knew love could be like this. It's you I want, Medoc. No one else."

"We've already come to terms, Victoria. Once decided, you can't run back and expect acceptance. I will always be an outsider, looking in."

"I keep telling you, I don't care about that. I love you."

"We agreed on September," Medoc said firmly.

When it was time for Victoria to leave, Medoc reminded her of their agreement.

"I still don't understand. It's been well over a month and I still want you in my life. Why can't you stay with me? It can't be my money. You have wealth of your own. Winifred had you investigated. Why didn't you tell me?"

"There was no need. I was your hired bodyguard and you had to pay the expenses. That was the arrangement. We just happened to fall in love along the way," he said sadly, "and that presented a problem. It's the type of life you're accustomed to. You need people, activity, things, Victoria. I'm satisfied with just having you with me on an old crappy boat. We're worlds apart."

"September first, noon in the park," she said. "I still think it's a dumb idea, like that stupid movie."

"This is not about a movie," Medoc said, with a sorrow he found hard to hide. "If you should fall in love with Winifred, you have my blessing. I know your life would be wonderful with him. I love you, Victoria. Always remember that. But do not call me again."

When she embraced and kissed him for the last time, a surge of passion raced through her body. Tears streamed down her cheeks. She clung to him and pleaded, "Don't make me leave, Medoc." The tears washed her face. "Please," she begged. "Can't you see this is tearing me apart? How much I need you? People who love each other don't do things like this." As hard as she tried, Victoria couldn't convince him a trial separation would not alter her love for him, nor give more importance to her lifestyle. However, he stood firm on their conditional contract.

Remaining silent, he led her to the door and watched her drive away. It was only then, after she had gone, that he threw himself across the bed and cried. Medoc hadn't lost her: he never had her to begin with. If he never had her to begin with, then how could he have fallen in love with her?

***

It was sometime in June when Victoria joined her golf group for lunch at the country club. Her presence filled the women with questions, since she normally left after playing nine holes.

"Where are you sitting Saturday night? What table?" A woman her age looked pointedly at Victoria and waited for the answer to her question. "The Charity Ball," she said, reminding her.

"I don't know. I'm coming with Winifred. I'm sure he's made all the arrangements."

"Oh, that explains it," a second woman mused. "He seems so different these days, much more personable. He's such a handsome blue-eyed devil. I'll say that for him. I wish my husband had his silver-colored hair."

"Maybe, he's over male menopause," the first woman said, causing them to laugh. "That could explain the difference in his behavior," she added, then changed the subject. "Your golf game seems to be improving. Are you taking lessons?" She caught Victoria's nod. "Is everyone still going to Melody Fair next week?" she asked the group. "My house at five for drinks," she said. "Are we renting a limo or coupling up for the play? I know Winifred likes going alone. I'm sorry, Victoria. But you know what I mean."

Victoria thoughts raced as she drove home. This was her life, one of endless parties and functions: golf twice a week, standing hair appointments, dinners at the club, tickets to sporting events, opening plays in New York, and of course, the local theater and opera her friends always programmed-in between charity functions. This was not living. Her shallow life was a series of scheduled events she usually attended alone. The names of the functions changed, but in the end, it was all the same. This was the life she had known and enjoyed. These women were her friends. They talked of parties, plays and the latest gossip. It was the continuous swirl of calendar dates that had made their social life so bearable, and yet so envied, by those poor unfortunates who had not yet materially arrived. But this was before Medoc entered her life and gave her what really mattered…the love between a man and a woman…meshing their lives into one.

She turned the car around suddenly…away from the city…away from her friends…to the park in Tonawanda. She sat on a bench, reflecting her life and the pain of heartbreak: a solitary figure with tears streaming down her face. This was not the life she wanted. She wanted her soul mate. She wanted the only man she ever loved: the first man to show her the physical side of love and the emotional pain of it. Tears continued to flood her cheeks. The life she was living was not the life she wanted.

A figure, who had followed her, stood hidden in a clump of trees. He, too, was alone...and watching…

Chapter 24
Death

The phone call came as a shock. They were not prepared for that kind of news. But with death, no one ever is. Janice was busy stocking the new collectibles that came in that day, while Peggy ran to answer the phone. It was Merton, Fred's boss, at the Planning Department.

"We found him slumped over his desk. I called 911 but it was too late to save him. I know this is going to be hard on Janice, but we need to know where to take him: what funeral home to call."

Peggy set the phone aside and approached Janice slowly. She took the gentle woman's hands and carefully explained the death of her husband and the prevailing circumstances at Planning. Only someone like Janice, with her kind of inner strength, could have steeled herself for the unexpected moment of death.

She took the phone, gave Merton the necessary information and made him understand that she would be at Planning in a matter of minutes. She would meet the undertaker there to sign the necessary papers.

Janice spoke quietly as she cradled the phone. "He had heart problems. The doctor couldn't seem to regulate the Coumadin, so I knew Fred's heart would give out sooner or later. There won't be an autopsy," Janice said, indicating she knew his time was near. "I'll call Amy." She stood by the gift shop door, holding her cell phone, and began to speak.

While Janice talked with Amy, Peggy called Megan and gave her sister the sad news and a full set of instructions. Peggy knew Amy would not arrive until much later that afternoon, so this was not the time for Janice to be left alone.

"Janice, wait." Peggy's voice rang out sharply when her partner gathered her belongings. "I'm coming with you. Don't argue with me." She grabbed the store's 'closed' sign and posted it on the gift shop door.

Peggy was glad she decided to drive Janice to Planning. Her partner needed the support of family and friends to help her through this very difficult period. She knew Megan would contact Ben and Seth with the sad news, before stocking Janice's refrigerator with groceries. Megan mentioned seeing Janice's house key in Peggy's cutlery drawer, so entry would be no problem. Peggy also told Megan the kinds of food to buy for serving those friends and neighbors who came by to express their condolences. Peggy had been quite explicit on that point. She knew Brad would help Megan arrange the food trays and felt secure knowing she could depend on them. They would be willing to do anything to help Janice in this difficult time.

Peggy's thoughts shifted to Ben Burrows. He would join them as soon as possible. His would be the steady hand in this time of sorrow and the one whose shoulder the family would cry on. Ben would help Janice through this. He would waste no time after receiving Megan's phone call.

Peggy thought about their unique friendship. The detective had been close friends with Fred and Janice for years. They were there for Ben at a very bad time in his life…when he too was struggling to survive…when life wasn't worth living without his wife. Then later, Fred became a charter member of Ben's monthly poker game. That was months after Julie's demise.

Of course, when Julie was still alive, the four of them went everywhere together. She and Janice were extremely close. As Peggy recalled, they met at a library function and became fast friends. After they brought the husbands in socially, the friendship just seemed to grow from there. If memory served her well, Janice took care of Julie when she was ill, when she was dying of cancer.

Her thoughts flashed back years earlier. Ben's sister also helped care for Julie…when she could. But for much of the time, Clarisa and her husband, Poag, were busy running a motel. There was always something going on, guests checking in or checking out, maintaining the rooms and the outside yard work that was not under monthly service contract. After all, this was their business, their livelihood. And although Ben's sister came when she could, the full brunt of caring for Julie fell on

Janice. Ben would phone after being called on a case unexpectedly, and Janice would rush to his house, so Julie would not be left alone.

Strange, how life turned out. Peggy never put it together at first. Although Janice would mention Ben's name occasionally, she would always refer to Clarisa as Ben's sister. Janice would say, "Ben and Julie are spending the holidays with his sister."

Of course, things changed drastically when Julie became ill and needed help. Although Janice never discussed the care she provided, no explanation was necessary. Peggy gleaned all she needed to know through snippets of conversation about the woman's deteriorating condition. Peggy remembered watching Janice pack the trunk of her car with plastic containers of frozen food and buckets of cleaning rags and detergents. It wasn't hard to determine Janice's dual role of caregiver and housekeeper in order to keep the everyday routine as normal as possible. However, her thoughts were cut short as she pulled into a parking space in the back lot of the Municipal Building.

"You will stay with me…I mean now, while…," Janice said, crossing the lot to the building entrance.

"Of course. Ben will be here too. I had Megan call him," Peggy replied, walking beside her.

Janice sighed. "I told Amy to go to the house. She'll be in late this afternoon. We'll go to the funeral home tomorrow to make our selections."

"I'm here for you, if you need me. For anything." Peggy emphasized her statement. "I know you and Amy have a lot of things to take care of, but food won't be one of them. I told Megan to stock your refrigerator. I gave her a list. I'm sure the neighbors who come by will not be empty-handed either."

"Oh, Peggy." A tear slid down her cheek. "How am I going to get through this?"

Peggy held her friend gently. "It will be hard, Janice, but remember, you won't be alone." Just as she released Janice from her arms, she turned her attention to the man shouting at them.

"Janice!" Ben Burrows rushed to embrace the woman. "I am so sorry." He drew her to him. "Merton called me with the news and I rushed right over. I knew you would be here." He took her arm as they walked inside the building. "Megan called." He addressed Peggy who trailed behind them. "She and Brad are at the supermarket with your list, whatever that means."

"Food for the house, Peggy...," Janice began.

"That's good." He understood, but his thoughts turned in a different direction. "Does Amy know?"

"She'll be in later," Janice answered quietly, and then catching Ben's strange expression, added, "Amy said she'd pack her things and leave immediately. Although some of the roads are torn up with construction, she thought flying would take longer than the drive from Ithaca."

Ben agreed silently with Amy's assessment as he guided Janice into the Planning Department. "Will she be coming alone?" The woman's stony silence told him Janice was uncertain of her daughter's plans. "I'm staying with you," he whispered before talking with Merton.

Sitting in Merton's outer office almost seemed surreal to Janice and Peggy. They listened to a flurry of activity before being ushered down the hall into a room that held a draped figure lying on a gurney. Seeing the exposed head of her husband brought the usually composed Janice to burst with uncontrollable tears. Peggy stood quietly, her arm around Janice, tears streaming down her own face, while Ben slipped a handkerchief into the widow's hand.

Janice's eyes shifted from her husband's face to that of the undertaker who held a signature form in his hand. Her eyes shifted once again, locking them on Ben, who completely understood her non-verbal request. Now, it was his turn to care for her, as she had cared for him, at the moment of Julie's death.

"We should leave." He waved Merton, the undertaker and Peggy out of the room and closed the door before addressing them. "She needs a private moment to be with Fred. This is her time to say those things she needs to say to him. This is their moment of parting...of one being left behind." His thoughts centered on Julie as he spoke. It was like yesterday. He remembered sitting at her bedside, holding her hand, watching her slip quietly away and feeling the dread of living without her.

Ben's words had a profound effect on Peggy. Never, in all her time of knowing the detective, did she realize his sensitivity or his complete grasp of Janice's needs. The longer Peggy knew him, the more impressed she became with the man.

They waited silently in the hallway at Planning, until Janice returned to them and signed the papers granting Schlatley's Funeral Home possession of her husband's body. After Janice signature barely dried, Ben quickly took her arm and led her to his car in the back parking lot.

"I'll meet you at the house." He told Peggy as he helped Janice into his car. "I'm totally available. I took the week off."

Peggy followed them out of the parking lot but turned in the opposite direction. A frown crossed her forehead. There was the matter of Janice's parked car at the gift shop. Never mind that now, she told herself, upon entering the store. Below the 'Closed' sign on the door, Peggy posted another one in large letters: 'Death in the Family.' Peggy took a cursory look around the shop before making a phone call.

***

"I never gave it a thought." Janice told the group that gathered in the family room. "Seth dropped by for the car keys and took Brad with him."

"I thought it best to have the car back at the house." Peggy dropped the subject. "Have you heard from Amy?" Although Peggy focused on Janice when she spoke, her peripheral vision caught Ben's hand slicing his neck, signaling her to talk about something else.

"You might want to check the fridge." Megan came to her sister's rescue. "If you think we need something else, Brad will take me to the store when he gets back."

"Tomatoes." Peggy wanted the conversation with her sister to continue on the safer subject of food.

"I put them in the crisper with the lettuce. The deli stuff's in the meat drawer, but we made two trays of lunch meat and cheese."

"Perfect." Peggy's response was cut short by Brad's sudden appearance.

"I parked your car beside Ben's on the driveway." Brad slipped the car keys into Janice's hand. "Seth parked next door."

"Are you sure there's enough room?"

"Peggy parked in her garage. I can do the same with yours if you need more space."

"Ben." Janice rose from her chair to give Ben her car keys. She walked out on the driveway with him, passing Seth who was just entering the house. Janice followed Ben into the garage after he parked her car.

"What's going on?" Seth seemed to address no one in particular.

"Ben signaled me to avoid mentioning Amy," Peggy answered. "Do we know what happened to her?"

"If there's a problem, Ben will tell us, so we'll know how to comport ourselves, particularly now, with Fred's demise," Seth said. His response seemed to meet with their approval.

"I'm definitely for comporting." Megan snickered but immediately changed into serious mode when she caught her sister's daggered looks. However, she knew Seth thought her remark was funny. He understood her well.

They heard voices coming from the basement and, for some unknown reason, felt an announcement was forthcoming and all conversation suddenly stopped.

***

"Janice wanted me to make an announcement before Amy arrives, so you don't ask questions that would embarrass her. To put it simply, Amy has broken her engagement and cancelled the wedding. She is taking it very badly."

The room fell silent with the announcement.

"Of course, you want to know the reason for this," he added, "but Janice has no information. Amy refused to elaborate. I think she will talk about it when she's ready, but this is not the time."

All eyes were fixed on Ben Burrows. They were trying to digest his announcement when the telephone and doorbell rang simultaneously. Ben ran to answer the phone, while Peggy ushered a tall handsome man with dark brown hair and equally dark eyes into the family room. Ben signaled Peggy and took Janice into the living room for a phone conversation with the funeral director.

"Who the hell is he?" Ben whispered to Janice, referring to the stranger.

"I thought he was your friend," she answered softly.

"Not likely. I know all the men on the force, and he's definitely not from the funeral home. You just talked to those people."

"Maybe he's some religious nut who heard about Fred."

"Don't worry." He took her arm. "I'll handle it."

"I don't think we know you." Ben addressed the young handsome stranger.

"Janice, Ben, this is Paul Langdon." The man stretched his hand outward as a friendly gesture when Peggy made the introductions. "Janice is Amy's mother and Ben Burrows is our close family friend. Paul is looking for Amy."

The young man took Janice's hand. "I was teaching a computer seminar in Rochester when I heard the news. I am so sorry to learn of Mr. Sommers' death. I want to help in any way I can."

"I apologize." Janice maintained her soft genteel manner. "I don't believe Amy spoke of you to me. I would have remembered your name."

"She has a lot on her mind right now," he sighed. "Where's her room? I left my luggage in the car."

"Just a minute." Ben halted him. "Before you move one more step I need to know your relationship with Amy. What are you doing here?"

"You're the detective." Paul extended his hand to him. "I heard how close you are to the family. I'm here to help my mother-in-law in any way I can. I'm Amy's husband."

The room fell silent again. This piece of shocking news left everyone speechless.

"The short of it is, we both got drunk at a conference in Vegas and ended-up married. Her fiancé and his parents were very upset with us, but shit happens." His upbeat manner and comments caused the whole group to snicker. "I don't mean to make light of what happened. But truth be told, I'm glad it did. I've loved Amy ever since we met and I know she loves me. Although I am ecstatic, she's very disappointed in herself. Getting married like that was unsettling, so unlike her…hurting her parents, her fiancé and his family. I guess, I'm asking for your understanding and support…particularly with Amy when she gets here. She is very broken up by the way we got married. And now, with her father's death, she's devastated emotionally."

"Did she ask for an annulment?" The question came from Megan.

"Annulment was not the solution: forgiveness was. Gerald Price and his family could not bring themselves to understand how something like that could happen."

"You're saying her fiancé called the whole thing off," Peggy interrupted.

"Not exactly. They had a heated conversation after learning what we had done, and, of course, sleeping together. Naturally his side of the family was angry and humiliated. Amy certainly understood the error." He laughed at the terminology. "But Gerald made the big mistake of looking down on her as a fallen woman and told her so. But you know Amy. She takes no prisoners. She told him to go…well." He stopped talking and ended the conversation by closing the front door behind him, knowing there would be a quick discussion while he got his luggage.

"Ok." Ben told the group. "We tell Amy we met her husband and were breaking bread together. So let's get some food on the table and follow through with our story." He noted Janice's nod of approval.

***

Within the hour, Amy walked through the front door expecting to throw herself into her mother's arms. Instead, she stopped at the dining room entrance and spotted Paul.

"What are you doing here?" She demanded of the man who rushed to embrace his wife and kiss her longingly. "What?" She melted in his arms momentarily and brushed his lips. "Did you…all of it?" she whispered.

"I told the family we got hammered and married in a single shot. They congratulated me on your behalf and wished us happiness." Paul released his hold on her.

"Mother." Amy hurried to sit beside her at the table. "I'm so sorry." She began to cry. "I made a mess of it. Not my marrying Paul. We are so good together. I wish dad could have met him. It's just with dad passing away and humiliating you and Gerald's family…I'm so ashamed of my actions, but not of marrying Paul."

Janice placed a loving hand on her daughter's arm and wiped her tears with a paper napkin. "If you and Paul love each other, your father would have been happy for you, regardless of anything else that transpired. Now, have something to eat. You've had a long trip."

"How long have you been here?" Amy asked her husband. "I did call the office."

"I know. Kiki called with the news. I knew you couldn't wait for me so I drove to Amherst from Rochester. I'm not worried. Kiki will take care of the business."

Amy caught the strange expression on her mother's face. "Kiki, short for Kathleen, is Paul's mother. I don't know if he told you about his computer business. In the office, his mother is called Kiki. At home, he calls her Kiki mom or just mom."

"Having your mother work the business is a smart way to avoid theft," Peggy said.

"Or cook the books," Megan added, causing everyone around the table to laugh.

"In any event, I am happy for you, Amy." Ben was the first to offer his best wishes and congratulations with a hug and kiss on the cheek.

Everyone around the table soon followed Ben's congratulatory lead.

"How about me?" Paul asked. "What do I get?"

"What the hell more do you want?" Seth offered. "You got Amy."

"I am really going to like living in this family." His smile encompassed everyone in the room.

***

On the day of the funeral, Ben stood with Janice at the cemetery, while Paul held Amy's arm throughout the final blessing. The limousine brought the foursome back to the funeral home where Ben's car sat in the parking lot.

"The group will meet us at Alexia's." Ben informed them as they entered his car. "Peggy and Megan made all the arrangements. I noticed Clarisa and Poag at the cemetery. We'll see them at the restaurant."

"Is Clarisa your sister?" Paul asked, catching Ben's nod. "So I get to meet the whole family. That's perfect. I have always felt that the bond of friendship is sometimes stronger than the bond of blood."

Ben listened to the young man and wondered if he and Megan were related. She had been singing that same song to Ben ever since they met.

"Ben, I feel I should be paying for the funeral lunch at Alexia's," Janice said in her own quiet way. "Between our group of ten and the neighbors who attend, this will be very expensive for you."

"You did so much for me with Julie. I could never begin to repay you. But for today, I think Fred would have appreciated a nice gathering at lunch, and that is exactly what we're doing."

Chapter 25
Janice

It was almost four o'clock on a Saturday afternoon in August, when Janice answered the gift shop phone and waited for the caller to ask a question concerning their merchandise. Peggy watched her partner silently, knowing she might be asked to check the price or availability of an item, while Janice continued her conversation with the customer.

"Oh." Janice's facial expression changed radically. "You don't have to go to all that trouble. I was just dropping it off," she said, and noting Peggy's quizzical expression, raised her index finger indicating a conversation was forthcoming. The woman listened to the caller's explanation and then said, "That would be lovely. I'll see you at five." She placed the phone back into its cradle.

"That was Ben," Janice explained. "He wants me to stay for dinner when I drop off his jacket. What's with the look?" She gave Peggy a piercing stare. "The jacket's been at the house since Fred's wake. He never picked it up, and now, two months later, he can't find my cell number, so he used the shop phone."

"He's busy." Peggy reminded her. "He probably had Fred's and couldn't call you on that."

"Hardly," she said. "I disconnected his cell shortly after…." She stopped. "The bills kept coming in and I had to notify every business I could think of to cut costs. And, of course, there was Amy, urging me to move closer to her. As if I wanted to…or needed to. Thank God for the shop." She gave her partner a winning smile. "The shop is good for me. I'm with people. I have you." Janice stopped speaking momentarily. "Maybe, I should go home and change."

"Why, for heaven's sake?" Peggy studied her partner's coordinated outfit. Soft spoken Janice always reminded her of a poster girl for genteel women who attended expensive finishing schools. Her hair was never out of place; her nails, neatly manicured; and her deportment led one to believe she may have been a model in her younger years. "Your silk blouse and skirt are perfect," Peggy said. "Just freshen up and leave. Go a little early. Maybe you can help Ben cook dinner."

"He's just throwing a few steaks on the grill. So, I'm assuming we'll have corn on the cob and a salad. Ben never cooked; Julie did it all. After she passed away, I think he ate out a lot, beef on weck, most likely. He never puttered around the kitchen like Fred did."

"Then go help him with dinner," Peggy urged. "You need to see a different face for a change. Frankly, I'm glad Ben thought of it."

Taking her advice, Janice freshened-up in the lavatory and left her business partner to visit an old friend.

***

When Janice pulled into the driveway of the red brick bungalow, she remembered with great fondness the back yard barbeques she and Fred enjoyed with Julie and Ben years earlier. Now, only Ben and Janice were left. Had it been seven years already since Julie's demise? It had only been a matter of months since Fred... Nothing ever stayed the same. Life was never constant. It was fluid… always moving forward…

Ben watched Janice slide out of her car and pull a hanger holding a man's sport coat from the back seat car hook. As she walked up the driveway toward him, he greeted her from the doorway and quickly ushered her into the house. He felt relaxed with the woman. They had been friends for years, when their spouses were alive…when the four of them went everywhere together. There was no pretense with her. No necessary preparation. No getting dressed-up. None of that. He wore a simple blue-collared tee shirt and a pair of brown slacks.

"It's a lot more comfortable in here," he said, taking the jacket from her and placing it in the hall closet. "I just had the air conditioning checked."

Janice turned from him and automatically crossed the living room into the kitchen. Two mismatched place settings rested on a semi-wrinkled white tablecloth that covered an oval kitchen table. In the exact center of the table sat a bronze sleigh with two red candles surrounded by Christmas greenery. It was not the customary center-piece arrangement of gorgeous-looking flowers, permeating the air with some heavenly floral scent. Instead, the smell of fried garlic and mushrooms flooded the entire house.

Ben watched Janice view his artistic effort and hurriedly informed her of his inefficiency at entertaining. "These were the only candles I could find," he said, pointing to the centerpiece. "They are connected somehow to the sleigh. I guess I could have bought some…if I had thought about it." He sighed in resignation. "You always had candles on your dining room table when we had dinner."

"No. It's fine," Janice insisted. Inwardly, she was smiling from ear to ear. It was obvious Ben did not entertain a lot. A lot? No. Ben didn't entertain period. He played poker with the monthly group at his house. But, that was cards, not entertaining. Fred had told her all about it.

"I found the sleigh combination on a shelf in the hall closet. I don't have a need for candles. I use a flashlight when I lose power." He explained in detail. It was more information than he intended to give. There was no need for it.

"Ben," Janice said very clearly, "I like what you've done. Really, I do. It's festive." Like celebrating Christmas in August, she thought. Janice let the candle discussion drop and changed the subject. "Now, what can I do to help?"

Ben walked to the refrigerator, pulled out a plate with two steaks and a magnum of 2010 Clos du Val Cabernet Sauvignon, and placed them on the kitchen counter. He uncorked the Christmas gift from Megan then placed the bottle on the table.

"Are we going to drink all that?" Janice eyed the huge wine bottle.

"I've been dying to try it since the holidays and I needed some-one to share it with me," he said. "I cleaned four ears of corn. Check the kettle to see if they're done. You can pour the wine while I grill the steaks out back." Then he started to chuckle. "I always have a job for you, don't I?" He nudged open the screen door to the covered patio.

Within minutes, Janice joined him with two glasses of wine. She placed them on a side table and watched him carefully grill the steaks. She offered the wine at the precise right moment.

"I'm glad we're doing this." Ben toasted her glass. "Here's to old friends."

"And old friendships." Janice dinged his glass once more.

"That too," Ben added, sipping his wine. "This wine's excellent. Tastes good chilled. What do you think?"

"You should turn the steaks, unless we're eating charcoal with our corn and salad."

"You checked the refrigerator," Ben said. "Now, you know the whole menu."

"I didn't see dessert." Janice shook her head. "So, I guess I don't."

Ben checked the steaks, tossed them onto a platter and walked inside the house. Janice followed, holding the empty wine glasses, which she promptly refilled at the table. She removed the corn from the kettle to a serving platter while Ben placed the steaks, salad and garlic mushrooms on the table. They stood looking at the food first, and then, each other.

"I think we should eat before it gets cold." Ben held her chair.

"Would you mind?" Janice asked, as she sat down. "You went to all this trouble, Ben. Could we close the blinds and light the candles?"

Ben began to chuckle. He closed the blinds, drew the living room drapes and darkened the whole house before lighting the two red candles. In the eerie glow, the two friends clinked their wine glasses once again, and began to eat a wonderful dinner while catching up on mutual friends, store happenings and the fact that Janice's daughter, Amy, was about to become an assistant professor at Ithaca College. They talked about her marriage to Paul and how much happier she seemed. Her whole personality had taken on a new transformation, now that her old fiancé, Gerald, was out of her life completely.

After a lot of wine and almost three hours later, Ben brought out an apple pie which he placed on the counter and cut two serving pieces.

"Ice cream?" he asked

"Sounds good."

"Wine or coffee?"

"Is there any left?" Janice slurred her words ever so slightly, as she measured the contents of the almost empty wine bottle.

"I think we should finish it," Ben said. "We're both off tomorrow. I've got two days and your shop's closed on Sunday. So, if we celebrate, who cares?"

"Good idea." She held up her empty glass, having him refill it. Janice sipped her wine slowly and watched Ben place the pie covered plate in front of her.

"Wait." Ben removed the plate. "I forgot the ice cream."

With his back turned away from her, Ben had no idea her condition had deteriorated so quickly, until he heard a cracking noise. When he turned to face Janice, Ben noticed that the side of her head was smack-down on the tablecloth and her body looked rigid.

"Janice." He hurried to her, but found his own movements increasingly slow.

"Whaat?" She slurred her question.

"I think you should lie down." He tried to get her out of the chair, moving it sideways, but she seemed unwilling to help. "C'mon, Janice." Ben pulled her upward, his hands firmly under her arms. He tilted her toward him, and almost falling backward himself, noticed one of her high-heeled shoes had fallen off her foot. He had the presence of mind to blow-out the melted candle puddles, before dragging and weaving Janice across the darkened living room toward the guest bedroom.

"I'mm...soo… in trouble," Janice began lamenting. "Somessthing's happened to my leg."

"What?" he answered.

"It'ss shorter than thiss other one." She stopped suddenly, moving his body somewhat. "I have to go."

"You're in no condition to drive."

"I'm…I have to peeh…" She gave a huge sigh, correcting his statement.

Ben's head started spinning. He knew from experience, he had to get to bed before the whole room started to rotate. He dragged Janice as they zigzagged safely to the bathroom.

Facing her directly, Ben continued to hold his hands firmly under her arms as he guided her to the toilet.

"Pull up your skirt, Janice and bend forward a little. I'll pull down your panties and put you on the pot."

"Yuu wil not." The drunken woman became indignant.

"Either you sit on the pot or you wet yourself." Ben pointed out the alternatives.

"Shuut yur eyes," Janice insisted.

"Then I won't be able to see. As it is, I don't know if I have 20/20."

"Shuut one eye and you'll hav 20." That seemed logical to her.

Ben sat her down on the commode and totally removed the underwear hugging her ankles.

"Where'ss my pannts?" She demanded of the man sitting on the rim of the tub.

"I took them," he said, but did not mention removing her other high-heeled shoe.

"Thaas okay. I have lotss more at home."

"You done?" he said, sounding like a father asking a child he was trying to potty train.

Catching her nod, Ben tried pulling her up off the commode, but found he couldn't move her. She was dead weight. He bent down once again and, pulling her upward with such a force, backed into the wall holding the towel rack and heard the thundering clamor of metal hit the floor. "Shit," he muttered, as he dragged her into the guest bedroom and listened to her mumble about the miraculous healing of her leg.

Ben sat Janice on the side of the bed, pulled a section of covers down and began undressing her. Since the room was already dark, he felt little embarrassment.

"Sstop that." She slapped him, as he undid her blouse and bra, and then in a cosmic second, fell back onto the pillow and was in another world of her own.

After removing her skirt, Ben covered the woman, placed her clothes on a chair and zigzagged to his own bedroom. They would feel hammered in the morning and it would not be a pretty sight. For either of them. He threw his clothes on a chair near his bed and slid under the covers.

***

Somewhere in the middle of the night, Ben was awakened by moaning sounds coming from the next bedroom. Fearing that Janice fell out of bed in her drunken stupor, he rushed to her side and found her sitting up in bed, crying and moaning profusely. He took her into his arms and held her. Although he could feel her breasts rubbing against his chest with every loud gasp she heaved, it was of no consequence. His friend was experiencing the grief that comes after the death of a lifelong partner. A grief, he knew so well: that empty longing for the companion, so sorely missed. Ben was familiar with her crying jag. He had suffered the same symptom, many times over.

"I'm not going to make it." A dam of tears rolled down her face. "I miss him so much. Why did he leave me behind, Ben? I'm so lonely without him," she wailed, sobbing in his arms.

"Give it time, Jan." He pushed her hair away from her face, somewhat surprised that he never noticed the length or softness of it before. "You have a lot of very caring friends."

"I'm sorry to bother you, Ben, but would you mind staying with me for awhile?" she asked, feeling safe in his arms. "Just for a little while."

Ben rested her head back against the pillow very gently and slid under the covers. "It's going to be ok," he said, holding her in his arms. "Go to sleep. I'll be here when you wake up."

In the stillness of the night, the two figures soon came to realize the intensity of their bodies lying against each other; and, whether planned or not, a hungry force, between two grieving people, took over before the sounds of sleep flooded the room.

***

"Oh, God," Janice moaned a few hours later, then turned, feeling somewhat shocked to find Ben's face nestled close to hers. The room was still very dark, and yet, she knew his bulging eyes were staring at her.

"What's wrong?" he asked. "Are you ok?"

"I feel like someone hit my head with a hammer."

"Aspirin," he offered a remedy. "I'll get it." Ben left the room hurriedly and returned with the aspirin and a glass of water. He snapped on the night light and sat at her bedside.

"You're naked!" Janice expressed shock.

"Take the pills," he said dryly, and then placed the glass on the dresser before turning off the light and slipping back under the covers. He moved toward her and slid his arm under her back.

"Ben, did we…?"

"You don't remember?"

"Don't tell Amy…," she groaned.

"That could be grounds for blackmail." He pulled her gently to him.

"What are you doing?" she whispered to his kiss, aware that his fingers were slowly inching down her body.

"I'm giving you something you will remember," he said, feeling her readiness before going deep inside her. She moved to his rhythm, her soft moans increasing with the speed of each penetration. He continued the rocking motion and judging the nearness of her peak, gave her one deep final thrust. She gasped loudly and clung to him, unwilling to release his body from hers, until her spasm ebbed and the pounding of her heart returned to normal. And yet, she wanted to relive that moment again and again.

"Jesus, Ben." She took a deep breath, still clinging to him. "I wasn't sure."

"Meaning?"

"You know exactly what I mean. You certainly are…endowed. I noticed when the light was on."

"Are you going to tell Amy you think I'm hung?" He snickered at the thought, "Or that we got hammered and had sex?" Then, holding her gently, Ben kissed her tenderly. "We need to get some sleep." He pulled the covers over both of them and closed his frog-like eyes.

***

Janice awakened to see the sun's rays framing the blinds in the darkened room. Her clothes rested on a chair near her bed. Ben had folded them over the chair back and placed her underwear on the chair seat. Her heels sat directly centered on the floor between the front chair legs. She dressed quickly, crossed the hall to the bathroom and took her morning pee.

When she sat on the commode, Janice noticed the broken towel bar and the wall inserts connected to its installation laying on the floor adjacent the tub. Had she broken the metal rack in her drunken stupor? Should she say something to Ben about paying for it? Maybe it was broken before she arrived. Still, something in the back of her mind told her a different story.

She spotted a few towels resting on the sink vanity and realized they were meant for her use. But knowing she would feel better showering at home, Janice did the ordinary thing one does as a guest. She washed her hands and face, and knew it would take all of her resolve to face the man she had sex with hours earlier.

"Hey!" Janice greeted Ben, who sat in the living room reading the Sunday paper. She hoped the friendly tone of her voice would mask her nervousness.

"Hello. I didn't want to wake you," he said, tossing the paper aside. "I made breakfast."

Janice quickly noticed the absence of the sleigh and melted candles. A gross looking tablecloth with a fruit mixture of apples and pears replaced the white wrinkled one from the previous night. On the hideous looking tablecloth sat two place settings, a carafe of coffee, milk, sugar and two glasses of orange juice.

"Bacon or sausage? One egg or two?" He watched her pour coffee into her cup.

"Two slices bacon, one egg, one slice of toast." Her breakfast order was simple.

"Same old, same old," he said. "Nothing's changed. Once over easy?"

"Please," she said, flattered that he would even remember how she liked her eggs.

Ben placed the plates of food on the table and sat down. He fashioned the bacon, egg and toast on her plate to make her meal look complete. He did this deliberately, not wanting to move from the table to get some other necessary breakfast item.

Janice played with her meal. Food was not paramount in her thoughts. She felt awkward. "Ben." She raised her eyes from her plate.

"Twice." He responded to her thoughts.

"Was I a positively drunken wretch?"

"Well, you offered to let me keep your underwear."

"Oh, no!" She was both mortified and hysterical with laughter. "Then, how did…" She left the question unfinished.

"You woke up crying in the middle of the night and asked me to stay with you."

Janice stared at the peppered-haired man with big bulging eyes and remained silent. What could she say? She had asked him to stay with her. She needed him to comfort her. And apparently they comforted each other. Throughout the years they had been such close friends. Would this romp ruin their friendship?

"I broke your towel rack, didn't I?"

"Actually, we did a backward fling against the wall and broke it."

"I want to pay for that, Ben," she insisted.

"No. I'm thinking of redoing the whole house. It's past time. One gets accustomed to a house and doesn't really see how stale it is. I need a fresh pair of eyes."

"I like the granite countertop. I thought you had Formica."

"Burned it with a frying pan and had to replace it."

"I'm sorry, Ben," she whispered, heaving heavily and fighting back the tears. "I didn't mean to burden you."

"Janice." His strong voice brought her up short. "Did you have a good night's sleep?"

"The best since…," she answered honestly.

"I'm glad. It's a very good bed. Now, eat your breakfast. I need to talk with you about Clarisa. My sister's birthday is around the corner and I have no idea what to get her. I also need your cell number. You already have mine. There's a blank card and pen on the window sill. Write it down, now."

They spoke for over an hour at the table and, before long, they stacked the dishes in the dishwasher and tidied-up the kitchen, joking and laughing over old times.

Janice took her handbag from the seat of a kitchen chair and crossed the living room to the front door where Ben stood watching her. She moved to the open doorway, but Ben pulled her back against the wall and kissed her.

"I'm glad you came," he said and watched her car leave the driveway.

***

When Janice pulled into the garage of her house, she was taken by surprise with an item left in her car. She marched into the house, dropped her purse and immediately dialed a number on her cell phone.

"Ben," she began, "I found your sport coat in my car."

"Really," he said, expecting her call.

"Why did you do that?" she challenged.

"Why do you think I did," he rebutted.

"Because you're attracted to drunk and disorderly women."

"True, but only when their clothes are easily removable."

"Was I that much of a problem?" Janice questioned her memory lapse.

"Only when you snore." Ben snickered with his answer. "I'll call you for my jacket. The one you brought isn't mine."

"Oh, my God!" Janice screamed into the phone. "It must be Paul's," she said, referring to her son-in-law. "I gave the other one to Goodwill! I thought it was Fred's."

"You are going to owe me big time, lady. I bought it at Roneker's Men's Store, so you know it wasn't cheap." He pressed the end button, terminating the call.

Janice stared at the dead phone, totally embarrassed that she had given away his jacket. Saying she was sorry wouldn't cut it, although he didn't seem angry. Owing him big time could have meant a lot of things. She couldn't worry about that now.

She raced upstairs to her bedroom, threw off her clothes and jumped into the shower. The warm, flowing water seemed to soothe her. It took the edge off her conversation with Ben. What did he say when she asked the question over breakfast? Actually, she didn't ask. She just mentioned his name…but he knew exactly what she meant. He told her, "twice." That was the end of it. He never referred to their sexual encounter again. Like it never happened. As if it was meaningless. What kind of man was he? *One who your how to push your buttons,* an inner voice told her, as she toweled the water droplets from her body.

She needed to piece the evening together. After the wine, everything that happened was a blur. According to Ben, the story was very simple. Somewhere in the middle of the night, she began crying for Fred and awakened Ben by her outburst. When he held her in his arms to comfort her, she asked him to stay with her for a while. That's when he crawled under the covers with her. It had to have happened that way. That must have been the first time. But, it was still a blur. However, later, when she woke up with a headache, she caught Ben's stare. Even in the dark, she knew those bulging eyes were locked on hers. He gave her aspirin, after turning on the night light…catching her by surprise. Her startled remark of his nakedness was stupid. His nude body had been cuddling hers when she woke up. No. She was shocked by the size of him. *"Face it, girl, you were comparing,"* the inner voice captured the essence of her thoughts.

She remembered their encounter vividly after that. The foreplay drove her crazy. She loved him touching her all over. With their bodies locked together, she relished every thrust of his penetration, driving her to that moment, as she held on, never wanting to let go.

She couldn't remember feeling that way for a long, long, time. Months, perhaps, even years. Suddenly, she felt a betrayal. How could she feel that way? Her marriage had been wonderful. Fred did everything to please her. Their sex life may not have been exciting as they aged, but it was certainly satisfying. *Not like last night*, her inner voice spoke once more. Well, she didn't need that. Her memories of Fred were enough. She would revere them, forever.

Janice didn't need some short, pudgy, gray-haired detective playing jacket games for sex. Still, she was having second thoughts. Was she being unfair to Ben? He didn't ask for sex. *She asked him to stay with her.* Maybe, the best course of action was inaction. Ben never dwelled on the encounter. He just said, "She snored." So, in the end, she should just forget about having had sex with him. Obviously, he had. Suddenly, Janice had another thought. Maybe, he was disappointed in her performance. What performance? She was drunk. Then, she had a headache. No. It wasn't about sex. He was playing mind games with the jacket. Damn him.

***

A few miles away, Ben was having a few thoughts of his own. He knew Janice would call him when she found the jacket in her car. He predicted it. She would be confused at first. Then she would suspect he wanted another sexual encounter. When her thoughts cleared, she would realize it wasn't the sex at all. He was pushing her buttons, playing the game. Now, she knew the jacket wasn't his. Would it have made a difference in the outcome of the previous night? The woman was his first and only since Julie died. He thought about that fact for a long, hard moment. He had been celibate like a non-fucking monk for the past seven years now. "Why?" he asked himself. "Too busy, unless forced by a situation?" Hell. He was lucky the thing still had life in it... lucky that it could still function that way. *Face it. You weren't interested, after Julie.* Still, he did enjoy sex with Janice. "You dumb shmuck," he said to himself. "You were almost as drunk as she was. You should have taken the jacket and been done with it. All you have now is a broken towel rack and dirty laundry."

So, if he hadn't have told her, what exactly would have happened when Janice returned the jacket? Would he have made dinner or taken her to the bedroom while they were both sober? One thing was certain: he would not have had to put her on the pot.

***

Later that night, Ben called her. "I just called to tell you something. When you want sex, you know where to come."

"When I want sex, I'll call my lawn boy." Janice referenced Peggy's playful thought of having their little old lawn man service her after divorcing Jeff.

"Is he better than I am?" Ben interrupted her.

"I don't know. I never tried him."

"Sometimes a known quality is better."

"And sometimes a known quality is a pain in the ass!"

"I love it, when you talk dirty." She heard him chuckle.

A second later, Ben was staring at a dead cell phone. Janice had pressed her end button and terminated the call.

Ben's face broke into a wide grin. He knew what buttons to push with this woman. He paused, as if deep in thought. Was he actively pursuing Janice or did having sex awaken something inside him, something he had been missing for years? Ben disliked both thoughts. He had been in the company of many women over the years, not dating, but in meetings, gatherings, and weddings; however, no one turned him on, so to speak. So why was he so interested in Janice? Was it because they were the only two left from their foursome? Or was it because he knew her so well and was comfortable with the woman?

He pulled a bottle of scotch from the cupboard, drank what amounted to two jiggers and went to bed. "Maybe I just don't want to sleep alone anymore." He told his pillow.

***

"He's got a nerve." Janice told herself. "If I want sex, I should call him. The whole night was a total mistake. We were both drunk. That's the excuse and I am sticking to it. Still…I enjoyed our romp together. If nothing else, we certainly know each other a lot better now. Looking at him though, I never would have guessed." She pulled the bedcovers up around her and snapped off the bed lamp. Within minutes, soft staccato-like sounds filled the room.

Chapter 26
Kismet

Ben called Charlene Winter for an early lunch on Tuesday at Sessions Restaurant where they had met months earlier. When he made the call to Medoc Hast, he asked for the same suave bodyguard that he used on the previous assignment. Under no circumstances did he want Clayson Black to appear. That would have spoiled everything.

Ben and Charlene sat at a corner table facing the front door in Sessions Restaurant, slowly sipping coffee.

"Okay, so what's the big surprise? Am I ripping off someone's house or is Cal back?"

With Ben, Charlene never knew what to expect. His mind seemed to work twenty-four-seven and he always had something going on. So she wasn't surprised when Ben waved a tall handsome man to their table.

"I thought the two of you should meet." Ben introduced them, before turning his full attention to Medoc. "Charlene can tell you about our first meeting later. I thought she might be useful and fulfill a need."

"I beg your pardon," she groused loudly, interrupting Ben. "With his looks, getting someone to fulfill a need should be the least of his problems."

"I didn't mean it that way." Ben apologized.

"Well, whatever way you meant it, his makeup's on crooked."

"What do you mean?" Medoc became distraught by her comment.

"Look, honey, your wearing makeup doesn't bother me," she said evenly, paying no attention to Ben's snickers. "I want to know if you're just plain queer, gay or want to be incognito."

Now, Medoc and Ben shook with a laughter that was uncontrollable. Within seconds Charlene joined them. They were still laughing when Medoc brought out a bottle of facial lotion for sunburn, which of course, Charlene took for makeup. When Ben got up to leave, they were still laughing.

"So why was Ben so insistent that we meet?"

"I have no idea," he replied.

"Let me tell you something. Ben Burrows brought us together for a reason and it's not a matchmaker kind of thing. No. You must be into something, but what?" she asked. "Does your job require the need for an actress?"

Medoc stared at the woman, his mouth agape, and then he broke into another round of laughter. "I have no idea what Ben's thinking, but I can't remember having a crazier time."

"What is it you do, then?" she asked.

"I'm a deck hand." He stretched the truth. "I go with a crew to the Caribbean. They hire out to tourists."

"Is this year-round?"

"Depends on hurricane season," he replied readily. "And you're an actress." Medoc turned the conversation around to her. "Do you travel much?"

"Summer stock usually, but other times I often appear at the Lancaster Opera House."

"Are you performing there now?"

"I'm emceeing with someone at a charity auction this weekend. I've done it before, but I don't think Winifred has."

"Winifred?"

"Winifred Pitts is doing it this year. The ones asked are usually well-heeled, if you know what I mean."

Although somewhat taken back by her statement, Medoc never acknowledged meeting the man. "Will he be your escort for the evening?"

"God. No. I'll be going alone. There is speculation whether or not he will be with Victoria Reynolds."

"I don't understand what you mean."

"It's just as well. Nobody really knows where she is," Charlene replied and rose to leave. "Nice meeting you. I have to go…an appointment with Jonathan, my hairdresser. He's a real shit, but does great work."

Medoc watched her leave, paid the check and drove to the police station. Had he arrived any earlier he would have met Megan.

***

"Months ago, you told me not to call her. I understood it then. Now I'm confused." Megan slid into a chair facing his desk.

"Why is that?" Ben asked, needing clarity.

"She didn't answer her cell. I've called so many times, so I went over. The doorman told me she went to a spa and left no word on her return."

"If Victoria's at a spa, she may be taking an extended stay. I don't see a problem."

"It's almost like she vanished."

"I'm sure she's okay. I know it's one of the things she wanted to do." He reassured her.

"You always make me feel better." She hugged him. "But then, that's who you are. Peggy told me you grilled Janice a steak. That was nice. You should take her out sometime."

"What is that supposed to mean?" He took a defensive tone.

"She's not the kind of woman who goes searching for companionship. I understand you helped each other when the spouses died. You've been friends for a long time and I'm sure she gets lonely. That's all I meant. I'm not trying to fix you up, although it would be nice if you took her to a movie or out to dinner sometime."

"Go home, Megan."

"Lunch tomorrow for beef on weck…please," she begged. "I won't talk about women. I promise."

"Noon, here." He caught her nod.

"I wish you were my biological dad." She hugged him again and walked away.

He watched the young woman exit the building. It was best to leave some things alone. Ben understood the extent of Megan's emotional turmoil, just as much as that of Victoria Reynolds'. In the latter case, he understood, but could not talk about it. He had promised confidentiality.

***

"Am I supposed to thank you?" Medoc sat across from Ben in the small windowed office.

"Meaning what?"

"Winifred," Medoc answered.

"What did you learn?"

"Not much. I got the impression Victoria is missing. Where is she, Ben?"

"What makes you think I know?"

"Trust. You're the one person she would go to."

"If Victoria came to me for advice, I would give it freely, but the final decision would be hers."

"What are you suggesting?"

"Go home, Medoc. You set the rules, now you'll have to live with them. You're allowing your past to devour the present. You gave up a long time ago, after being thoroughly heartbroken. You're reliving your past, even to the point of a park meeting. But Melissa didn't come, did she? She gave you her answer by marrying your brother. And maybe, you're betting on a repeat of sorts. But you're wrong. Victoria is not Melissa. She's a woman who loves you, not some sweet thing that jilted you years ago. Stop repeating your past mistakes. You have someone who wants a life with you, and you are in love with her. Face it. That kind of love rarely happens at our age. If you're smart you'll make the partnership work. She is willing to give up everything for you, which I think is unfair. You both need outside intervention and attending one or two functions can hardly be problematic. You have not given this enough thought."

That Victoria confided in Ben was no surprise. The lines had been drawn and Medoc was the responsible artist. Her social life held no interest for him. He had been there, done that. He wanted a lifestyle without commitment. He had made his position clear.

"Words mean nothing. It's what's in here that counts." Ben pointed to his heart. "But you have to come together. It won't work, if you don't meet half-way, no matter how much you love each other."

"No. I made that decision before I came," Medoc said quietly. "I've been given a second chance and I'm not going to screw-it-up. You're right. It doesn't come around again at our age. But there is something else I hadn't realized. I miss not waking up to her, having coffee and laughing together. I never realized how lonely I've been. I finally found someone I want in my life; things we can share together. I don't want to be alone anymore." He shook the detective's hand and left his office.

Ben watched the dejected man leave the building. How strange life was. Only months earlier, a self assured Medoc Hast stood before him. That was before he fell in love and his world fell apart.

***

Danny Boyle knocked on Ben's door and shook him out of his reverie. "I'm setting up a table for the Policemen's Benefit. Want to sit with us?"

"I hadn't thought about it. When is it?" Ben looked at his calendar.

"Two weeks from Saturday, September eighth. Are you taking your daughter?" He met Ben's stare. "Or not," he added.

"There will be two of us," Ben replied, marking his calendar. "I'm sure I can scout the prison cells for a date."

"Good one." Danny Boyle laughed, leaving Ben's office.

Ben watched the young police officer disappear before closing his office door and dialing a number.

"I need a date for Saturday, September eighth. It's the annual Policemen's Benefit," Ben said. "No, I'm not calling to see who you have on your registry," he growled. "Yes, dammit, I'm asking you to go with me." He listened to her side of the conversation. "I'm out of prac-tice with that kind of thing," he said, and started over. "Janice, I would like you to accompany me on September eighth for the Policemen's Benefit." He listened to her response. "Thank you. I will pick-you-up at six-thirty. Usually, it's cocktails at seven and dinner at eight. If that changes I'll let you know. Do me a favor. Don't wear panties, in case I have to put you on the pot again." Ben checked his phone. Janice had pressed her end button and hung-up on him.

***

The leaves of the tall elms and mighty oaks took on the red and gold tones of an early fall season as their majestic colors embellished the park grounds. Even the clumps of split birch seemed more polished with their silvery sheen. They glistened in the autumn sunlight mirroring the hues of nearby trees. The somewhat crisp September air seemed pure and fresh, giving rumor to all, that life still continued in its vibrancy. However, the blades of grass in Tonawanda Park had lost their tonic and, bending to summer's end, hinted the coming of a dormant sleep, one that precludes the deathlike state of winter.

Far into the park, near a bench whose paint had been forgotten long ago, a man stood waiting. He was not one to pace nervously. He had learned long ago, pacing was a wasted effort. He checked his watch, noting his early arrival and began to stroll around the park. After a fifteen minute walk, he found himself back beside the same paint-worn bench. He checked his watch again. The noon day sun streaked through the trees, signaling a path for a new beginning. Would it come to pass or would the past be repeated?

Medoc Hast stood tall and waited.

A woman dressed in a tailored pantsuit raced into the park and stopped dead center before the waiting man, her eyes never leaving his.

He opened his arms to her and as she stepped into them, a tear spilled from her cheek. "Tell me it's real, Medoc. Tell me." She began to cry, a torrent of tears flooding her face.

"It's real, Victoria." Medoc looked deep into her eyes and kissed away the tears, before melting his lips with hers longingly. A glowing expression of love crossed his face, his eyes falling on hers as he held her.

"What we have is very real," he said, pledging himself to her. "I felt it when we met; I knew when we made love; and I ached when you were gone. More than anything else, I want you in my life, as a part of me, and a beginning of us. Whatever you want, wherever we go, we'll be together. You belong with me, Victoria. You are my world now. I love you."

He held her in his arms and heard her whisper softly, "This is all I ever wanted…I love you, Medoc."

***

The night of the Policemen's Benefit went extremely well. Danny Boyle was on his very best behavior. He knew Ben Burrows and Fred Sommers had been friends for years. And with Fred's subsequent death, Ben was around, as a family friend, to reciprocate for Janice's help with his own wife's demise. It was general knowledge that Ben never dated as such. If he were with a female, other than his 'adopted daughter,' there was always a good reason. So when Ben arrived with Janice Sommers, no one at the table thought much of it. He was just being a kind friend. And since Janice knew most of the couples seated there, she felt very comfortable during the entire affair. The conversations went smoothly, the food was delicious and the speeches, short.

At the end of the evening as Ben was driving home, they spoke about the dinner, until Janice realized Ben was pulling into the driveway of his house.

"What are we doing here?" she asked, taken by surprise. They had not seen each other since…the jacket return.

"I thought we could have a nightcap," Ben said casually.

"As long as it isn't wine." The last thing she wanted was a repeat of her drunken stupor.

"Scotch, ok?" He caught her nod.

Ben walked to the passenger side of the car and escorted her to the front door.

As soon as they entered the darkened house, Ben took Janice into his arms and held her close, his need growing stronger as their lips met with a prolonged kiss. "Should I switch on the lights? Would you like something to drink?" he asked quietly, his breathing becoming heavier.

She could feel his growing readiness and felt a pulsating surge of her own rush through the lower depths of her body. Her lingering silence gave Ben all the response he needed, as he led her into the guest bedroom.

Within minutes, they were on the bed, locked in each other's arms and moving in sync with each undulating motion. Ben listened to the increased frequency of her soft moans, knowing she was near peak. He moved deep inside her with one final thrust and felt her fingers digging into his back as she clung to him, never wanting to let go of the moment. Seconds later her struggle for breath had ebbed.

"Oh. Ben," she whispered softly. "I never expected it to be like this... with us. But is it right? I mean so soon after..."

"I think he'd want me to look after you. You are too perfect to be alone. But are you disappointed?" he asked, needing her reassurance.

"With your size and the way you move, I'd be the envy of the Smorgasbord Ladies."

Although the room was dark, Ben Burrows was glowing inwardly. Megan, his chief promoting yenta, must have reported on the number of women vying for his attention at the Croft New Year's party. Now Janice knew they considered him, "a catch."

Of course, Janice was having a few thoughts of her own. "Too perfect to be alone." What did he mean by that? "It's his way of saying he cares for you, but don't push it," an inner voice whispered. Her thoughts, however, were brought up short when Ben moved away from her and drew the bedcovers up around them.

"I think we should sleep-in tomorrow and have a late breakfast," he said sliding his arm around her.

"I'd like that." She curled into him and felt his lingering kiss, before closing her eyes.

Although Ben couldn't see her expression, he knew they were on the same page. A wide smile crossed his face as he slowly fell asleep.

###

www.ingramcontent.com/pod-product-compliance
Lightning Source LLC
Chambersburg PA
CBHW070318260626
47160CB00003B/880